FEEDER

PATRICK WEEKES

FEEDER

Margaret K. McElderry Books
New York   London   Toronto   Sydney   New Delhi

MARGARET K. McELDERRY BOOKS
An imprint of Simon & Schuster Children's Publishing Division
1230 Avenue of the Americas, New York, New York 10020
This book is a work of fiction. Any references to historical events, real people, or real places are used fictitiously. Other names, characters, places, and events are products of the author's imagination, and any resemblance to actual events or places or persons, living or dead, is entirely coincidental.

MARGARET K. McELDERRY BOOKS is a trademark of Simon & Schuster, Inc.
For information about special discounts for bulk purchases, please contact Simon & Schuster Special Sales at 1-866-506-1949 or business@simonandschuster.com.
The Simon & Schuster Speakers Bureau can bring authors to your live event. For more information or to book an event, contact the Simon & Schuster Speakers Bureau at 1-866-248-3049 or visit our website at www.simonspeakers.com.
Book design by Sonia Chaghatzbanian and Irene Metaxatos
The text for this book was set in ITC Slimbach Std.
Manufactured in the United States of America

10 9 8 7 6 5 4 3 2
Library of Congress Cataloging-in-Publication Data
Names: Weekes, Patrick, author.
Title: Feeder / Patrick Weekes.
Description: First edition. | New York : Margaret K. McElderry Books, [2018] | Summary: Lori Fisher hunts monsters, aided by an interdimensional creature called Handler, but when she stumbles across the Nix, a kidnapped group of mutant teens, she becomes the hunted.
Identifiers: LCCN 2017017802
ISBN 9781534400160 (hardcover) | ISBN 9781534400184 (eBook)
Subjects: | CYAC: Monsters—Fiction. | Ability—Fiction. | Brothers and sisters—Fiction. | Orphans—Fiction. | Science fiction.
Classification: LCC PZ7.1.W4284 Fee 2018 | DDC [Fic]—dc23
LC record available at https://lccn.loc.gov/2017017802

For my boys—
I love who you are, and I will love
whoever you grow to be

CONTENTS

MONDAY

LORI

The message about the new feeder came while Lori Fisher was trying to get her brother, Ben, to eat his breakfast.

"This is what you said you wanted," Lori said, putting the toast down in front of him.

Ben, seven years old and blessed with a complexion that made him look perfectly tanned, while Lori herself just looked sallow, glared at Lori and let out a put-upon breath as he pushed the toast away. "I said toast. I didn't say toast with butter!"

"Toast implies butter, though. Toast comes *with* butter," Lori said, and then she looked down as her phone buzzed.

Handler: New feeder. Taxi will pick you up.

"I didn't want the butter part!" Ben insisted, playing angrily with a Lego figure on their large and cluttered kitchen table as the toast sat uneaten in front of him. "I just wanted the toast part!"

"Okay, but the butter is on the toast already. I can't take it off.

Can you eat it just today for me?" Lori gave her brother a hopeful smile, then looked down at the phone again and tapped in a response.

Lori: I was going shopping with Jenn.

Handler: Sorry. And client wants to consult.

"No! I only want to eat what I said I wanted to eat, and that was toast, and not toast with butter!"

Lori looked at the clock on the microwave of their small kitchen. It read 7:17, which meant it was actually 8:21 because she had never reset it after the time change in the spring, and it had been four minutes slow before that. The ferry came by at eight thirty every weekday to take Ben to day care, and while the schedule wasn't quite as strict during the summer as it was when she was trying to get Ben to school, Lori still got dirty looks from the day-care people if she brought him in late.

The plan had been shopping with a friend, partially school supplies for Ben and partially a new back-to-school outfit for her. Instead today would be spent dealing with feeders . . . assuming Ben ever left.

"Ben, we are almost out of time."

His eyes brightened, and he pointed above Lori's shoulder at the sign that hung over the sink. "'Our family might get there late!'" he read.

"'But we'll get there together,'" Lori finished without looking back at the stupid sign, which had an overloaded car covered with luggage and a bike and a surfboard, "and that doesn't mean we can miss the ferry!"

Ben *was* dressed and was even wearing an appropriate pair of shorts and T-shirt instead of the long-sleeved shirt and heavy sweatpants he'd put on the last time she let him dress himself. He still had to brush his teeth, though. The time it would take to make toast again and convince Ben that it was in fact new unbuttered toast was not time they could spare.

Ben saw her look at the clock, then saw her look at him, and changed his expression from angry to pleading. "I would eat a granola bar?"

Lori sighed. "Superfast?"

"Superfast," Ben said immediately.

"And a banana," she added as she reached up into the pantry over the fridge and grabbed a granola bar.

"I will eat a banana if you open it for me."

Lori tossed him the granola bar, grabbed a banana from the bunch on the counter by the fridge, and peeled it for him. "Deal, little guy," she said, and put it on the plate next to the awful, terrible buttered toast, which she grabbed for herself. "Superfast. I have to go to work, so I'm going to get dressed. Brush your teeth as soon as you're done, all right?"

Ben was already chewing on the granola bar, and nodded as he read a page from a comic that had come free with one of his Lego sets and coincidentally included characters from a lot of other Lego sets available for purchase.

Lori's bedroom was down the hall from her brother's. She pulled off the long nightshirt she'd slept in and tapped another message at Handler while hunting for a clean bra.

Lori: Consult on-site or over phone?

Handler: Mainly phone, but on-site possible. Grown-up clothes, plz.

She scarfed the toast, pulled on dark gray slacks and boots she could move in, found a bra, and tugged it on. "You still eating?" she called back out into the kitchen.

"Almost done!"

"You promised me superfast," she called with a note of warning in her voice, and pulled on a purple blouse that looked like it was silk but was in fact a high-quality stain-resistant polyester. The outfit made her look like she was in her early twenties instead of sixteen.

"The banana had a dark spot on it!" Ben called back from the kitchen.

Lori glanced at her phone: 8:25. "Okay, leave the rest of the banana and brush your teeth."

She heard the sound of the electric toothbrush while she pulled her dark hair back into a ponytail and put on just enough makeup to look like an adult—a bit of eyeliner to accent the big dark eyes she shared with her brother, some blush on her cheeks, lip gloss that didn't actively work against the purple blouse.

It was 8:27. "Shoes on," she called, and grabbed her wallet and keys.

Ben came out of the hallway with a handful of Legos. "I just remembered, today we're supposed to bring—"

"No time," Lori said, cutting him off.

"But—"

"Shoes!"

Ben's face screwed up into a knot of misery. "It's not fair! You always want me to go fast, and I never go fast enough, and if I don't bring it, I'll be the only kid at day care who didn't bring a Show and Share toy, and . . ."

Lori sighed again and looked at the microwave clock, which now read 7:24 and *meant* 8:28. "Fast, please?"

Ben grabbed the rest of his Legos, shoved them into his backpack, and got his shoes on with remarkable speed. One minute later, she was hustling him out the apartment door, down the stairs, and out onto the sidewalk, where other children were already waiting. Most of them had long pants. A few had sweat-shirts.

Lori looked at Ben in his T-shirt and shorts, and then at the overcast sky, and then at the ferry already puttering up the canal toward their stop. "Are you gonna be warm enough?"

"I'm fine."

"Okay, but it's a little cooler than I—"

"I'm *fine*," Ben said again, as though Lori were the biggest idiot in the world, and Lori let it drop.

The ferry was a stubby boat with old rubber tires hanging from its sides and "Santa Dymphna Eastern" stenciled in above the waterline. Its horn blasted once as it navigated the tricky final turn—their street had been narrow before the rising water turned Santa Dymphna into a canal city—and pulled to a stop at the dock.

"Have a great day," Lori said as they joined the line of people boarding. "Good listening and good attitude, right?"

"Right. Love you." Ben hugged her. "Can you pick me up right after day care today?"

"I've got work, so go to day care, and we'll see if I can get you early." Lori returned the hug, then stepped back and waved as the ferry pulled away. Ben was already chatting with another kid, probably about Legos.

The ferry puttered down the canal, reached the old corner intersection, and chugged carefully through a turn better suited to cars than boats.

Then it was gone, and Lori dug out her phone.

Lori: You know I hate consults.

Handler: S'why it's called a job, kid. Let's go kill some monsters.

Handler: Least you're not missing school for this, right?
Handler: Get it done fast, maybe you can still hang with Jenn in aft.

Lori sighed, then switched over to contacts and found "Vickers, J." She dialed.

Jenn picked up before the second ring. "What's up, Lorelei?"

"Hey, Jenn. I just got a consult job, and it's a rush. They need it this morning."

"Your consult job *sucks*," Jenn said in a disgusted but supportive way, and Lori smiled despite herself. "Front Row's sale is today only!"

"What if we go in the afternoon?" Lori asked as a public ferry came to the dock. She hurried toward it. "Consult might go quick."

"Sounds like a plan. You're going back to school fashionable this year, Fisher. No cop-outs. This is the year the boys notice you on the very first day."

"Sounds good." Lori rolled her eyes. "I'll talk to you later, Jenn."

By agreement with Handler, the private taxi would pick Lori up in a public location halfway across Santa Dee, to avoid any possibility of feeders tracing her location back home. Lori hung up and hopped onto the public ferry that would take her there, flashing her monthly card at the driver and searching for a free seat inside. They were all taken at this time in the morning, with commuters in business clothes holding briefcases and phones. Most of the kids Lori's age were either at work already or sleeping in because it was summer. Lori sighed and found a good spot to lean against the railing on the deck as the ferry chugged into motion.

She watched the buildings go past, the salt-spray smell mixing with the sweet vanilla scent of the ferry's fuel. This boat had been converted, unlike the old one that took Ben to day care, which still ran on gasoline. The water below the railing churned with the ferry's passage, but the clear water farther away was gray-green, catching the light of the cloudy sky overhead. Below the sidewalks, Lori saw the lower stories of the old buildings, the ground level before the water rose. They were mostly covered with seaweed now. Here and there, Lori saw the telltale golden glimmer of the miracoral shining from a wall near the floor of the canal.

"I hear they're encouraging more growth through the canals," said someone standing nearby. Lori looked over and saw a bearded man in a blue business suit looking down at the miracoral, like she had been. "Maybe engineering a new, hardier strain. If they can get more of Santa Dee energy independent, they can export energy to the mainland."

"And then we all get rich?" Lori asked.

The man smiled and shrugged. "That's the hope. More miracoral, less need for oil, anyway."

The man's beard was neatly trimmed, and he stood with the easy grace of someone who had lived in Santa Dee long enough to get his sea legs. "It's lucky that scientists came up with it right as the water rose," Lori said.

"Luck, or preparation?" the man asked, and shrugged again.

"You mean that the scientists who invented the miracoral might have known the water was going to rise?" Lori added.

And just like always, the man's face went blank, and he said the same thing they always said. "Guess it was just one of those things."

"Okay, but why?" Lori pressed. "Why did the water rise?"

"Guess it was just one of those things," the man said. The casual tone was exactly the same as the first time he'd said it. It could have been a looped recording.

He turned away from her and looked at his phone, seemingly forgetting she existed. A moment later, Lori's phone buzzed.

Handler: Ever get tired of doing that?

Lori: It's weird.

Handler: Lots of things are weird, kid.

Lori got off the ferry at a downtown stop, grabbed a coffee, and waited until a small private taxi pulled up at the dock. A thin dark-skinned man poked his head out of the cab. "Angler Consulting?"

"That's me!" Lori poured the rest of her coffee into the trash, then tossed the cup into a recycling bin. The last time she'd drunk coffee while wearing a nice outfit, the taxi had hit a wave, and she'd dumped it all over herself.

The driver gave her a hand as she climbed down into the cab. The taxi itself was dark and sleek, and the cab was clean, with leather-backed seats that cupped her body like the ones in nice cars on the mainland. "Any bags, ma'am?" the driver asked. From his accent, she guessed that he was from Africa.

"No, thank you." Lori flashed him a smile. "You can just call me Angler."

"Okay, ma'am," the driver said, smiling back, and settled into his seat. "Just a few minutes to the Lake Foundation shipping center."

Lori assumed that was where they were supposed to be going. "Great."

The taxi pulled out, zipping around a ferry. Lori caught a vanilla-scented whiff of a new engine as they pulled around a corner.

"Very busy, the shipping center," the driver said. "All the

traffic, all day. Even for me, and this is not a cargo ship."

"Lot of people coming in and out?" Lori asked.

"Very much." He eased around another corner, muscled the taxi ahead of someone's private boat, and pulled into open water that had once been a large plaza or other low area with no buildings. He opened up the throttle a little, and Lori bounced in her seat as the taxi cut through another boat's wake. "Oh, they have contact information for you." He passed her back a card, only half looking at the chaotic wave of boats zipping through the choppy water.

Lori took the card and pulled her phone out again. "Thanks. You're really good on the water."

"I drove on rivers back home." He smiled, caught the sweet spot of another boat's wake, and eased into a groove. "When my family moved out here, I heard there were good jobs for drivers."

Lori's phone buzzed in her hand.

Handler: And here we go.

She ignored it. "So why *did* the water rise, anyway?" she asked. "Did you hear a different explanation back in—"

"Guess it was just one of those things," he said, and turned back to the front as Lori's phone buzzed.

Handler: You happy now?

The connection setup was easy enough. Lori joined the private network, popped her earpiece free from her phone, and hooked it over her left ear. She heard a crackle as it came to life. "Hello?"

"Hello, is this Angler Consulting?" came a friendly woman's voice that sounded like it was coming over a speakerphone. "This is Diane Tucker with the Lake Foundation."

"You can call me Angler," Lori said. "It's nice to meet you."

"Oh, you too, Miss Angler!" Diane Tucker with the Lake Foundation said with a lot of enthusiasm. "I tell you, we are so grateful to have you here. This is not the kind of thing we're used to dealing with at all."

"That's how it goes with most people," Lori said, trying to sound reassuring. "Why don't you tell me what happened?"

"Well, it started with some of our workers disappearing a few days ago." Beneath the voice, Lori heard the sound of paper rustling, as though Tucker was turning pages. "Several of them, from the cargo dock. Our security people investigated, and they said it was nothing to worry about, and then the security people refused to leave. All they'll say is that they'd like to stay. It's been a few days now, and, well, it just doesn't make sense. I . . . So that's when I decided to get in touch with Angler Consulting."

Tucker's voice went flat on the last sentence. Lori noticed that people tended to react to questions about how they'd gotten Angler Consulting's number the same way they reacted to questions about why the water had risen. She knew for a fact Angler Consulting wasn't listed on the web.

"Well, we're here now to help," Lori said as the taxi pulled off into narrow canals again. They were headed toward the western edge of Santa Dee, where all the cargo ships docked, circling around the island to avoid disturbing the great miracoral reefs in the shallow waters between Santa Dee's eastern edge and the mainland. "How do the security people sound? Did it sound like they'd been drugged, or . . . ?" Or brainwashed or mind controlled, Lori didn't add.

"Not really, Miss Angler. I mean, they sounded happy. They all just sounded very happy."

"Okay, but . . . they sounded happy about refusing to leave the cargo docks?" Lori looked down at her phone and typed, *"Shells or puppets?"*

"Well, that does sound odd, now that you say it like that," Tucker said, just as Lori's phone buzzed.

> Handler: Money's on shells. Puppets wouldn't have blown cover that easily.

"All right, Ms. Tucker, we're going to go in and take a look," Lori said. "As soon as we have any information, we will get right back in touch with you." Her phone buzzed as she said it.

> Handler: Oh yeah, btw.

"Oh, I was told you'd have a channel open the whole time," Tucker said.

> Lori: Seriously?

Lori glared down at her phone while saying, "Of course, I'm so sorry, I'll be happy to keep you on the line while we take care of this."

"Thanks so much," Tucker said apologetically. "I know it's a pain, but my boss, Ms. Lake, really wasn't sure about bringing in outside consultants."

"We totally understand," Lori said. "It's not a problem at all."

> Lori: I hate you so much.

> Handler: If it helps, we're getting paid a LOT.

> Lori: It does, actually.

The taxi pulled out of the canals of Santa Dee into open water. Looking out through the window, Lori saw the water go dark as it deepened beneath them. The taxi turned hard to starboard, and the driver opened up the throttle. Ahead, Lori saw the massive wharfs where shipping freighters brought Santa Dee everything it needed to survive.

They docked at a wharf that was empty but for them. Lori saw corrugated steel cargo containers stacked on huge pallets, but everything was still.

"Here we are, ma'am," said the driver, and opened the cab. He started to get out, and Lori waved him back.

"I'm fine, thanks. You go ahead, and have a great day," she said, and stepped out. She looked back. "Stay safe."

The driver nodded and smiled, then closed the cab. A moment later, the taxi hummed to life and pulled away from the dock, leaving white water and the scent of vanilla behind it.

"All right, Miss Tucker," Lori said, "let's see what we're dealing with."

The dockyard was silent as she walked. She kept her steps light, the heels of her boots barely making a sound on the concrete. She slid her phone into her pocket. If Handler had anything else that needed saying, Lori would've heard it already.

"Do you see anything yet?" Tucker asked in Lori's ear, which really helped Lori stay focused and stealthy.

"Not yet," Lori said, still keeping her steps light. "You wouldn't happen to have security cameras for the area, would you?"

"Oh, yes! Yes, I do. Here, I'll call them up, and I'll be able to watch everything." Lori heard the sound of fingers clacking on a keyboard. "Here we go. There you are, clear as day. I can see you walking toward the cargo containers."

"Great," Lori said. "That's great, you being able to see me and everything. That's perfect."

Her phone buzzed twice in her pants pocket, a special double buzz that Handler used for *"No"* when Lori was on a job and needed her hands free.

"Wait," said Tucker. "Something happened to the cameras. How odd. They were working just fine until—"

"That happens a lot in cases like these," Lori said. "I wouldn't worry about it."

Without warning, a voice came over the dockyard loud-speaker.

"Heyyyyyyyy," said someone who sounded about Lori's age. "Heyyy hi how's it going?"

Well, it knew Lori was here.

"Hey so it is supergreat that you're here," said the voice, light and breezy and flirty and feminine. "Supergreat and not a problem at all for either of us, neither of us is in any danger right now, especially you."

"Do you see anything?" Tucker asked over the earpiece.

"Give me just a sec, Miss Tucker," Lori said brightly, and began to run.

"Hey so listen," the voice came over the loudspeaker, "do you want to hang out, because I have some friends here who would love to hang out, all of us just hanging out and getting relaxed and not doing anything harmful to each other, and I don't suggest this to like everyone, but you seem superchill, so if you want to hang out, just find some of my friends, and they'll bring you to me and not hurt you at all."

Lori came around a corner formed by a stack of cargo containers and found what was left of one of the security guards.

He'd been a tall, thin man before the feeder had killed him. He was a tall, puffy shell of a man now, his body expanded grossly under his uniform, green-tinged skin visible where his blue shirt strained against the buttons. His pants and shirtsleeves looked like they'd been filled with great thick pool noodles, perfect cylinders that bent like an old rubber doll. His face was a swollen parody of itself, leaking green gas from the mouth and nostrils.

"Hhhhhhey," the shell said with more breath than he needed, coughing out with more of the green gas, and as he raised the gun in his hand, Lori moved.

She sidestepped the gun, checked his wrist to stop him from tracking the motion, and punched him in the face as he fired past her.

"Oh my god!" Tucker yelled in Lori's earpiece.

The shell's face sprayed green gas where Lori's punch had connected, and she slammed a chop into his hand, sending the gun clanging to the concrete, and then kicked him in his puffy cylinder of a knee, twisting the arm to send him sprawling. She came down on him knee first, another impact that spat puffs of green gas out from between the buttons of his shirt, and then punched again and again.

"Was that a gun?" Tucker shouted.

Finally, something gave, and the body hissed, then sank and yielded underneath her as though it were an air mattress whose cap had come off. She rolled off as it deflated beneath her, trying not to breathe the gas, and the skin itself flaked and crumbled as green cloud ate through it, and then there was nothing but an empty security uniform lying on the ground with a dark little smudge where the head had been.

"Miss Angler, say something!" said Tucker, which was nowhere near as important as the "Hhhhhey" Lori heard from right behind her, along with the sound of *another* gun's safety flipping off.

She felt Handler *pull* her, and for a moment, she was—

Pretend for a moment that you're looking down at a microbe smeared on a microscope plate. The microbe has lived its entire life stuck between those two planes of glass. As far as it's concerned, there's no up or down. Everything in its world is forward, backward, left, or right. Pretend that you took away the top slide, got an eyedropper, and put a tiny liquid blob of something the microbe would find interesting right in front of it.

What would that be like to the microbe? It never thought to look up—it never thought of much at all, really, being a microbe. As far as it's concerned, that little blob of something interesting just magically appeared in front of it out of nowhere. Maybe it moves forward to eat it, since "eat it" is the primary mode of interaction microbes have going for them. You don't want that to happen, though, so you take the eyedropper, suck the little liquid blob up, and lift the eyedropper away. Then, just to mess with the microbe a little, you dab the eyedropper behind the microbe and squirt the little interesting thing back out onto the plate.

For you, this is trivially easy, albeit still more trouble than most people would go to in order to play a prank on something that lives on a microscope plate. But for the microbe, what has just happened is an impossibility. There's no up in its world. There's no frame of reference for what it just saw. To the best of its knowledge, the interesting thing just vanished, and then reappeared, impossibly, behind it.

Now let's say you're the microbe.

—somewhere else, and then she was back, herself again, behind the second shell as it fired at the spot where she had been. She kicked him in the back of the knee, grabbed his collar as he fell, and slammed the heel of her palm into the base of his skull once, twice. He tried to point the gun back behind him, and Lori got hold of his chin and jaw and twisted, and she heard the crunch of what used to be bone and then a whoosh as the neck snapped, and her hands stung as the gas slid through them.

She stepped back as the increasingly empty uniform crumpled to the ground. Her skin felt clammy, and everything was a little brighter than it should be. That happened when Handler pulled her to another place. It took her a bit to fit back in again.

"Miss Angler, are you there?"

"Yes," Lori said. Her voice sounded wrong in her ears. "I'm here. The guards are dead." The words were cold, but that was normal, too, when Handler pulled her.

"Miss Angler?"

The wisps of gas were trailing back around a corner, and Lori followed them. She no longer tried to be stealthy. It knew she was here.

"Heyyyyyyyyyy hi again hello," came the girl's voice over the loudspeaker, "I am superglad you weren't killed by those guys who I don't even know how they got in here, and it's clear that you are more than strong enough to deal with anything you run into, so there's no reason for you not to come forward and see me and we can get to know each other, because you're already so close, and you're not dating anybody, I can tell that, it's this funny thing I can do, like a party trick, and you and I can be the party, and I can be that thing you don't have in your life, because I bet you're pretty lonely, right, aren't you, I mean if you didn't want to be with me, why would you be here?"

Lori felt herself coming back. The heels of her boots clacked on the concrete with each bold stride as she came down the path between two rows of corrugated steel cargo containers.

"It's a feeder," she said to Tucker. "It lures them in, and then does something that hollows them out and leaves the shells to help it get more prey."

"What are you talking about?" Tucker asked, her voice high-pitched and loud in Lori's ear. "This is like a monster? You're saying there's some kind of, of, of monster in our shipping yard? There are no such things as monsters!"

"Then why did you hire me to come take care of it?" Lori snapped.

"I . . ." Tucker paused, the idea slipping through her brain. "I can't actually remember. But why would a monster be in our shipping yard?"

Lori blinked. That was a good question, actually.

Then something rapped on the corrugated steel of the cargo container next to her, and she dove to the side, hands coming up ready.

There was nothing.

The bang came again.

It was coming from inside one of the containers.

"Is that you?" Lori asked.

"Noooooooo?" came the voice over the loudspeaker.

"Is what me?" Tucker asked.

Lori's phone buzzed twice in her pocket.

"Tucker," Lori said, "something is banging inside one of the containers. It's . . ." She looked over at it, one of the few standing on its own. The others were all dark red or yellow, but the one that something was banging inside was black, with no logo and no numbers on the side. "It's an unmarked black shipping container. The feeder says it isn't her."

"The feeder says . . . ?"

"Okay, but she's—*it's* been pretty honest so far, for one of them," Lori said, which made feeders sound a whole lot nicer than they in fact were, "so do you know anything about this black shipping container?"

Keyboard keys clacked in Lori's earpiece.

"I don't . . . hmmm." Tucker paused. "I'm going to contact Ms. Lake. She might know about it."

Lori looked at the container, and then up at the loudspeaker.

"Soooooo you're still coming, riiiiight?" the voice came over the loudspeaker. "I was getting all bored here by myself, and I know you're lonely, and there's a part of you that thinks you don't deserve to be with somebody, that it's better for you to be alone, but you know that's not true, right, we all deserve someone, and you deserve me, and you can just come and find me and we will be together and it will be so beautiful and wonderful and not dangerous for you at all, I promise."

It didn't seem like the feeder was in the container. Something *else* was, and that was bad, but whatever the thing in the container was, it was probably better dealt with after Lori had taken care of the feeder.

Stepping quietly again, back to herself as the last echoes of Handler pulling her faded, she came around the corner, stalked down a lane of containers, and found the clearing.

And there it was.

The concrete had been corroded away, leaving a black-edged pit that opened to the dark water below. And hunched over the edge of the pit was a mass of slick glowing tentacles that—

a beautiful woman, her skin pale as moonlight, facing away from Lori with her dress sliding down so that the muscles and bones of her sexy back played under her skin, and her hair tumbled down in a cascade of shimmering black, and Lori could just see the bare edge of her face, and if Lori just came closer, she'd be able to see her perfectly, and it would be so worth it to see such

—almost looked like a human form when they coiled a certain way and blinked their strange lights.

Lori walked forward.

"Oh, hey, you can actually see me," the feeder said. Its voice was still coming from the loudspeaker, which hardly seemed necessary anymore.

"And you can read minds," Lori said, still walking forward. "Messing with the loudspeaker, so maybe you do things with electricity, and that includes reading how the neurons in my brain fire?"

"I can't help people find true love unless I can read their desires," the feeder said, "and as a magical creature who travels the world helping people find love, that's totally something that it makes sense that I need to do, and wow you don't even believe that a little bit, and most of you just thinks that's a dumb idea because you know about feeders, but there's a tiny part of you that just thinks no magical love-creature would ever come to you, because you don't deserve anyone, and that is so tragic and sad that even though I was okay yes going to eat you before, feeling someone who is this down on herself makes me think that today, just this once, I should try to use my powers for good, and maybe in the process learn a valuable lesson—"

"Is there *anything*," Lori cut in, "coming from my brain that makes you think I am in any way believing this?"

"No, but that's all right," said the feeder, "because even though you're really actually pretty good at this whole not-believing-me thing, you are still coming closer, and that's all that matters, because all of this, the talk and the pheromones I'm pumping into the air and the hallucinatory lights and the mild manipulation of your nervous system to adjust what you see—"

"It's all a lure," Lori said, taking the last few steps toward the feeder.

"Right, that is supergood thinking for a human, but see once you're here, all I have to do is *this*—"

A tentacle snaked up and coiled around Lori's arm.

Lori smiled through the sudden pain of whatever venomous ichor stung her wrist. "Okay, but did you ever wonder what the perfect lure for one of *you things* would look like?"

Pretend you took that microbe on the plate, dabbed something interesting in front of it, and then, as it oozed forward in its own primitive way, pretend you bit down into the plate. Feel the glass crunch and crackle beneath your jaws along with the wriggling whispers of the little microbe who only now realizes what is happening to it, caught by an enemy it never saw coming because it came from a dimension for which the little microbe has no frame of reference. Pretend you are that enemy, no, not an enemy, that hunter, and that you are grinding the glass away as the juices of your maw begin to digest the still-struggling microbe that thrashes, speared on your jaws. Pretend you drag the microbe down into depths it cannot even imagine because the direction has no meaning for it, and that it will vanish forever from that little plate.

Pretend that this is how you feed.

The fangs came out of nowhere as they always did, spearing through the feeder as they clamped down. The loudspeakers shrieked and the tentacles flailed, but the great fangs, sprouting from nothing in an oblong elongated fashion that made Lori's eyes water to look at them, held firm, and after a few frantic wriggling moments, the tentacles went still.

"When you think about it," Lori said, "the perfect lure for one of you would be *something that looked human*, wouldn't it."

The jaws receded without losing hold of their prey, pulling up or away or somewhere that made them look as though they were getting farther away without actually moving backward. The feeder, still pinned, went with them.

In a moment Lori was alone on the dockyard, still massaging her stinging wrist. It was red and puffy where the tentacles had touched her. If she'd been a real person, her internal organs would probably be liquefying already, but she healed quickly from just about any injury, and attacks from the feeders themselves could barely scratch her.

And *that* was why, however nice Handler was in the little texts, Lori never made the mistake of thinking of it as a person.

"Hey, Tucker, good news," Lori said, hoping that maybe Tucker hadn't been listening to all of what Lori had been saying for the last little bit. "Your feeder is all taken care of." With the feeder itself gone, the residual evidence would slide out of this world as well, and once Lori and Handler had gotten paid, even Tucker would probably forget any of this had happened. "You'll want to have a team clean the area thoroughly in case there are traces of whatever toxins it was using, but most of the danger is over."

"I'm so very glad to hear it," said a low, smoky voice that was in no way Tucker's. "Tia Lake. Thank you so much for all your help."

"Oh," Lori said, connecting *Lake* to *Lake Foundation* in her head. "It's nice to meet you in person. Is Ms. Tucker—"

"This is hardly personal," said Lake with a little laugh. "What do we call you again?"

"You can . . . Angler," Lori said. "From Angler Consul—"

"But what is your first name?"

Lori's phone buzzed twice.

No kidding, she thought, and then realized that she was already opening her mouth to answer, and she thought of ten different names, but her mouth couldn't work the words.

Susan, Samantha, Sarah, Sally, Lee, Laura Laurie Lori Lori LoriLoriLori

Something in her twisted, and at last, pulling her phone from her pocket with her wrist still stinging, she said, "I'm not supposed to use my name," and that at least she could get out. "There are privacy concerns."

"Of course, dear, how very prudent," Lake said reassuringly. "Now, speaking of privacy, you asked about that container, the black one. Have you opened it?"

"No," Lori said, *but now I have to*, and her mouth opened like it wanted to say the words. She clapped her free hand over her lips and looked at her phone in desperation. Past all of the *No* texts that a double buzz from Handler signified, she saw a new note.

Handler: You can't lie to her?

"That's good, dear," Lake said. "In that case, we have nothing to worry about. The taxi should be there for you shortly."

"I hope you're satisfied with our services," Lori blurted on autopilot, because this was what she always said, and it was true even, "and if you ever run into any trouble like this in the future, please consider using Angler Consulting again."

"I will, dear, I absolutely will," said Lake, and Lori pulled her earpiece away, turned it off, and began typing furiously into her phone.

Lori: What is this?

Handler: No idea! Why can't you lie?

Lori: You have no idea?
Lori: YOU have no idea.

Handler: Kk, stay calm, don't freak out.

Lori: I am not freaking out. I am justifiably concerned.

Handler: All right, you can lie to me, at least. Good to know!

Lori: Did the jellyfish thing hit me with truth serum?

Handler: Nope. That was a sihuanaba. Your basic sexy-lure feeder.
Handler: Some people say it has a horse head, tho. Kinda makes you
    wonder.
Handler: We can figure out what's going on once you're out of here.

Lori left the pit where the feeder had been. She started walk-ing back toward the dock, where the taxi would be waiting. Her wrist was almost back to normal already, with just a few little red bumps to mark where the tentacle had grabbed her.

She saw the black shipping container.

There were a lot of things Lori didn't know. Most of them were things she didn't want to know, the little blessings still lurking in the shadows next to the pile of horrible awful things she *did* know.

Her phone buzzed.

If she looked down at it, she'd see whatever it was that Handler wanted her to know. An order, for example, like, *for the love of all that's holy, don't open the container, that's a terrible idea.*

Handler was always very nice to her. It told jokes and gave her friendly grief and reminded her when Ben needed to take his pills in the morning. It didn't hurt Lori at all.

But she bet if she'd asked those shells that had once been security guards, they'd have said that the sihuanaba was very nice to them, too.

Lori wasn't entirely sure she *could* do something Handler had told her not to do. She thought of her mouth working soundlessly, trying to talk to Lake, but nothing coming out, like her lips and tongue and vocal cords weren't even hers to begin with. Could Handler do that? If it did, would she even remember it later?

She didn't look at her phone.

She ran to the black cargo container, flipped the latch, and slid the bolt loose. The door opened with a low creak.

A handful of teenagers blinked at Lori from the darkness inside. They were all locked in restraints, more restraints than normal people would ever need, straitjackets and handcuffs and straps that kept them locked into their chairs.

The nearest one, a boy with light brown skin and dreadlocks and eyes that glittered in the dark of the shipping container, had somehow gotten part of one hand free from his restraints, although the rest of him was still strapped into his chair. The container wall behind him was dented. His fingers twitched as he saw her.

"Hi!" said the pretty blond girl behind him. "I'm Maya, it's great to meet you!"

"I'm not here," Lori said. She stepped over to dreadlocks boy, grabbed one of the straps, undid the latch, and pulled it free. "I wasn't here, I'm not here, you never saw me."

"Is she hypnotizing us," the blond girl named Maya asked another girl with a warm tan complexion and bright green hair, "or is she supposed to be invisible?" The girl with the green hair shrugged.

"Hey, Not-Here, I'm Shawn," said the white guy to her left with a little grin. He was pulling against his restraints. "If you could maybe undo my strap as well while you're not here . . . ?" From his voice, she thought he was from the South, maybe Georgia or the little bits of Florida that were still left.

Lori stepped over and undid the straps on his chair as well.

Dreadlocks boy was pulling himself free. She was already regretting this. Five teenagers—Maya, green-haired girl, dreadlocks boy, Shawn-from-Georgia-or-Florida, and a small, dark-skinned boy Lori thought might be Filipino—all in a shipping container at a site that already had a feeder and whatever was going on with Tia Lake.

"Okay, you can get yourself out the rest of the way," Lori said, and stepped back. "And help the others."

"I'm on it," Shawn said, still grinning. "Thanks for the not-help. Tapper, you pop Hawk, and I'll get the girls."

"I'm actually good," said Maya, and slid her fingers out from where the straps crisscrossed under her chin. "I'm flexible." She waved at Lori.

"Why did you not do that *earlier*?" the girl with the green hair demanded.

"Well, the door was latched shut from the other side, so . . . ?"

"I was never here, okay?" Lori said again.

Then she ran to the dock.

The taxi was already waiting for her when she got there. It was the same driver, and he smiled and helped her into the cab, *ma'am*ing her as he did.

Lori settled into her seat, smiled, and asked him to go. She didn't look at her phone. She didn't look back to the dockyard. She didn't look at anything.

"Yes, ma'am. She's aboard now," the driver said, and Lori froze.

The taxi exploded, a big greasy fireball that spat shards of metal and fiberglass into the water and across the dock, leaving only smoke and charred debris floating in the flaming wreckage.

Cold and clammy from Handler's pull, Lori watched the flames die on the water, now a hundred meters away, from the safety of the cargo containers.

Lori: Can she find me

Handler: Lot of dummy accts. Will take time.

Lori: She finds me she finds ben
Lori: How long

Handler: Hard to say.

Lori: How long

Handler: Three-ish days.

It was Monday morning.

Lori came around the corner of the black shipping container. The kids inside were still pulling free and helping each other.

"Hey," she said. "I have to destroy the Lake Foundation before Thursday, and I need your help."

02

MAYA

Maya had mostly slid out of the restraints when the pretty girl with the silky dark hair who'd opened the door for them came back, and she waved again. "Oh hi, I'm Maya. I'm introducing myself because you *weren't here* before," she said, and winked. "That's Tapper helping Hawk, who's been kind of in and out."

"I got electrocuted," Hawk muttered, groaning. "You all just got drugged."

"And Shawn is helping . . ." Maya paused and then took a good run at it. "Eeeyara?"

"Iara," said the girl with the dark red skin and the green hair. She'd said she was from Brazil, and Maya, who was from Nebraska, was still having trouble with the name. The accent was cute, though.

"Right, and that's Shawn helping Iara."

"I need your help," the girl who'd rescued them said again.

"And why do we care about what you need?" Tapper asked,

tearing the straps free from Hawk. Hawk began to untangle himself, still dizzy. "You were scared to stick your neck out when we
needed you, but now we drop everything—"

"Tapper!" Iara said sharply.

"I *did* help you, though," the girl said. "And now I have three
days before the Lake Foundation finds out who I am and comes
after me and my brother, so I need to take them down before
that."

"Okay," Maya said.

"Speak for yourself," Shawn said, still fiddling with Iara's
restraints. "What makes you think the rest of us can help?" He
shot Maya a look, which seemed really unfair, because they had
all been talking ever since they woke up, and they had all agreed
that they were in this together.

"Because Lake locked you up," the girl said, looking at all
of them. "She got suspicious when I asked about the container,
and she asked if I'd opened it. I took down a feeder out there,
and if Lake wanted you enough to kidnap you and lock you in a
shipping container . . ." She swallowed and her hands tightened
into fists. "I'm guessing you're not completely human."

"And you wouldn't be bringing it up if you were completely
human yourself," Tapper said, glaring at the girl. Now that they
weren't sitting in complete darkness like they had been ever
since they woke up, Maya realized that Tapper's default state
seemed to be glaring.

"Guys," said Hawk, and Tapper looked away from the girl and
grabbed hold of Hawk as he stumbled. "She's on our side. We
probably wanna chill and hug this out later."

"Deal." Shawn finished with Iara's restraints and slid them
free. "'Sides, taking down the Lake Foundation works for me."

"And me as well," Iara said, pushing the restraints aside
and flipping her wavy green hair back out of her face. "Let us

escape, and then destroy our enemies!" She slammed her hands down fiercely on the armrests of her chair.

The chair slid forward, and as the fabric of the straitjacket fell away, Maya realized it was a wheelchair.

"Oh, shoot," Maya said, "that is going to make it *super*hard for us to get away. Um, no offense."

"None taken," Iara said, and smiled, her lips curving wickedly on her heart-shaped face. "Get me to the water before their boats arrive, and I will show you my world."

"Boats?" Hawk asked, looking around.

"Wait," Maya said, "what does showing me your world mean? Was that like flirty or threatening or . . . because I'm okay with either, I mean obviously the first more—"

"Seriously?" Tapper said. "We're doing this right now?"

"Sadly, *alemā*, I only like men," Iara said.

"Someone said something about boats?" Hawk asked.

"See, that's perfect," Maya said, "because I only go for girls."

"Excellent!" Iara slapped the arm of her chair. "Divide and conquer. The women are yours, the men are mine, and the world falls before us!"

"What was it you said about boats?" Hawk asked, and then turned, stepped away from Tapper, and squinted out to the open water visible through the row of shipping containers. "Wait, hang on, I see 'em."

He took a couple of steps toward the water, and then stopped.

A moment later, a sharp whistling sound like a steaming tea-kettle zoomed in.

Then an explosion slammed Maya to the floor of the cargo container.

Amid the terrible cacophony of blinding light and roaring noise that shook the metal around them, Maya looked up, blinking. The girl who'd freed them was gone—not dead or anything, just *gone*—and most of the others were on the ground like Maya. Iara's chair was on its side, and Iara lay beside it, her green hair covering her face.

The only one still on his feet was the little guy, who stood in the middle of a bunch of scorched concrete. Little bits of flaming debris were scattered around him.

He looked back over his shoulder, completely unharmed as far as Maya could tell. "Dudes," he said, "I think maybe they know we're free."

HAWK

"Boat's coming in," Hawk called, and started walking toward the water. He was finally feeling steady again. Being electrocuted had messed up his balance.

It was a small speedboat, dark and unmarked, like a corporation would have. The pretty girl with the dark eyes had said they were after her. They'd gotten Hawk and the others, so that stood to reason.

Something flashed in the corner of his vision, and he blinked, and then looked down to see that the guys on the boat had arrived at the dock, and now they were shooting at him. Little bullets or casings or whatever it was that actually came out of guns? Bullets, right. Bullets were sprinkling on the ground around him. They were all messed up and flattened, and he almost bent down to check them out, but then he realized that if he did that, the bullets might zip past him and hit somebody.

"Oh yeah, they're shooting at us too," he added over his shoulder, "so if you've got, like, any powers that help with that . . ."

More bullets *bipp*ed off him. A couple dinged his head and made him flinch. He wondered what'd happen if they caught him in the eye. He probably didn't have, like, supereyes. That didn't make sense.

Of course, it wasn't like his throat was reinforced by a lot of muscle or bone either, and as a shot dinged his Adam's apple, all that happened was he started hiccupping, so maybe he should stop trying to make it all work by science.

He squinted, though. For safety.

There were three guys, all grown-ups and all white and wearing dark suits with ties. They were all pretty big and ripped, and they looked like when the guys on the football team dressed up for a game, big shoulders poured into business wear. Their guns were assault rifles, and apparently they held a lot of ammo in each clip, because they were still firing as Hawk came out into the main docking area.

"Dudes, be cool!" he yelled. The guys kept firing. He hiccupped again as bullets bounced off his throat.

"They're puppets!" yelled a girl's voice off to Hawk's right, and he turned to see the girl who'd freed them crouched on top of a stack of containers.

"Puppets?" Hawk looked back at them, hiccupped yet again. "Where are the strings?"

"Probably inside them!" she shouted back, and then ducked down as a bullet plinked off the container where she was crouched. Then she sucked in on herself really fast and was gone, and Hawk looked back at the guys with the guns, and there she was, unfolding out of nothing superfast behind one of them and slamming her elbow into the back of his head.

The guy fell, and the other two spun toward the girl, and *then* something whooshed past Hawk, and *another* guy fell with a sudden crack and a flash of light, and Tapper was standing over him with one fist extended, the air around him shimmering like hot pavement.

By now Hawk had finally reached the third guy, who turned toward Tapper. Hawk grabbed the gun, reached up, and punched the guy in the jaw.

The guy's head came off.

Hawk stumbled back. "Oh, dude, I didn't . . ."

There was a lot less blood than in the anime Hawk watched. Hardly any at all, in fact, which seemed unlikely. The head bounced back into the boat like a lopsided football, and something wriggled at the top of the headless corpse, and at first Hawk thought it was some kind of automatic movement of the spine or something like in the French Revolution when people got guillotined, and Hawk's stomach lurched like he was going to be sick.

It wasn't the spine, though. It was some kind of worm-snake thing, yellow and slick with slime, slithering out of the man's torso, and as Hawk tried not to throw up in front of Tapper and the cute girl, the thing slid into the water and vanished.

"S'messed up," Hawk said instead of puking, and he thought of when he was a little boy, and Nanay had told him and his brothers and sisters stories about the *aswang*, the ghouls that changed their shape and ate people, and she had always finished by hugging them all and telling them that monsters weren't real, and he really wanted his *nanay* right now.

"Puppets," the cute girl said, stomping hard on the throat of the guy she'd taken down. The guy didn't make any noise, but the thing *inside* him did, and then the guy's head split open like a chopped watermelon, and another worm-snake thing slipped out and flopped into the water. "They work the body from inside. Like the hand inside Kermit the Frog."

"That's . . ." Hawk hiccupped, almost lost it, and then finished with, "Those are Muppets, that's totally different."

"*That's* what bothers you about this?" Tapper glared at Hawk. "Pull yourself together. We aren't all bulletproof."

The guy Tapper had taken down shifted, and Hawk saw a worm-snake split the guy's head open. Then Tapper was there, a blur of motion striking down, and the worm-snake was crushed under his work boots, its head exploding in a spray of green slime.

"These weren't from the feeder that was here," said the girl who'd rescued them, whose name Hawk realized he still didn't know. "Those were shells, with no living human left. These are—"

"Stop! Shut up!" Tapper yelled. "What do I even call you? What are you?"

"Boat," she said, and pointed. "They knew they couldn't stop us with just one." Her voice was dead calm, as it had been since the fight started. It wasn't calm like she was a cool badass who fought sick monsters all the time, and this was no big deal. It was calm like she wasn't even paying attention, like she was an action figure and someone had pressed a button to make her say one of seven prerecorded phrases. "How did they catch you before?"

"Drugged my drink," Tapper said, "and I woke up tied too tight to get free."

"Oh yeah, I thought that tasted funny," Hawk said. "Didn't knock me out, though. I don't think I do poisons anymore." The water was bubbling near the dock.

"So that's when they electrocuted you?" Tapper asked.

"Yeah. Ran the current through a big fishing net," Hawk said as a big metal tube rose out of the bubbling water. "Hey, what do you think—"

The net exploded from the tube and covered them with a giant wave of black.

SHAWN

The giant net sprang out of the water and *fwomp*ed down over Hawk and Tapper and whoever the girl who'd rescued them was, and Shawn shook the last of the dizziness away and stumbled to his feet. It was time to tag in.

Wheelchair Girl—wait, no, *Iara*; Shawn felt like a jerk, because now he was just gonna think of her as Wheelchair Girl, and that sucked, because the accent had been hot for the hours they'd been sitting there talking before they'd gotten free, and she had *been* superhot before he had seen the wheelchair, and Shawn knew he shouldn't make it a thing—was crawling back toward her chair. She crawled in a weird way, hunching her legs together and sort of sliding.

"We gotta help!" Shawn yelled, and scooped her up. She was warm and soft and smelled good even after being stuck in a straitjacket for a long time, and her arms slid up and over his shoulders as he lifted her.

"Next time, ask first," she said, shaking her head. "Ears still ringing. Get me to the water."

He started running. He couldn't move at a blur like Tapper— or whatever it was the girl who'd rescued them did, if she was moving at all or teleporting or something—but he'd been strong even before the change, and now he could carry Wheelchair-Girl-no-wait-Iara like she was nothing. "You can swim?" he said between breaths.

"Watch and see." She shook the last of the dizziness away and gave him a wicked smile.

He was totally gonna get past the wheelchair thing.

Men were pulling themselves up onto the docks from the water, water dripping from their wetsuits. The net was moving around, with the people caught in it struggling, and then one of the men in the wetsuits pressed a button on his wristband, and the net crackled and sparked.

Shawn kept running. The guys in the wetsuits didn't have guns. Another boat was coming toward the dock, and the guys in the boat *did* have guns, and Shawn had figured out some cool tricks since the change, but he was pretty sure he didn't have anything that stopped bullets.

The guys in the wetsuits saw him as he came out onto the main dock. They had face masks and scuba gear that made it hard to see their expressions, but they were pointing his way.

"Throw me!" Iara shouted, and as Shawn adjusted her from carrying position to something like a shot-put position midstride, she unhooked her arms, and then Shawn launched her with all of his strength just as she pushed off him, and he had a moment to think that wow, she had a *fantastic* butt.

Then she torpedoed into one of the wetsuit guys, and both of them went into the water.

Shawn spun to the second wetsuit guy, who *did* in fact have a gun, some kind of weird, clunky toy-pistol-looking thing made from black plastic, and Shawn wasn't sure if it was a speargun or what, but he knew he didn't want it pointing at him, so as the wetsuit guy brought it up, Shawn lunged in, fingers tightened to a spear point.

His hand punched clean through wetsuit guy's chest and out the other side. He saw the man's eyes go blank behind his mask, and as Shawn yanked his arm back out, the man's mask ripped off, and some kind of horrible snake-worm slithered out and slid into the water.

Which was good, Shawn decided. It was definitely good. He slid the blood off his hand—not that there was much; whatever he did to make himself sharp made the blood sheet right off him. If wetsuit guy had a snake-worm inside him, he wasn't really a person, so Shawn wasn't a murderer, and that was good.

He heard the crack of gunfire and saw that the boat was drawing closer. After a second of staring like an idiot, he realized they were firing at him, and he dove to the ground beside the giant pile of netting.

"No, no, no." He needed to get into the water. A bullet spat off the concrete beside him, and he rolled away, behind the netting now.

The netting.

"Hang on!" Shawn shouted. "Get down!" He thought, *scissors, scissors, scissors,* as hard as he could, and then held his hands out like a karate expert doing a chop and sliced into the netting.

His hands sheared through the heavy rope like it was overcooked pasta, and he slashed it free, then hauled it apart with all of his strength.

Under the giant net, Tapper and Hawk crouched. Tapper was twitching. Hawk was blinking a bunch.

"I g-got el-l-lectrocuted ag-g-gain," Hawk said.

"Where's the girl?" Shawn asked. "The one who got us out?"

"She got out," came a voice from behind him, and Shawn turned to see her crouched by one of the containers. She didn't look good—she was pale, and her blouse and pants were wrinkled, but the weird part was her face. Normal girls freaked out when their nice clothes got messy, or they were too angry to worry about it, sometimes, but she was just . . . blank.

Then gunfire cracked again, and he forgot about Creepy Blank Lady and dove to the concrete. He peeked around the pile of netting to see if the guys in the boat were shooting at him.

They weren't. Their guns were pointed down into the water on one side.

A moment later Iara leaped from the water on the *other* side, punched one of the gunmen at the top of her arc, and dove cleanly back into the water like a kung-fu mermaid.

Shawn grinned. "Get them out!" he called back to Creepy Blank Lady. "I'm going in!"

He heard the cry behind him as he scrambled forward, but then he was in the water.

His element.

He sucked in a lungful of cool water. The shock of it always hit him like a jolt of adrenaline, the heavy coldness as he went from air to water, the taste of sea salt in the back of his throat. He thrust his arms out to either side and thought *wings* and pushed and surged through the water faster than any Olympic medalist.

There were more wetsuit guys under the water, holding on to a big machine with a propeller and a bunch of handholds and the tube where they'd shot the netting out. The water here was a dark blue, the wetsuit guys just shadows themselves, and they hadn't seen him yet.

He glided forward with another flap of his arms, then thought *spear point* and stabbed at the nearest man. His fingers punched through the guy's chest, and he flailed as blood clouded the water. Shawn tasted it and freaked out for a moment, kicking away as the man thrashed.

The second wetsuit guy turned and raised one of the toy guns, and there was a bubbling pop as something like a needle or a nail hissed past Shawn's shoulder with a little buzz of pain. Shawn shouted in surprise, surged forward, and stabbed the man through the chest.

This time he kicked off and out of the blood cloud before he tasted it.

He saw when the snake-worm ripped out of the dead guy. It moved fast in the water, as fast as Shawn, and Shawn stabbed at it on instinct, but the snake-worm curled around the thrust, and

Shawn felt its slimy skin around his wrist as it slipped away and wriggled down into the darkness below.

The heck with that. It was time for some answers.

Shawn made his arms into wings again and surged down after the thing that had used the wetsuit guy like a puppet. He stroked down, pulling himself into the dark water. It was deeper than it ought to have been this close to shore. That must be where the snake-worms lived, down in the dark water.

Up above, he saw splashing and the gray-blue silhouette of water rippling on the surface, and then he heard, "Wait!"

It was Iara, her voice cutting through the water with the perfect clarity of a bell. Shawn looked up and saw her shape in the splashing. She glided through the water even faster than he could, her muscular arms pulling her forward with each stroke.

"You take the ones on the surface!" Shawn called up. Unlike her perfect clarity, his voice burbled in the water like a normal person's, and he wasn't sure if she could understand him. Still, she was smart. She could figure it out. "I'm going after them!"

He flapped down into the darkness again, ignoring her cry. He'd lost the snake-worm he'd been trailing, but he could still sense the little bubbles of its wake, disturbances in the water that would probably have been invisible to him before but were now as clear as footprints. There were other bubbles too, big green ones floating up from the dark water below. Shawn wasn't sure where they were coming from.

The snake-worm's trail led down into the deep, though; maybe there were more of them down there.

He swam down, eyes straining. The blue-gray faded to washed-out black below, and he felt the water grow hot around him.

Then it moved, and green bubbles surged up all around him.

He thrust out blindly through the sudden heat and felt his hand hit something, and then something hit him.

He thought *spear point* and then *wings* and then *help help help no no help*.

As he tasted his own blood in the water, his scream came out as bubbles.

LORI

Lori's phone was buzzing almost constantly now. Lori hadn't looked at it.

Hawk and Tapper, the two boys on the ground in the pile of netting, still weren't moving. Shawn had dived into the water.

Lori had yelled at him to stop. He hadn't.

She wasn't sure why she had yelled.

Everything was cold and clammy. Nothing directly threatened Lori right now. She had seen something in the water. No. She had *felt* it, or Handler had felt it and Lori had felt it because of what Handler had felt, like your fingers imagining the heat of a hot stove because your eyes had seen that it was turned on. She had yelled for the boy not to go in. He had gone in anyway.

Buzz, buzz, buzz, went her phone.

Too many jumps in too short a time. The girl who couldn't take care of herself had let the monster save her and, as punishment, was now having to remember that she wasn't really a girl. She was part of the monster, and it was having trouble making her act real.

A bullet panged off a cargo container beside Lori. She looked at the boat with the two gunmen in it, but they were still shooting at the water where Iara, the girl with the green hair, was hiding.

She looked around.

Three gunmen in wetsuits had come around the corner.

Lori remembered the hole the feeder had made in the concrete, opening it up to the water below.

She was moving on instinct, sidestepping the gunman at the front and checking his gun with one hand even as her other fist jabbed into his throat. He stumbled, and she saw another gunman aiming at her and ducked down under the *first* gunman's gun to put his body between her and the others, then punched him in the crotch.

His head and chest spat blood as bullets ripped through him, clanging off the cargo containers over Lori's head, and Lori shoved the dead man into the other two.

She didn't need to fight. Handler would pull her again if she was in danger. She'd lose more of herself, and that would have bothered her before, but Lori didn't see why it mattered right now.

Still, it was what she did.

But there were still two of them, and they shoved the man they'd just shot to death aside and aimed at her with their pistols.

Then a section of the cargo container beside them came to life and wrapped itself around one of the men like a giant snake. The corrugated red steel—no, an arm, Lori realized, stretched out longer than any arm and twisted like a bendy action figure and somehow colored to match the pattern of the shipping container, but still with fingers at the end—choked the man and twisted his arm away from Lori. His gun went off pointing at the *other* man, who went down with his chest bloody, and then the man turned his gun back toward himself, shooting behind him. Lori heard screaming, and part of the shipping container fell off, and then Lori realized it was Maya, the corrugated pattern rippling back into the normal shape of the willowy blond girl holding the man in a chokehold.

He was trying to fire behind himself at her, and Lori stepped in, grabbed the gun hand, and punched him in the throat until he collapsed.

"Oh gosh oh gosh oh gosh, I wasn't trying to kill that first guy," Maya said. "I just saw them pointing at you and I wanted to help. I did a season of wrestling. You punched him in the throat. He's not human either, is he? I mean, not that we're not human." Maya smiled hopefully at Lori. "Mostly human? Ish?"

Lori's phone buzzed again. She took it out and looked at it.

Handler: RUN
Handler: NOW
Handler: They are trying to herd you toward the water.
Handler: It's in there and we are not ready to fight it yet.

"So should we help Iara and Shawn?" Maya asked. "Or . . . I brought her wheelchair, which, I don't know, it seemed like she wouldn't want to leave that behind."

Handler: Shawn is dead.

"What?" Maya said, and Lori realized that she'd said it aloud. "Did he like text you to tell you that? Should we share numbers?"

Handler: Lori. Lori, focus.
Handler: If it gets us, it will still finish tracking accounts.
Handler: IT WILL GO AFTER BEN.

It was like pins and needles as Lori came back to herself, and it hurt, like biting a sore on the inside of your cheek, all the anger and fear and frustration that make people *people* rushing back in at once.

Lori felt hands on her shoulders and realized she had stumbled. Maya was steadying her. "Are you okay? You got weird. Did I trigger you? Was it phone numbers, because I don't know why it'd be phone numbers and not like being shot at or whatever those snake-worm things are that just crawled out of those guys' heads, but I am totally not judging your trigger—"

"I'm Lori." Lori stood up straight and squeezed Maya's hands before pulling them away from her shoulders. "We need to run *now*, or we're all dead. Grab the wheelchair."

"On it!" Maya nodded brightly and looked down at the things slithering back toward the docks. "Oh yeah, you meant *literally* on both *now* and *run*."

Lori dashed back to the edge of the dock, where Hawk and Tapper were slowly getting back to their feet. "We're leaving," she said. "Can either of you drive a boat?"

"I can," came a voice from nearby, and Lori looked up to see Iara driving a now-empty boat. Her eyes were large, and her legs splayed out awkwardly in the chair, but her hands were steady on the wheel. "There's something in the water."

"Yes, there is," Lori said.

"It killed Shawn," Iara said. "I don't . . . I don't know what it is."

"I don't know what any of us are," Lori said. "Would you like to find out?"

"I have your chair," Maya added softly.

"Thank you." Iara swallowed as the boat bumped gently against the dock. "Let us get out of here, then. I wish to call my parents and go home."

03

LORI

Lori was mostly back to herself by the time they reached the downtown docks and abandoned their stolen boat. She looked at her phone to check the time. It was only a little past noon.

"Give me a minute," she said to the others, and pointed across the canal to a large water-level shop whose logo was a big friendly manta ray. "I'll meet you guys in there."

Without waiting for a reply, she stalked off, then dialed Ben's day care.

"Sandee Day Care, this is Maura," came the voice of an older lady. Maura was a genial woman who didn't give Lori grief when she had to bring Ben late after he missed the ferry.

"Hi, Maura, this is Lori, Ben's sister. I got a missed call?"

"Oh, hello, Lori. Let me give you to Mister Barkin," Maura said.

Argh, Lori thought. "Thanks," Lori said.

"Hello, Miss Fisher." Mister Barkin was a big man who, as far as Lori could tell, was pretty sure everyone was raising children wrong. "We've had some trouble with Ben today."

"I'm sorry to hear that." Lori kept her teeth ungritted. She was pretty sure Barkin could hear when she grit them. "What's wrong?"

"He's been very disruptive and has had a hard time following directions."

"Okay, so he's seven," Lori said, and immediately knew it was the wrong thing to say.

"When we invited Ben to share with us why he was so upset, he said that you had yelled at him this morning."

I am going to kill that little jerk, Lori thought. "Ben sometimes has trouble getting ready on time in the mornings," she said instead. "It's honestly a challenge for both of us, and I'm sure Ben read my . . ." Her phone buzzed, and she pulled it away to look.

Handler: . . . attempt to set a consistent schedule to help him develop a
    routine . . .

". . . attempt to set a schedule to develop a routine," Lori finished, "as being grumpy with him."

"Ben also said that you didn't give him his ADHD pill this morning," Barkin went on, and Lori winced and swore silently at the phone. "An important part of children's development is establishing a routine, including regular and appropriate medication."

"No, of course." Lori didn't care if he could hear the gritted teeth this time. "I completely understand. I was trying to get Ben out the door, and it completely slipped my mind. Since it's summer, we haven't been worrying about his medicine unless he's going on a field trip." This was true-ish.

"We at Sandee Day Care can't give any medication ourselves

without authorization, and if you don't think that you can commit to giving Ben his medication when he needs it—"

"If he's becoming disruptive without it, then of course, I'd be happy to see that he has it every morning," Lori added. "Ben's doctor wanted us to avoid overmedicating him, you understand." Because she'd had a lousy morning, she added, "Especially during the summer, the doctor really assumed he'd be getting enough exercise at day care that he wouldn't need medication. Does Sandee still have outdoor playtime? Because I've heard horror stories about those day cares that just put the kids in front of the TV all day."

After a thoughtful pause, during which Lori remembered why Mister Barkin made her nervous, he said, "We'll keep an eye on him this afternoon. Based on his behavior—"

"I'll be by in a little while to pick him up, anyway," Lori added. "My work has finished up early for the day. Thanks so much for calling. I really appreciate you keeping me up to date on how Ben is doing."

"We'll see you soon, Miss Fisher," Barkin said, and hung up on her.

Lori sighed, took a breath, and then dialed again. A moment later Jenn picked up. "Lemme guess."

"I'm sorry," Lori said. "Go without me."

"We were supposed to figure out a plan for which guy you were gonna get this year!"

Lori sighed and gently head-butted her phone. "I can't even manage a trip to the mall, Jenn. I think dating is going to be a stretch."

Her phone buzzed, and she glanced at it.

Handler: Or you could tell your friend the truth.
Handler: About your noninterest in guys, I mean. Not about us.

It wanted her to be honest. That was rich.

Lori glared, even as Jenn said, "Come on, Fisher. That stuff might fly freshman and sophomore year, but it's time to make a play."

"I know. I'll, um . . . I don't know. This consult might run a couple of days. I'm sorry."

"Okay, Career Woman, but if I get you something, will you try it on?"

Lori found herself smiling despite everything. "Sure."

"Oooh, this could work. I can pick out something so much hotter than anything I'd've been able to talk you into buying in person!"

"Good-*bye*, Jenn," Lori said, and hung up and went inside PortManta, smiling a little bit now.

Part coffee shop, part juice bar, and part general hangout, Port-Manta was where Lori spent a lot of her summer afternoons when Handler didn't have a job for her. The walls were painted in various eye-searing pastels, and the manta-ray logo smiled and waved in old photographs to which it had been digitally added. Sometimes she was there with Jenn, gossiping about classmates and checking out new bands on their phones over PortManta's Wi-Fi. Other times she would hang out on her own and just enjoy the silence.

Anna, a tiny little red-haired girl with a face full of freckles, smiled from behind the register as Lori came in. "Hey, Lori! Nice outfit. Work day, huh?"

"Yep. Early one."

"Be glad you don't work here," Anna said, rolling her eyes. "Six a.m. opening. You want your usual?"

"Please." Lori used her phone to pay while Anna rang in the fruit smoothie order. "Hey, did a new group come in? One skinny black guy with locks, one short guy, pretty blond girl, and a green-haired girl in a wheelchair?"

"*Pretty* blond girl?" Anna asked, and grinned at her.

"Um . . ." Lori felt herself starting to blush, and Anna laughed out loud.

"You probably could have led with the green-haired girl in a wheelchair," Anna said, and pointed at the service elevator. "They're on the roof. Or at least most of them are. The green-haired girl came back down and said she'd be right back."

"Thanks. Guess there aren't too many wheelchair users here in Santa Dymphna." Lori glanced outside. "The city's still a few years away from having access ramps everywhere after the water rose."

"Guess it was just one of those things," Anna said without missing a beat, and Lori winced. She hadn't meant to trigger it that time. She hated doing it to people she liked. It made them seem like *things*, which was unfair to them. She was the weird one, after all.

A moment later Lori's juice came up. She grabbed it and shoved a straw in. "Have a good one," she said to the now-silent Anna, and went up to the roof to get some answers.

IARA

Iara rolled into the electronics store and smiled at the balding shopkeeper who looked down at her with undisguised surprise.

"Don't get a lot of handicapped in Santa Dymphna," he said thoughtfully.

"The sidewalks are very well maintained," Iara said, still smiling, because he was an old man, and she had been brought up to respect her elders.

"Gotta be hard getting into the boats and all," the shopkeeper added. "Can you swim?"

"Yes," Iara said, still keeping the smile. "I wished to buy a new phone."

"And you can use the phones all right?" the shopkeeper asked doubtfully.

The shopkeeper was now beginning to vex her, but as he was one of the innocents that she would be protecting in her new role as Fighter of Eel Monsters, Iara simply gave a tiny sigh and said, "Unless you operate them with your feet." As she said the words, she added a tiny little *click* from the back of her throat.

The shopkeeper looked at her feet. "Your feet don't look different," he said, and his gaze trailed up her legs to the hem of the formfitting black skirt she wore.

"I am pleased that you noticed," Iara said, and wheeled herself a few meters forward and *clicked* again, looking back at the shopkeeper as she did.

She shut her eyes and let out a long breath.

"Are you all right?" the shopkeeper demanded, coming around the counter to her. "Listen, I can call a doctor if you need help."

"I need a phone," she said, eyes still closed.

She felt the words bounce off him, sensed the vibration and the echoes forming a pattern that her mind turned into the shape of the room. Past that—

It was not sight, although that was how her mind processed this new sense. Instead, it was as though her sense of balance, the tiny little reactions to movement that let her body know when she was upside down or leaning to the left, had been made a thousand times more sensitive and then somehow tangled up with her sense of touch. She could feel the electric hum of the machines in the shop, the laptops and tablets and phones and fitness trackers, all of them buzzing against her skin. She could feel the wires running through the walls, power cables and Internet lines and security feeds.

She could feel the electromagnetic field buzzing around the ignorant and prejudiced shopkeeper's body, and with her two little triangulating *clicks*, she had a picture of his brain.

"You have five new phones for me, already paid for," she said, and hummed underneath the words, a subsonic vibration that took her words and carried them through the air and into the shopkeeper's brain. The right frequency, keyed to the shopkeeper's distance from her and his own natural electric field, kicked it into a different part of his brain.

With that little hum, Iara turned it from a thing he was *hearing* into a thing he was *remembering*.

Her words, no matter how beautifully phrased, could not create a memory from whole cloth, but she didn't really have to. The human mind, Iara had learned, liked to correct errors. Given a false positive for a memory of her buying the phones, the shopkeeper's mind was busily cobbling one together from the view he had of her now and a thousand past transactions.

"Oh, right!" the shopkeeper said. "Just be a minute. Sorry, I should have boxed them up for you earlier."

It was not the power Iara would have asked for, but then, most of her heroes had been the same way. Peter Parker had wished for popularity, not spider powers, but fate had given him what he had *needed*, not what he had *wanted*, and she assumed that the same was true for her. She might have wished for Captain Marvel, but she *got* Professor X.

Iara smiled as he scanned the phones, bagged them, and passed them down to her. "Thank you."

"You know how to use them?" he asked. Bless him, he sounded honestly concerned.

She smiled and patted the bag. "Since I cannot walk, I have had much time to get very good with electronics."

She wheeled out of the shop and back to the juice bar with the manta ray logo.

∷ ∷ ∷

HAWK

"So you can like Jedi mind meld people?" Hawk asked as he sipped his strawberry-acai-matcha smoothie with soy protein and watched his new phone sync up his apps. They'd all gotten each others' contact information when Iara had passed out the phones, and all that was left now was to download old app info over PortManta's Wi-Fi.

"Mind *trick*," Tapper muttered, more to himself than Hawk. Whatever he was drinking had many shots of espresso in it. The guy's jeans and T-shirt had dried off really fast too, which Hawk thought might be because Tapper was always kind of vibrating.

"Not quite," Iara said, blushing prettily and running slender fingers through her wavy green hair. "I only plant memories. I cannot force them to do anything."

"Jedi mind trick, Vulcan mind meld, that's *basic* information . . ." Tapper thumbed his phone, glaring intently at the glowing screen.

"And you can swim," Maya added. "You and Shawn were really good swimmers."

"Were," Tapper muttered. "We even sure he's dead? All we have is Lori's word on that."

"And mine," Iara said, and looked away and sipped the apple-berry smoothie she had said reminded her of some kind of soda they had back in Brazil. She had really pretty lips, and Hawk realized he was staring at them like a doofus and looked away instead.

They were up on the roof, which had a little patio. Hawk had visited family on the cluster of high-rise islands that was all that was left of Houston after the water rose, and they'd had the same kind of thing there. No room to grow out, so people grew up instead. PortManta had chairs and tables, all made from the same grayish-pink plastic that came from miracoral oil.

Across the canal, Hawk saw little gardens, barbecues, and even tents made from plastic sheeting. In Santa Dymphna, the poor moved up, not down. A narrow woven-plastic footbridge connected PortManta's rooftop to the building next door. The bridge swayed in the breeze. The Santa Dymphna locals walked across them without a second thought, but they creeped Hawk out. Partly the height, even though being indestructible now probably shouldn't make that a thing, and partly the way the braided ropes of gray-pink plastic looked like a spider's webbing.

"What happened to him?" Hawk asked. "Iara, you saw it?"

"I heard it," Iara said, and put her drink down. "I do not know. I could not hear its shape, but it was very large."

"*How* very large?" Tapper asked.

"Larger than the Hulk," Iara said thoughtfully, "but smaller than Galactus." She grimaced. "Shawn had no chance."

Tapper grunted. "Locked in a stupid crate with all of you, and now one of us is dead, and we still don't know what's going on."

"He helped save us," Iara said, lowering her eyes. "He carried me."

"We'll make it right," Hawk said, and sipped his smoothie. "After we figure this out, we'll make it right."

"Hawk?" Lori asked, and Hawk looked over at her. "It was your turn." She was apparently only sixteen, like him? She'd looked older in her nice blouse and slacks. She was pacing around the edge of the table while the rest of them sat. Iara looked comfortable in her wheelchair, Maya was kind of splayed sideways across the chair like it was a very small resting couch, and Tapper was hunched over like he'd rather be anywhere else.

"Turn?" he asked, and saw that Lori looked older when she glared. She could probably use a smoothie. Something chill, anyway.

"We were sharing our stories of how we all ended up in the cargo container," Maya said, "like how I got a scholarship from the Lake Foundation, and then when I came out here, I got drugged during my interview and then woke up in the cargo container." She sipped her smoothie, which was only technically a smoothie instead of a chocolate shake because she'd let them throw in some whey protein. "That's actually pretty much my whole story."

"Probably call it a Force nerve pinch . . ." Tapper glared at his phone. "Aw, that is some garbage."

"Well, I mean, I was giving the TL;DR version," Maya said, "like, I mean, also they asked about doing wrestling and football and swim team and what I thought about rising sea levels and a time in my life where I had to overcome adversity, but I thought the part where my drink tasted funny and then I could taste my own happiness and then I lay down under the table to hug the floor was the part we cared about . . ."

"Not that." Tapper waved his phone. "TidePool suspended my posting privileges again. Said my account is locked."

Iara raised an eyebrow. "Do you believe it is tied to what happened to us?"

"I don't think so," Maya said. "I just reposted a kitten video!"

Hawk had just finished installing the TidePool app on his phone. "Mine's okay too." He reached over for Tapper's phone, and the other guy jerked his hand back faster than Hawk could follow, then glared and flipped his screen around so that Hawk could see. "The following post was flagged as . . ." He squinted at the quoted post. "Oh, dude, you can't write that! That's somebody's mom!"

"Somebody's mom should've raised a guy with smarter opinions about whether anime is better subbed or dubbed," Tapper said grimly.

"So they *haven't* locked your social media accounts," Lori said. She hadn't looked at her own phone. "That's something. So, Hawk?"

Hawk grinned at her. "Yeah?"

She did not grin back. "Your story. About ending up in the cargo container."

"Oh, right, yeah. So it's basically same as Maya's. I've lived in Austin for about eighteen months—after the water rose and Houston was underwater, the military moved their big base there, and my dad got transferred."

"Where are you from originally?" Iara asked, taking another sip of her drink.

"Born on a base in the Philippines," Hawk said, "but we moved around a lot, but because of the navy moving my dad around, I've lived in pretty much every US state that has a naval base."

"You can't be Filipino," Tapper cut in. "Filipino guys are big. Like the Rock."

"The Rock is Samoan," Iara said. "He did a Samoan dance for his grandmother out of respect on her birthday."

"Oh yeah, I remember that!" Maya said, tapping on her phone. "I reposted the picture and everything, and I mean, I don't do guys, but that grin plus him doing it for his nana, that was hot."

"Superhot," Iara added. *"Gostoso."*

"Right? Anyway, Filipino guys are like tiny." Maya looked over at Hawk. "Wait, sorry, no offense!"

"My feelings are also mostly invulnerable," Hawk said, grinning back at her, because at five foot three, he couldn't exactly argue about it, and also she might not go for guys, but she was still a very cute blond girl.

"And *then*?" Lori asked Hawk, and Hawk almost asked *and then what?* and then saw the look in Lori's eyes and realized that she might actually kill him and remembered what they'd been talking about.

"*And then* it was the same as Maya's story, with a scholarship offer from the Lake Foundation. I flew out and did the questions and all. The poison didn't work on me, so they used a net and then hit me with a stun gun or something." Hawk shrugged. "That's it."

Lori frowned. "Tapper?"

"Hang on, I'm making a new account." The guy's thumbs were moving faster than Hawk had ever seen anyone's thumbs move. He hadn't even known the phone could keep up.

"You know, you can unlock your account if you apologize and remove the offending post," Maya said.

"I will delete that post when a dubbed anime carries the same level of story and voice performance as a sub," Tapper said, thumbs blurring, "which will be never."

"What about *Avatar: The Last Airbender*?" Maya asked. "That was pretty good."

"That wasn't even—" Tapper stopped as his phone made a little click, and then he sat back slowly, leaving his phone on the table in front of him. The screen had a long crack running along the bottom right-hand corner. "I'm not talking to you. I do not acknowledge your opinions." He looked up at Lori. "Same story, 'cept I'm from Vegas." He gulped down his espresso-whatever-it-was.

"Dude, do you really need more caffeine?" Hawk asked.

"Bite me, Pint-Size."

"My story is also similar," Iara said. "The Lake Foundation said the scholarship was for international students with disabilities."

"And they flew you all out here, to Santa Dymphna," Lori said, tapping her phone on her leg as she thought. "And drugged you." Her phone buzzed, and she glanced at it. "Hm. But they didn't drug you right away. They interviewed you." She looked at Hawk. "Did they do anything to you first? A medical procedure? Something that could've given you . . ." She paused, shook her head.

"Our superpowers?" Iara asked.

"They're *not* superpowers," Tapper snapped. "They're mutations."

"The X-Men gain superpowers *through* mutation," Iara pointed out, "unless you believe that our origin is tied to super-science, like the Flash or Spider-Man." She smiled. "Or unless you believe we are all children of Krypton or Asgard."

"Or Tír na nÓg, or however you say it with the accents and stuff," Maya said. "That's where fae come from, and they sometimes swap babies with humans, so I think we're maybe changelings."

"You also think *Princess Mononoke* was better with Claire Danes," Tapper muttered. "You've forfeited the right to an opinion."

"I was kind of hoping we were angels," Hawk said, and he said it quietly, just in case it sounded really dumb once it came out of his head, but Tapper was still ranting about anime, or possibly manga now, and nobody caught it.

"Regardless of what they are," Lori snapped, "none of you . . ." She paused. "None of *us* are normal. Did the people at the Lake Foundation do something to you all that made you like this?"

"No. My powers came almost a year ago," Iara said. "I do not know why. Nothing happened that would mark it. One day my senses were stronger, and while my legs were no different, my arms could pull me through the water faster than ever before."

"So they didn't give you powers," Lori said. "Or at least not then. Why not drug you as soon as you arrived, then? Why the interview?"

"They had to be sure," Iara said softly.

"Like about a time when I faced adversity?" Maya asked.

"It's obvious." Tapper finished his drink. "Their questions were to confirm that we had powers, that we were the right targets."

"Because I just made up a thing about stealing bread to save my starving family," Maya added, "and then turning myself in to save an innocent man my parole officer mistook for me, and I'm not positive, but I *think* I got that from a movie."

"Could you . . ." Tapper placed his hands on the armrests of the chair. Hawk saw that the guy's fingers were tapping a furious little rhythm on the plastic. "Could you *please* stop talking?"

"Tapper, do not be rude," Iara said, and then smiled at Hawk. "What questions did they ask you?"

"Same as you guys, I guess." Hawk sipped his smoothie and thought. It had been yesterday, but yesterday was a kidnapping and several weird monsters ago. "Influences, what I wanted to be when I grew up, what Maya said about adversity . . . ?"

Maya's hand shot up, and she fidgeted in her seat.

Lori sighed. "Yes, Maya?"

Maya looked over at Tapper, who rolled his eyes and waved at her to go. "Plus sea levels."

"Hunh." Hawk nodded at the blond girl. "Yeah, they asked me that too."

"Why they rose," Tapper added. "Why all the coasts were underwater now."

Lori was standing very still. "And what did all of you say?" she asked quietly.

"I said I thought it was global warming," Hawk said.

"Ah yes, I suggested soil erosion." Iara sipped her smoothie.

"That's stupid." Tapper shook his head. "Neither of those would account for the sea level rising this much in just a few years. I told them it had to be a chemical attack."

"I said that I guessed it was just one of those things," Maya said, "right? Because that's what everyone says whenever I ask about it, so I thought that was what I was supposed to say, but then the interview lady got disappointed, so I added some stuff about how it could be the same crustal displacement that sank Atlantis, and she seemed happier."

"Maya's right," Hawk said.

"What? No." Tapper glared. "Crustal displacement is pseudo-science—"

"About that being what everyone says," Lori said. She stepped toward them, and Hawk hadn't realized until then how she'd put herself a little ways apart from the group. "*Guess it was just one of those things*. Those exact words, every time, no matter who it is."

"Or how many times you ask," Iara added.

"Their eyes always stop moving too," Tapper said, fingers clicking a staccato rhythm on the plastic. "It's like they go blank. Like they were programmed." He pointed at Iara. "Like one of the Girl from Ipanema's Jedi mind melds shoved the answer into their brain."

"I thought it was a Jedi mind *trick*," Maya said. Tapper glared at her.

"That's what the feeders—the things I hunt—that's what they do," Lori said, frowning. "They change people's minds, and people act like that when their mind hits something artificial that the feeder put in. But none of *you* acted like that. You showed them you weren't . . ."

"Controlled?" Iara asked.

Lori nodded. "That's when they decided to take you."

Hawk's phone chirped, and he looked down at it, then let out a big sigh, tension he hadn't known he'd been carrying melting from his body. "It's finally hooked up to the voice lines," he said, and began dialing. "My parents can get us, and then we can go to the cops—"

"What?" Lori said, seeming more alarmed than pleased.

"Do you think the police will be able to deal with creatures like the eels?" Iara asked.

"Dunno," Hawk said, "but my dad's military. Maybe they've heard of these things."

He heard the phone ring, and a moment later, his mother picked up. "Hello?"

"Mom," Hawk said, and realized as he said it that she must have been wondering where he'd been for most of a day. He pictured her calling the Lake Foundation and the hotel frantically, worried out of her mind. "Mom, I'm sorry, it's me, they got me, but I got free—"

"Oh, hello, dear," his mother said. "I hope you're having a good time at the Lake Foundation."

"No, Mom, I'm not." Hawk found himself fumbling for the words. "They're, like, bad guys. They're trying to do experiments or something on us . . ."

"I hope you're having a good time at the Lake Foundation," his mother said again.

Hawk's mouth worked for a moment, but nothing came out. He looked over to see the others staring at him sadly. "M-mom?"

"I hope you're having a good time at the Lake Foundation."

"I'm . . . yeah." Hawk shut his eyes. "I'll see you soon." He hung up the phone and looked at Lori.

"I'm so sorry," she said, and he blinked and shook his head.

"Can I get her back? Like . . ." He gripped the arm of his chair. "Like if something is messing with her head, and we kill it, she's okay, right?"

"It's impossible to . . ." Lori's phone buzzed, and she glanced down at it. "Yes," she said. "Yes, if it's one of those eels, and we get it out of her soon, she should be fine."

Hawk looked over as Tapper said, "Mom?" and realized he was calling his family as well. "Mom, it's me. If you were worried about . . . No. No, yeah, I'm having a good time. I am. I'll call you back." He hung up, scowling at the ground, and shook his head.

"What are these things?" Hawk grimaced, and the chair squeaked. He looked down and saw that the plastic had curled in where he'd gripped it too hard. "The eels, the feeders, whatever you call them?" He looked at Lori, realized he was almost shouting but didn't care. "Whatever killed Shawn? How do they do this to people's minds?"

"I don't . . ." Lori looked down at her phone like she was waiting for a text. "It's hard to explain. But maybe I can show you." She looked around at all of them. "If you want to know what they are, I know something that can sort of explain it."

"Not like we have anywhere else to go," Tapper muttered. "Blondie, Ipanema, you gonna call home?"

"I do not wish to hear that my family has been affected by these creatures," Iara said grimly.

"My parents aren't, uh . . ." Maya shook her head. "If they got yours, they probably got mine, right?"

"Right." Hawk shoved himself to his feet. "If you've got something to show us, show us."

IARA

Lori took them out of PortManta and along the sidewalk. It was busy at this time of day, and people bumped into Iara's wheelchair as she rolled along with the group.

No one ever bumped into Professor X's chair in the comic

books. Sometimes he even had a chair that levitated. She would not have minded that.

She grimaced as a man jostled her, and then smiled as Hawk moved him out of the way with a little "Scuse me."

"Oh, sorry," the man who'd bumped into her chair muttered, and went back to looking at his phone.

"Is it always this bad?" Hawk asked her.

"It is an annoyance," Iara said. "At least here in Santa Dymphna, they apologize."

"Where are you from in Brazil?" Hawk asked. "Rio, São Paulo?"

"Rio," Iara said, and smiled at him. "I do not know many Americans who could name more than one city in Brasil."

"The navy sent my dad all over the world to help with relief efforts after the water rose," Hawk said. "When we weren't with him, I liked to read up on wherever he was."

"So many areas flooded." Iara loved to swim in the rivers, but some of her friends had swum in the lakes that had once been parts of the city. They liked the clear water and the glow of the miracoral, but to her, it had seemed like swimming over a grave-yard, looking down at the drowned buildings below. "How could the world forget? Or not notice?"

"No idea," Hawk said. "Guess Lori's gonna show us." He looked up ahead, and Iara saw that Lori and the others were heading up a ramp that led to an overpass made from the gray plastic of the miracoral. "Hey, you need a push?"

Iara could push herself, but Hawk had a nice smile, small and a little uncertain but honest, and Iara smiled back and shrugged her shoulders and said, "Well, if someone with superstrength wishes to *volunteer* . . ." and then sat back contentedly in her chair as the nice boy pushed her up the ramp.

They headed up and over the canal, and Iara pretended not to notice Hawk glancing down anxiously as they crossed the bridge, because he was being chivalrous. On the far side, Lori and the others headed down a ramp. Iara reached up gently behind her and said, "I have it from here." Looking back over her shoulder and up at Hawk from under her lashes, she added, "But I am *most* grateful." He flushed and stammered a bit, and Iara grinned as she wheeled down the ramp, letting herself whoosh past Lori and Maya and Tapper and catching a breathless laugh in her throat as her chair bounced at the bottom of the ramp. It likely looked uncontrolled to the others, but compared to the streets of Rio, this was nothing.

Lori had taken them to a large plaza. A sign guiding tourists read REEF SQUARE. One side of the square was a dock for ferries and personal boats that bobbed safely behind shiny white railings. The other three sides were high-end stores, glittering in the pale late-summer sun that was the best they were able to get this far north.

In the center of Reef Square, behind a little waist-high railing . . . Iara stared.

At first her eyes refused to make sense of it, and she shook her head to clear a sudden dizziness as she looked at the mass of metal. A pyramid of steel that shone with a different light, or no, a cone, no, a . . . In annoyance, she shut her eyes and *clicked*, and felt the echo, and when she opened them again, she could make sense of it.

It was a train car, or part of one. It had been whole once, a local line that carried people around this city. But something had caught it, and now half of it was not simply *gone* but *going*, stretched like taffy and pulled to a tapering point of infinite thinness, so that the overall shape was of a pyramid lying on its side.

"Will it ever disappear?" Iara asked.

"It's been like this ever since the water rose," Lori said. "Never changes."

"What is . . . I can't . . ." Hawk rubbed his eyes. "Why's the corner all red and stuff?"

"It's not," Tapper snapped. "That end is being pulled somewhere else. The light waves bouncing off it are pulled too. They take longer to reach you, and the frequency—"

"Dude, I just got a solid A-minus in physics," Hawk said. "I know what a Doppler shift is."

"Is that the one where a trumpet player on a train sounds one way coming toward you and another way going away?" Maya asked.

"Yyyysorta," Hawk said as Tapper snorted and shook his head. "I just didn't expect to see it, you know, right *here*."

"Walk around it," Lori said quietly. "It looks that way from every side."

"That can't be right," Hawk said, starting to walk. "If you go to the other side, it should be blue, because it's coming toward . . . hunh."

"It's being pulled away from us from every angle," Tapper said impatiently, "because it's being pulled into another dimension."

Iara cocked her head and wheeled forward, thinking about that.

"So, like, space?" Hawk asked.

"No," said Tapper.

"Sort of," Lori said. "That's what the feeders are. They come from someplace we can't understand, someplace outside of the universe as we know it."

"Someplace *wrong*," Tapper added.

"But how could this be in plain sight, and the world not alarmed?" Iara demanded. "This is proof of a world beyond our own, of dangers we must fight!"

Lori gestured, and Iara followed it. A mother wheeled her daughter past in a stroller. Behind them, two young men laughed at a joke together, holding hands and sharing a pair of earbuds. An older man in khakis and a button-up shirt talked in annoyance into a headset microphone, gesturing angrily with a croissant held in one hand and a cup of coffee in the other.

None of them looked at the train being pulled into a place that could not be.

"Some of it might be on purpose," Lori said, walking toward the train car. Iara wheeled along beside her. "Some feeders can affect people's minds. But I think we . . ." She grimaced. "I think the feeders are just too *different* for this world, and so sometimes, when a big one changes things, the world just sort of flops into a new shape around whatever they do, and then the whole universe tries to pretend nothing happened."

"People are good at seeing what they expect to see," Maya said from beside them, and then added, "except who put up the railing?"

Iara looked over at the blond girl in surprise. "Excellent question, Maya."

"There's a plaque." Hawk stepped to the little square of metal on the ground before the railing. "*Invisible Changes:* An art piece donated by the Lake Foundation."

"Like they weren't creepy enough *before* they drugged and kidnapped us," Tapper said, glaring at the plaque.

"And put monsters inside our families." Iara's fingers ached, and she realized she was clenching the armrests of her wheelchair too hard.

"This is what feeders are," Lori said. "This is what I hunt and kill, and this is what they do to the world, what they'll do to people if we don't stop them. They will destroy it and kill people, and no one will ever even realize what they've done."

"Then we will stop them," Iara declared. "Even if no one thanks us, even if no one but us can see what has gone wrong in this world, we will fight—"

"Hey," Maya said suddenly, "those two people can see it."

Everyone stopped and looked where Maya gestured. A little ways away, on the other side of the train car, an old man stood looking at the train car, with a younger man behind him, arms draped over the old man's shoulders.

The old man's lips were moving, and Iara focused and listened as only she could.

"What made the water rise?" the young man was saying.

"Guess it was just one of those things," the old man murmured.

And again, "What made the water rise?"

"Guess it was just one of those things."

And still again, "What made the water rise?"

"Guess it was just one of those things," the old man repeated, and Iara realized that the arms draped over his shoulders ended in frilly little claws.

MAYA

"It's a feeder," Lori said sharply.

Maya wasn't sure what she'd been expecting, but it wasn't for Iara to suddenly wheel forward with a yell of, "For humanity!"

She was maybe halfway to the old man and the feeder when a whoosh of air zipped past her, and then Tapper was by the old man and the feeder, and the feeder was falling away from the old man, who looked . . . wet or something? His clothes were glistening, and there was something around him that she hadn't seen before, a bubble that drew back toward the feeder as the man fell away from it.

Tapper's arms were a blur, and the feeder sort of danced in place. Maya realized a moment later that Tapper was hitting it a whole bunch of times really quickly. "Where am I supposed to hit it?" he shouted.

"Head usually works!" Hawk yelled back. He and Iara were almost to the creature.

"It doesn't *have* a head!" Tapper shouted, and Maya, who was still beside Lori, blinked and cocked her head, because, well, the feeder did *seem* to have a head.

"He can see it," Lori murmured, and then it clicked for Maya, that if she could see the train car going down a black hole but normal people couldn't, maybe Tapper could see something the rest of them couldn't, and Maya squinted as she jogged forward, trying to let it come to her like one of those 3-D-staring things she had never been able to make work.

The feeder looked like a normal man, pale and with brown hair, wearing a white dress shirt and a brown suit that hung on him loosely, with baggy pant legs and flowing sleeves. And then Maya thought, *It doesn't have a head*, because that was what Tapper had said, and let her eyes unfocus—

five brown limbs splayed out in all directions from a white maw in the center of the body, and on the underside of the limbs, little wriggling spines, and it curled forward even as Tapper kept punching, the spines grabbing hold

And Maya saw the normal-looking man fall onto Tapper, who shouted and yelled as the man hugged him with both arms and one leg, slowly but unstoppably.

At least, it seemed unstoppable until Hawk got there, grabbed ahold of the feeder, and then tore one of its arms off.

"Hey," said the feeder, "what made the water rise?" The arm Hawk had torn off flopped on the ground.

"Shut up!" Tapper shouted.

"What made the water rise?" the feeder asked again. "Do you know? Think about it."

"Get off of him!" Hawk added, and tore off another arm. It flopped on the ground next to the first one.

"This usually works," said the feeder. "Look at the train car. Look at it and think about the water rising."

"Ow!" Tapper yelled. "It's got something on it, acid or something!" He was a blur of motion under the feeder, and that same bubble of wetness that Maya had seen before around the old man was forming around Tapper now.

Maya looked at the feeder. Iara had reached it now and was punching one of the arms on the ground, which kept moving and was trying to grab her wheelchair.

Lori was there as well. She looked like she was about to grab it, but then she stopped and flinched, looking anxious. "What do I do?" she yelled.

"Hey, guys!" Maya called. "I think it's a starfish!"

In the sudden silence, the feeder added, "Okay, but have you thought about what made the water rise?"

"Like *Starro*?" Iara yelled.

Maya had no idea who Starro was. "I think more like the one on *SpongeBob*!" She ran forward. "Look, it doesn't have a head, and its arms still work if they're torn off, and when I went to the aquarium they talked about how starfish find stuff that can't move, and then they grab it and, um, shoot out their stomachs and digest stuff and then suck it into them."

"It's *digesting* me?" Tapper yelled. "Get it off!" He blurred *harder*.

"Hang on!" Wincing, Lori worked her hands in toward the

watery fluid that bubbled around Tapper. "I think I've got it. Hawk, *pull!*"

Lori pulled one way, hugging the water around her, and Hawk pulled another way, wrenching back on the main body of the creature, and Tapper whooshed out and was suddenly standing next to Maya, his clothes stained and in some places eaten through.

With a horrible *splortch* noise, the feeder came apart, the watery guts ripping away in one direction and the body going in another, and Lori and Tapper both flung away the parts they were holding.

"You tasted different," said the body from the ground. "You're from home. That's why thinking about the water didn't work. I forgot . . . how . . . delish . . ."

Then it melted away, hissing into a stain on the ground. All of it, all at once, seemed to just sort of give up on existing, and it flickered like it was falling away even though it was already on the ground, and then all the different pieces were gone.

"Touchdown, monster hunters! Are you okay?" Maya asked Tapper. He was still blurry, and she realized it was because he was moving fast.

"Had to get the acid off me," he said. "It hurts."

"It even hurts me," Hawk said, wiping his hands on his pants, "and I'm kind of indestructible. Lori, you all right?"

"Yeah." She held up her hands, which were unmarked. "I'm mostly immune to things like that. Sorry, Tapper. I couldn't get it without . . . The way I kill them would have hurt you, too."

"Yeah, well." Tapper sniffed. "Good thing Blondie was there to save my butt with *SpongeBob*."

"Indeed," said Iara, and Maya looked over to see that she was smiling broadly. "Now, shall we go fight Lake and banish her from our dimension as well?"

Maya looked down at the old man on the ground. He was breathing, but he still had slime on him from the feeder. "Wait, we need to help him first."

"I don't . . ." The old man was trembling. "It hurts."

"It's okay." Maya knelt down, careful not to touch him. "We're going to take care of you."

"It had me, and I couldn't . . . I couldn't . . ." The old man began to make a little noise in his throat.

"Um, it's okay, I think you're just confused," Maya said, and looked up at Iara. "I think you *maaaaaaaaybe* remember getting dizzy?"

"Aha!" Iara nodded and then did a little thing with her throat that Maya couldn't hear, but watching the muscles in her jaw and neck work was a little cute and distracting.

"Then you fell into the water by the docks," Tapper added. Everyone looked at him, and he patted his acid-stained clothes and glared. "Into all that nice clean salt water, where someone will come rescue him right away and give him medical attention?"

"Oh, dude, yeah, good." Hawk gently picked up the old man. People in the area were still not looking at them, caught in whatever field of not-seeing the feeder or the train car put around them. "Okay, hang on, sir." He looked over at Iara. "We chill?"

Iara wheeled alongside him. "One moment," she said, and then firmly said to the old man, *"There was no monster. You got dizzy and fell into the water."*

Hawk jogged over and very gently dropped the man into the water while everyone else followed.

After a second, since nobody else was doing it, Maya yelled, "Oh gosh, I think that man got dizzy and fell into the water!"

As if a spell had been broken, people looked down and began shouting and pointing at the man. Everyone still ignored the acid-stained ground behind them.

"That was a small one," Lori said quietly as they all looked down at the confused man splashing in the water. "The bigger ones don't just eat. They do things to people, or their bodies. Using dead bodies as shells or using living people like puppets, as they . . ." She trailed off.

"As they did to our parents," Tapper finished.

"I'm sorry." Lori shook her head. "I've dealt with that before. If we can kill whatever is controlling the eels soon . . ."

"The beast in the water," Iara said. "We should have fought it. Perhaps we could have saved Shawn."

"Wrong, Ipanema." Tapper shook his head. "We nearly got beat fighting SpongeBob just now."

"It would actually be SpongeBob's friend Patrick," Maya chimed in, since Tapper was the kind of person who liked specificity.

"Or Starro," Iara added.

"Tapper's *point*," Lori said sharply, "is that if we'd stayed, we'd have died." Tapper nodded. "Tia Lake is tied to the thing controlling the eels somehow—maybe a puppet, or maybe she's . . ." Lori swallowed and lowered her voice. "Maybe she's a fake person that the monster is creating like camouflage." Her phone buzzed, and she ignored it. "Before we do anything, we should try to get back into the Lake Foundation headquarters and find some answers."

"Tomorrow morning," Iara said, looking down at her phone, "Tia Lake is doing a live radio interview about new advances with the miracoral. It is very early, around six in the morning."

"Good." Lori nodded. "So Lake will be away, and the building will be mostly deserted. How about if you all meet me back at PortManta around five thirty tomorrow morning?"

"That is superearly," Hawk said.

"You can catch up on beauty sleep once the bad guys aren't trying to catch us and kill us," Tapper said.

"Are you okay to get new clothes and a hotel?" Lori asked. "I have to go pick up my brother from day care."

"Your brother?" Maya asked.

"Ben." Lori's lips curled into a little smile. "He's seven, and he's normal. He doesn't know anything about all this. I promised I'd get him today if my work finished early."

"I can ensure that the group is taken care of," Iara said confidently. "Go get your brother. And Lori . . . thank you. Thanks to you, we are free, and we have a chance to save our families."

"And it was nice to meet you too, even, you know, without all that," Maya added, smiling at Lori, who blushed a little and shifted her weight around.

"See you tomorrow," she blurted, and headed off without a backward look.

"She's a little odd," Hawk said, "right?"

"She fights monsters to protect the innocent," Iara declared, "just as we will."

Tapper snorted. "She's not like us. Not that we even know what *we* are yet."

Maya sighed. "What if the angels *were also* fae?"

LORI

From: lfisher@anglerconsulting.sea
To: jvickers@santadee.net
Subject: Obnoxious favor

Hey, Jenn,

Tried to call you but couldn't get through. The consult job needs me superearly tomorrow, before Ben's day care is open. I can't find a sitter. Is there any chance you could watch him for a couple of hours before day care?

I'd need you here at 5:15. Yeah, I know.

If you can, let me know. Stupid job.

-L

Ben was delighted to have Lori come pick him up early from day care.

She held him tight as they rode the ferry back home, half listening to what he'd built out of Legos and what his Pokémon had done to his friend Josh's Pokémon in what was either their card game or them acting out the battle or some excited seven-year-old combination of the two.

She got him back home and into the small kitchen with the garbage under the sink that she'd forgotten to take out because it was a monster-hunting day. She got him pretzels and cheese as a snack, took his lunch bag out of his backpack, took back the pretzels and cheese upon seeing his blueberry applesauce sitting entirely untouched in the lunch bag, had a short argument about whether Ben had or had *not* said that he liked blueberry applesauce at some point in the past, and eventually came to a mutually agreeable compromise of Lori swapping the terrible blueberry applesauce for *normal* applesauce that Ben would eat while watching streams of people playing video games, with pretzels and cheese to follow upon completion of this arduous task. She threw in some chocolate milk to seal the deal.

Only then, only when Ben had settled in front of the computer, happily listening to a stream of a man with a loud and dubiously British voice, did Lori look at her phone. She had e-mails, including one from her personal account, and she opened that first.

From: jvickers@santadee.net
To: lfisher@anglerconsulting.sea
Subject: re: Obnoxious favor

That is way too early, and you owe me big.
Seriously, no worries. See you there.

-Jenn

PS: Have coffee ready plz
PPS: Bringing what I got you today. You're gonna love the neckline!

Lori breathed out a sigh of relief for friendship. Then she went over and set up the coffee machine on a timer for tomorrow morning, so she wouldn't forget.

Then, and only then, did she look at the texts from Handler.

Handler: It's OK.

Lori: Like heck it is.

Handler: Nothing is gonna happen.

Lori: Not until Thursday.
Lori: Three days. We have three days to stop Tia Lake.
Lori: Whatever she is.

Handler: Prolly good to figure out what she is, then, huh?
Handler: Incidentally, I think Starro McSpongeBob might've been a
        kappa.
Handler: Google says they drown people and have water that pours out of
        their heads.

Lori: I am concerned that Google is our best source of information here.

Handler: We've got this, kid. I will not let anything happen to Ben.
Handler: Unless Josh upgrades his Charmeleon to a Charizard.
Handler: Ben's pretty much toast in that case.

Lori looked over at her brother as he laughed and shouted, "Oh no!" at something the possibly British game streamer was doing to an enormous pile of TNT.

"You okay over there, little guy?" she asked.

"Yep!" he called back without turning around.

Lori: I will kill anything that threatens him.
Lori: I need you to be okay with that.

Handler: Do I seem NOT okay with that?

Handler always seemed reasonable. It was so easy to forget that it also used her as a lure to catch and eat things. She wondered why it bothered.

Lori: How am I going to work with the others without showing them what you do?

Handler: Don't know if you can.

Lori: I need them to take down Lake.

Handler: Yep.

Lori glared at the incredibly helpful message on her phone screen. She thought about pretty blond Maya seeing the giant teeth come out of nowhere, of realizing what Lori really was.

Lori: Are they like me?

Handler: Definitely not.
Handler: Iara said she only goes for guys.

Lori: Like US. You and me.

Handler: Nope.
Handler: Dunno what they are. Exactly.

Lori: Would you like me to Google it for you?

Handler: Not feeders.
Handler: So take the help.
Handler: Plus I think Maya's maybe got a thing for you?

Lori blushed and coughed and put her phone facedown on the table.

So what was she supposed to do? If Handler ate another feeder while the others were watching, they would see. *Maya* would see.

No, that was dumb. Forget Maya. Maya deserved to be with a real person.

What really mattered was that if she refused, they wouldn't be able to stop Lake.

And they only had until Thursday.

Could she even refuse to do what it wanted? She'd never tried to *stop* Handler from eating a feeder before. It would be like Lori's hand telling her not to eat a sandwich. Could she, when it actually *mattered* and wasn't just banter over text messages, actually *do* anything, even have an opinion, that Handler didn't agree with?

Lori hadn't asked permission to open the container that the kids had been in, though. The phone had buzzed, but she hadn't looked. The message, whatever Handler had said as Lori had walked toward that container, would still be there if she scrolled up high enough. She could read it and know for certain whether she was actually allowed to do things that Handler didn't like.

She'd know for certain whether she was a real person.

She pushed the phone aside. Right now it didn't matter. She and Handler both needed to stop the Lake Foundation, her because of Ben and Handler because Lake was a threat to it. That was enough for now.

"Hey, little guy," she called, "when you're done with that video, I have a question about Pokémon."

That covered the hour until dinner nicely.

MAYA

"What do you think, Iara?" Maya held up the lime-green T-shirt with the smiley face on it, squinting and trying to imagine what it would look like in normal light and not the glare of department-store fluorescents. She wasn't good at trying on clothes. There was too much people-looking-at-Maya for it to be fun. "Also, am I getting your name right?" The others seemed to have gotten it okay, but Maya wasn't good with other languages.

"You are fine, *alemã*," Iara said, smiling. "You say it very well, and with more care than most."

"I just want to make sure I'm not calling you the donkey from *Winnie-the-Pooh*." Maya held up a dark red blouse with a little sweetheart neckline. "It matters what people call themselves." She sighed. "And I don't know which to get."

Iara had a blue sundress with pretty purple flowers sitting in her lap, and she grabbed both shirts from Maya and added them to her pile. "You will get both," she said firmly. "The green is fun and very pretty with your hair, and the red blouse will break the hearts of the ladies."

"Oh? Oh!" Maya went hot and guessed she was probably the same color as the blouse now. "I, um, I was thinking more for breaking into the building and looking harmless, right? Something that fitted in so that nobody would get suspicious of us."

She didn't think Iara was entirely listening, because she had wheeled over to a rack with jeans. She held up a baggy pair, held them out in front of Maya, squinted, and then tossed them aside with a sniff. "You have very pretty legs. You deserve pants that do them justice. Maya?" Iara's voice took on a concerned tone. "Maya, what are you doing?"

Maya looked down and realized she had inadvertently blended into a clothing rack of tan slacks, camouflaging perfectly. "Um, nothing, sorry." She slipped back to normal colors before anyone in the store noticed, although since most people were trying hard to look anywhere but at Iara, she was probably safe.

"You do not like shopping for clothes?" Iara asked. "Or did I give offense? When I shop with my girlfriends, we try to tell the truth about what will look good on each of us."

"I, um . . ." Maya ran her fingers back and forth across a soft blouse. "I didn't have girlfriends to go shopping with back home."

"Hmph." Iara grabbed a pair of very tight jeans, held them up in front of Maya, and added them to the pile. "You do now, *alemã*."

"Well, um, thanks. That sundress is good, then. It's, uh . . . it's a full-blitz sundress."

Iara looked at her blankly. "I do not understand."

"It means seeing it is going to knock some boy senseless," Maya said, grinning at Iara.

Iara smiled back and rolled out her shoulders, pleased with herself. "Good. It is good to hear that."

Maya looked at a little kiosk near the clothes and saw a pretty jeweled keychain that also had a USB drive and a flashlight all built into it. She'd had a keychain with Sailor Neptune on it once. A bunch of guys had taken it away from her, and she'd never gotten it back. This one was at least sparkly. "Um, if it's not too much trouble, we might want this to like copy data from the Lake Foundation tomorrow . . . ?"

"Of course!" Iara grabbed one. "Now come, we will pay before the boys arrive." She smiled. "I think I would like to surprise Hawk with what I wear tomorrow."

"Awww . . ." Maya followed Iara as she wheeled to the register, then hung back a bit of a distance to watch. Iara talked to the cashier, and then, after a minute, the cashier took the tags off everything, bagged everything, and passed Iara a receipt.

"Still messed up," Tapper muttered, and Maya squeaked and jumped a little and then tried to pretend she had realized he had come up beside her.

"Yes! Right. It is." Maya looked over at Tapper and saw that Hawk was there as well. "Wait. What is?"

"Her messing with people's minds." Tapper grimaced, his eyes glittering as he watched Iara wheel toward them. "Not much different from what the feeders do." He was tapping his fingers against the plastic of a clothing rack, fast little clicks.

"Can I help you find anything?" asked a smiling sales guy, a slender white man with short brown hair that flopped over half his face. Maya started to respond, and then realized that the sales guy was talking to Tapper.

"No," Tapper said, and then, "Thanks, though." His fingers went still.

"Just let me know if you change your mind," the sales guy said, still smiling, and wandered off.

"It's *totally* different," Maya said when he was out of earshot. "Deception is when the other team fakes a handoff. Strategy is when *we* fake a handoff."

"Maya's right," Hawk said, and then added, "and also more into football than I expected. Anyway, feeders do it to eat people. Iara's just getting us clothes."

"This time." Tapper shook his head, and the clicking noise became kind of a crackle as his fingers moved fast enough to blur. "What if she decides to do a bank next? What if she decides to make you remember kissing her?"

"Totally okay with that," Maya said.

"I would not do that," Iara said as she came over, and Tapper started, clearly having thought she was out of earshot, "because it would be wrong. With great power comes great responsibility."

"But you *could* do a bank if you wanted to, *Uncle Ben*," Tapper insisted.

Iara sighed. "I could," she said slowly, enunciating her words carefully like Tapper was being dumb, "but at the end of the day, when the bank did not have the right amount of money, the security cameras would show a green-haired girl in a wheelchair taking the missing amount, and I would be very easy to track, no? So I use it only for little things, when needed, and not when it will hurt people. You, though? You move very fast. You could run into the store, grab the clothes, and run out without the cameras seeing you."

"It makes a shock wave if I do it for too long," Tapper said irritably. "I'd probably break the windows."

"But you could," Iara said, looking up at him with a hard smile, "just like me. So we are not so different, you and I."

Tapper just glared, but Hawk was thinking. "What about plane tickets?" he asked. "Could you get us flights? I mean, we could all just fly home again and get away from the Lake people, right?"

"I could." Iara nodded. "But do you not wish to know what has happened to us? Do you not wish to save our parents?"

Maya still hadn't called her parents. She looked down and realized she was blending into the clothing rack again, and made herself go back to normal.

"Yeah, no, totally," Hawk said, stammering a little. "I just . . . I always like to sit facing the exit, you know? So if tomorrow goes wrong . . ."

"If we do not find what we seek tomorrow, I will ensure you get home," Iara said, and smiled up at him, her hair tumbling down to frame her face. "But for now, let us hope for good things instead."

Hawk blushed and grinned, and Maya smiled to herself. He wouldn't stand a chance against the full-blitz sundress tomorrow.

LAKE

Tia Lake, a tall woman with perfectly curled dark hair falling to the neck of her black silk blouse, sat in a black leather office chair and tapped at the polished mahogany desk with nails painted the same blood red as her lips.

"Four of them escaped," she said.

Tap, tap, tap went her nails on the hardwood.

"They haven't returned to their rooms at the office," she said, "and it's doubtful that they will. They're smarter than that."

Tap, tap, tap.

"Give me what you remember for their contact information," she said, smiling gently.

On the ground next to the desk, what was left of Diane Tucker twitched. She didn't do much more than that—nobody with that many eels attached to them could do much more than that—and her eyes were glazed, but there was enough of her left in there to twitch, still.

"This is just for information, Diane. You'd be surprised what can happen when it's for punishment."

Tap, tap, tap. Her nails gouged little crescents of white into the desk.

"Ah, there we go," she said a moment later, and the pile of eels flexed and writhed and bit in and took the right parts out. "Thanks so much, Diane. Now how about that thing calling itself a girl who worked for Angler Consulting? How did you get ahold of that number?"

Diane twitched again. This time her eyes darted to the ceiling. Diane had been a feisty one.

Tia let out a long sigh, and a pair of eels wriggled toward Diane Tucker's eyes.

Tap. Tap. Tap.

Finally Tia smiled. "You really don't remember, do you, Diane? Oh, that's helpful, even so. Here's why you don't remember, right here, and . . . ah yes, what a clever thing. So gentle." The eels began to take out what they needed, carefully this time, since Tia would want a closer look.

"The payment information is probably fake, but we should follow up just to be sure, don't you think, Diane?"

No twitch from under the eels this time.

"Diane?"

Tap, tap, tap.

Tia Lake cocked her head. "I guess I took out your name with that last bit. You don't even remember yourself, do you?" She smiled down fondly at the pile. "Lucky thing."

She sent out her orders from her phone while the eels finished what was left.

TUESDAY

04

MAYA

Maya wasn't expecting to have to be the motivating force getting everyone outside PortManta at five thirty in the morning. In Maya's experience, timeliness was something that happened to other people. Her dad had always gotten her up for morning football practice. He'd even woken her for swim practice after she left football, and he wouldn't talk to her much beyond that.

So when Tapper banged on the door to her hotel room at four forty-five (once she had looked through the peephole to verify that it was him and not some kind of horrible monster like the ones she'd been dreaming about all night, and then opened the door with the locking chain still on just in case it was a monster that could disguise itself) and said, "Nobody else is up. We can't be late on this," she was somewhat confused.

"Wurrrwha?" Maya said, squinting and blinking at the greasy light in the hallway. "It's not even five yet."

"Thought you'd wanna shower," Tapper said. He was wearing

the new outfit that Iara had gotten—well, stolen—for him, black cargo pants and a dark red sweater. "Girls take longer to shower. Before you hop in, get the other two up."

Maya started to wake up a little. "Why do I have to do that? You're already awake."

"I don't motivate," Tapper said. "When I talk, it just pisses people off."

"You're talking to me, though."

"Offending you is like punching a pillow." Tapper turned away. "I'm gonna break into the snack machine down the hall. Get Pint-Size and the Girl from Ipanema up."

And so Maya motivated Iara into wakefulness and pounded on Hawk's door until the half-asleep "Dude" responses turned to begrudgingly awake "Dude" responses. Then, because she *was* one of the girls who took longer showers, she hopped in and got cleaned up.

Forty-five minutes later, they stood outside the coffee-and-juice place, waiting in the darkness.

"It is *way* too early to be awake," Hawk muttered. He wore baggy board shorts and a gray button-up shirt left open to show a thin white T-shirt underneath, an outfit that would have probably left him cold in the chilly pre-dawn wind had he not been immune to everything except electricity. He was eating one of the snack bars Tapper had stolen.

"Today we take the fight to our enemies," Iara said. Her hair still somehow managed to look vibrant and bouncy (and green) despite it being way too early, and she rocked her chair back and forth. "Today the Lake Foundation learns to fear us!" She wore a nice black leather jacket, because she probably *would be* cold just wearing a long blue sundress with little purple flowers on it.

Maya was starting to think she'd played it a little safe with the green shirt with the smiley face, but she *had* at least gone for the skinny jeans Iara had picked out.

She watched the few ferries pass by in the canals, the gentle hum and the rushing of the water so much quieter than the gasoline-powered cars that were still all over the place back home in Nebraska. "Maybe the Lake Foundation could just forget us instead?"

"She said she'd be here at five thirty." Tapper glared at his cracked phone.

"She is," came a voice, and everyone looked as Lori came around the corner. Her hair was pulled back in a ponytail, and she wore a long-sleeved T-shirt and jeans today. It made her look much more like someone Maya's age. "Sorry. Had to get a sitter for my brother. Come on, let's grab a ferry."

LORI

At five forty-five, they stood outside the Lake Foundation's main headquarters, a tall building whose windowed walls gleamed in the predawn half-light, looking at the well-lit front lobby and the security guards inside.

"I thought they'd be closed," Maya said. "I mean, I thought we might have to sneak past janitors or something, but I didn't think we'd have to deal with security guys, and do they have guns?"

"Yes," Tapper said. He glanced over at Lori, his eyes shining. "You're Miss B and E. What do we do?"

Lori glared at him. "We don't stand out here looking suspicious. Come on."

She started walking, and they fell in behind her, giving her time to think. Her phone buzzed, and she glanced down at it with the sudden thought that something had happened with Ben, that Jenn needed Lori to come back home.

Handler: Circle the building. Gotta be some better way inside.

"I don't break into places," Lori said. The Lake Foundation headquarters took up the whole block, and she started down the sidewalk, glancing up from time to time at the chain-link fence topped with barbed wire that seemed to ring the entire place.

"Did you not break into the docks?" Iara asked as she wheeled herself along with them. Lori had expected her to need help getting her chair onto the ferry, but she'd navigated the narrow gangplank with amazing ease.

"I was *invited* to the docks," Lori said. "People hire me to hunt feeders." *They don't remember how they found me,* she didn't add, *and they probably don't remember me after I'm gone, because the thing that uses me alters their minds, just like every other feeder.*

"You know much about these feeders," Iara said, and smiled. "This is good. I look forward to destroying whatever commands these eels."

"Hey, why did we go with *eels*?" Hawk asked. "I mean, are they eels or snakes or . . . ?"

"No idea," Maya said, "but Iara lived near rivers, so she probably knows what eels look like better than we do."

"Also Ursula's minions in *The Little Mermaid*," Iara added.

"The *eels*," Lori went on doggedly, "are little bits that the bigger feeders have. Sometimes they're like larvae—its children. Sometimes they're more like extensions of the feeder, like it's . . . like it's this thing sitting in another dimension, and it just kind of pokes part of itself in, right?"

"Like space?" Hawk asked.

"No. Like . . ." She looked back and saw everyone staring at her. "So say we're all fish in a lake, and some guy is looking down into the lake, and none of us can see him, because we're the fish, and we never think to look up. He puts his fingers into the water, and we all look up, and as far as we can tell, it's like ten different creatures, like little worms, just came into the water, but really it's all one creature. You see?"

They continued to look at her blankly.

Lori looked away and kept walking. "Anyway, that's how it works."

"And the man whose fingers are the eels," Iara said, "he is the creature that killed Shawn." She was still rolling beside Lori, her hands flicking the wheels with tireless strength. "And he uses the Lake Foundation as his villainous lair?"

"Maybe. Tia Lake isn't human. Whatever the feeder is, it's using her and her company." Lori kept walking. As they reached a corner, it became clear that the Lake Foundation was more of a complex than a single building, large enough to fill most of the block with shiny gray structures.

"If this were Austin," Hawk said, "I'd say we try the parking lot. Tech companies always have weaker security by the parking lot, because that's where most of the normal folks come in."

"No parking lots in a canal city." Tapper ran fingers through his dreadlocks.

"Are they a tech company?" Maya asked. "I didn't really look at their website when they offered the scholarship. I mostly just went, 'Oooh, cool!' because when I switched to swim team, there weren't a whole lot of scholarships for that."

"They are the ones who harnessed the power of the mira-coral," Iara said, and made a clicking noise. Lori looked over and saw that Iara's phone, sitting faceup in her lap, was loading a page. "They learned to extract oil from the reef, and they learned how to capture the electrical discharges the coral generates."

"You can make your phone work by clicking at it?" Maya asked, eyes wide. "That is supercool."

Iara shrugged and continued wheeling herself forward along with the rest of them. "I needed my hands free." As her phone loaded its page, she added, "I have their office map."

"Nice job, Oracle," Tapper said.

Iara made a face. "I liked that she got to punch villains even in her chair, but then they made her get better for no reason. The office has no parking lot, but one of their buildings faces out onto the generator pool." She clicked at her phone again.

"The what now?" Maya asked.

"Big shallow pool with a bunch of miracoral growing along the bottom that supplies electrical power, like a wind or solar farm," Tapper snapped. "Did you do *any* homework in school?"

"The pool is open to viewing from the other side." Lori chewed on her lip, thinking. "I've been. The building side didn't look guarded, or at least not as heavily. People wouldn't expect anyone to swim across."

"Right, 'cause anyone who jumps into the water gets electrocuted," Hawk pointed out. "And guys, I'm pretty tough, but I *hate* getting electrocuted."

"You will not be in danger just from swimming," Iara said, smiling and shaking her head. "I have swum near little reefs in my home. The miracoral only shocks fish that get close enough to touch it."

"It could work," Lori said, and nodded to Iara. "Good thinking."

"Spent most of yesterday sloshing around," Hawk said, "and now the new outfit's gonna get wet too."

"I will get you more," Iara said, and smiled at him. "Perhaps a nice jacket. You need a nice jacket." Hawk grinned back and swaggered a bit as he walked.

They turned the corner and started down the sidewalk. The canal traffic on their left was light, just sporadic personal boats passing by quietly and the occasional ferry chugging from one stop to the next. The cool morning air smelled of diesel and vanilla.

On their right, the huge generator pool caught the streetlights and cast them back as pale orange reflections, while below, the miracoral's own natural radiance lit the water with gold. Locked off from the canals, the surface was smooth as a mirror, a massive stillness that had always seemed strange to Lori in the middle of the canal city. A ten-foot chain-link fence ran the length of the pool, with razor wire at the top to stop anyone dumb enough to try to climb over. On the far side of the pool, there was only a waist-high railing, and the Lake Foundation had a little patio with tables and chairs.

"Bet it was the parking lot before the water rose," Hawk said.

Tapper was glaring at the pool. "Problem. They've got motion sensors on the pool. We swim across, we'll trip an alarm."

"Where are the sensors?" Iara asked. Tapper pointed, and Iara squinted, then shut her eyes and cocked her head. "Ah, there they are," she said a moment later. "How did you know where they were?"

Tapper looked over at the rest of them, his eyes sparkling in the predawn twilight. "I can see the beams."

Lori's phone buzzed, and she looked down at it.

Handler: If he can see the beams, maybe we can avoid them?

"Yes," Lori muttered, "I was getting there."

A moment later, she became aware of everyone looking at her.

"Tapper," she said, trying to ignore the looks, "if you can see the beams, can you tell us how to avoid them?"

He jerked his head back to the pool. "Yeah. It's a grid. None near the wall on either side. If we go in without a big splash, we could swim across." He looked back at all of them, glaring a challenge. "Can you all hold your breath that long?"

"No," said Maya, "but I *can* breathe underwater, if that works?" Tapper rolled his eyes.

"That's even better, Maya," Hawk said. "I can do it for about an hour. How about you, Iara?"

She smiled. "Fifteen or twenty minutes. That should be enough time." She held up her phone. "It is good I got the water-proofing package for the phones, yes?"

"Pretty much a necessity in Santa Dymphna," Lori said, smiling back at her.

"How about you, Lori?" Maya asked. "Do you breathe under-water, or can you hold your breath, or are you gonna just teleport across?"

"It's probably best if I . . ." Lori's phone buzzed, and she glanced down at it.

Handler: You can breathe underwater.

". . . swim with you," she finished. "I can breathe underwa-ter." *Apparently*, she added in the silence of her mind.

"Great!" Maya beamed. "So you and me are water-breathing partners, and Iara and Hawk can be breath-holding partners, and Tapper can show us where to go." She looked over at the chain-link fence. "Once we figure out how to get through that."

"Any motion sensors or beams or anything on it?" Hawk asked Tapper. Tapper shook his head. "Sweet."

He stepped over, looked either way down the sidewalk, grabbed the chain-link fence with both hands, and pulled with-out any appreciable effort. With a squeal of protesting metal, the links tore apart in his grasp, and in moments, he had a gap large enough for a person to fit through at about waist height. "All right, that should . . ." He paused, looked over at Iara in her wheelchair, and then frowned back at the fence. "Hang on." He tore down and opened the gap to the ground, then pulled the edges away and curled them back gently. "That gonna be okay for you?"

"Let us find out." Iara smiled at him and held out her phone. "Do you mind? This dress does not have pockets." As Hawk took it, she wheeled forward to the gap Hawk had torn, shrugged out of her leather jacket to reveal deeply tanned shoulders left bare by her sundress, and then hunched forward and dove cleanly through the gap and into the pool, knifing into the water with barely a ripple.

In the light cast by the miracoral below, Iara was a dark silhouette twisting nimbly until she was looking back at them from under the water. She waved, her green hair fanning out like a halo around her head, and then tumbled back around and darted through the water with long powerful strokes of her arms.

"Daaang," Hawk said, watching her go.

"Right?" Maya said beside him. "I mean, I've liked mermaids ever since Ariel looked sad doing the song where she didn't know what forks were, but—"

"Can we *go*?" Tapper muttered.

"You guys first. I'll pull the chain links back together once we're through, so it's less obvious." Hawk gestured for them to go ahead.

Tapper went first, shoving the links aside and dropping into the water quietly. He hovered under the water and pointed at where they should drop in to avoid the beams. Maya followed a moment later, slipping through the gap in the fence with a twist of her shoulders that didn't seem entirely natural to Lori.

Lori slipped through the fence, then looked down at her phone. "I can breathe underwater?"

Handler: Yyyyyyup.

Lori: Since when?

Handler: Ever since we started working together.
Handler: Fringe benefit.

Lori: Were you ever going to mention this to me?

Handler: Hey jsyk, you're amphibious.
Handler: See how that doesn't come up naturally in conversation?

Lori: It would have been useful to know.

Hander: When have you ever needed to breathe underwater?
Handler: Figured I'd let you know when it'd help.
Handler: Btw, Maya is waiting for you.

Lori jerked her head up from her phone and looked into the pool. Tapper had swum off, but Maya was treading water a few feet below the surface, her short blond hair glowing in the water. She waved as Lori looked.

Lori felt herself blushing, and shoved her phone into her pocket.

"You okay?" Hawk called softly from back by the fence. He'd slipped through and was carefully pulling the chain links back together.

"Fine."

Then she slipped into the water, which apparently she could breathe.

It was going to be a day full of new things.

MAYA

Maya wasn't sure what people who knew they could breathe underwater looked like, but Lori wasn't one of them. She slid into the water holding her breath, and Maya watched the little bubbles spray away from where Lori's feet kicked as she scrambled against the wall to stop herself from floating back to the surface. After a moment, she let out a long bubbly breath, then inhaled with a kind of full-body shiver before settling down. Her long black hair, still in its ponytail, bobbed behind her as she shook her head.

Finally she waved back to Maya with a smile that looked forced, although it was hard to tell underwater.

Maya gave her an encouraging thumbs-up, then looked back to where Iara circled Hawk, who had splashed in after Lori, while Tapper hung in the water up ahead. Neither of them could swim like Iara could, but they were doing all right. Maya checked to make sure Lori wasn't going to die or anything—she was still flailing around a little bit like someone who didn't do a lot of swimming—and then Maya kicked her legs and headed after them.

Maya had done swim team back in Nebraska, which had been *so much better* than wrestling or football, and she'd known she could breathe water right after the change. She didn't know *how* she'd known. It had just been there, another skill she hadn't had before but was now available and as natural as anything else as a problem-solving response. *Make people laugh. Run away. Camouflage self. Go bendy. Breathe underwater.*

She had never gotten to swim in the ocean, though. And, well, the canals weren't exactly the open water, but they were seawater, at least. The pool was even more of, well, a pool than the canals were, but it was seawater as well. It felt different, feeling salt water in her lungs—it was like the difference between being in an air-conditioned room and being outside with the wind in her face. The water felt cool and thick and *right* sliding through her fingers.

Now that she thought about it, she thought she remembered that some fish could survive in only salt water *or* freshwater, but not both, and that would probably have been a good thing to think about earlier, but it wasn't killing Maya *now*, so she decided not to worry about it.

It was the first time she'd been in the water close to miracoral too, and as she swam in a nice lazy breaststroke, arms and legs flowing easily and maybe just a tiny bit more flexibly than they had before the change, she looked down at the stuff that was replacing oil all over the world.

Her first thought was that the miracoral looked like a brain. Maybe not what an actual brain looked like, but whenever you saw a movie with aliens who had creepy big heads and oversized brains visible, that kind of brain. Each of the brains was the size of a backpack, and there were clusters of them all along the floor of the pool, along with seaweed and little fish that were probably what the coral ate.

The miracoral itself gave off the golden glow. Maya had expected it to be like one of the old night-lights she'd had as a kid, like it was translucent plastic with a cheap bulb behind it, but it was sharper and clearer than that, as though the light was coming from the skin of the miracoral itself. It was bright enough that it *should* have hurt Maya's eyes, but instead the light felt warm and soft and kind, somehow.

The pool was around twenty feet deep, and Maya was swimming near the midpoint, deep enough that she wouldn't make big waves on the surface but still safely away from the miracoral itself, since everyone had been superserious about it giving you an electrical shock. Again, though, it didn't *look* like something that would shock her. The same feeling that had told her she could squeeze between the bars of the gate to get away from the guys at school was telling her that the miracoral was safe.

She looked back at Lori, who was catching up finally. Lori paused and raised her hands in a *what is it?* motion.

Lori's long-sleeved shirt was superclingy underwater, and Maya stared for probably just a bit longer than she had to, hoping the water hid her blush. Then she remembered about the miracoral and pointed down at it.

Lori gave Maya a blank look.

Maya decided to go with it.

Turning over in the water—and wow, the best part about being able to breathe underwater was not having to worry about water going up your nose when you did that—Maya kicked down toward the bottom of the pool. Behind her Lori made a warbly bubbly noise that was probably something about this not being a good idea, and darn, it was a shame that Maya couldn't hear it.

The glow was even brighter as she drew closer to one of the bunches of miracoral, bright enough that if it were any other kind of light, Maya would be squinting, unable to see anything, but here it was still just natural. If anything, she could see even *more* clearly, the little ripples and ridges along the outside of the coral that gave it the brainy look, the tiny motes in the water that caught the light, all of it. In fact, the light was changing on the patch she was approaching, moving from the steady gold into a friendly pink as Maya drew closer. Little fish darted out of her way as she eased down toward it.

Then a hand clamped down around her ankle.

Maya looked back—well, up—and saw Lori grabbing her.

"Wharbrrryoodoing?" Lori yelled. Even under the water, Maya picked that up.

"I think it's like us," Maya said, or tried to. It came out mostly as bubbles. She gave Lori a reassuring smile. "Look!" She grabbed Lori's hand and pulled her down. "It's okay!"

Lori flailed for a moment, but then she saw Maya's look, and after a long stare, during which Maya realized that Lori had really strong hands, Lori stopped struggling. Squinting against the light, she let Maya pull her down.

Hands linked, they moved toward the miracoral.

"See?" Maya said, or tried to, anyway, as they closed to within a few feet of it. "I think it knows what we are!"

Then the water went cold and sharp around her as the miracoral's glowing light went an angry red, and dozens of tiny lobster-scorpion things with angry-looking claws began to pour out of the ridges of the coral.

HAWK

Hawk didn't swim a whole lot faster than he had before whatever had happened to him, but now he really liked cruising. Back in Austin, he had loved to swim, and when his abilities had come to him, he'd started going through the reefs that had once been the southern edge of town. The cold hadn't bothered him—honestly, swimming in the gulf was barely what you'd call cold anyway— and the water hadn't stung his eyes anymore, and for like an hour, he could just drift under the water in silence.

That had been cool, but there hadn't been a hot green-haired girl swimming alongside him, either, so even though he was still a little nervous about the miracoral glowing down below him, he was counting this as a step up.

Iara was literally swimming circles around him, her arms pulling her through the water in an effortless glide. When she saw him look her way, she paused and waved. Her hair swirled around her sweet curving smile, and then she darted away to swim another loop.

Up ahead Tapper had reached the far wall already and was treading water and glaring Hawk's way. Hawk jerked his head to convey *sup, bro* in a way that was universal between dudes, but Tapper didn't seem to speak dude.

Maybe Tapper was into Iara and was one of those guys who had no chill when he had it bad for a girl. That might explain why he was always glaring at Hawk. Hawk, who had grown up with sisters at home, could at least *kinda* talk to girls like they were people, even if he did spend a lot of that time wondering what their necks would smell like right at that part where they met the shoulder. He looked over at Iara again as she swam by, grinning his way.

Her neck probably smelled really good.

Up ahead Tapper climbed out of the pool. Iara flitted forward, then circled back and waved for Hawk to go first. He nodded, reached the wall, and surfaced as close to it as he could.

"About two feet of clearance from the beams," Tapper muttered. He was already on the other side of the railing, and his cargo pants and sweater already looked dry. How the heck did he do that? "Security by the door, so try not to make noise."

Hawk pulled himself up, nearly slipped on the side of the pool, grabbed the railing, and splashed over awkwardly. "Sorry, dude," he said as Tapper shook his head in disgust. The guy's clothes *were* already dry. The sweater even looked fluffy, like it had just come out of the dryer.

"At least you won't be as bad as her," Tapper said, jerking his head toward Iara, who was circling in the water below.

"Dude," Hawk said, "uncool. She can't help needing a wheelchair, and she's better in the water than any of us." He waved down at her. "Also, just 'cause you've got it bad for her doesn't mean you've gotta be rude. Pulling the pigtails is, like, middle-school stuff."

"You think I—" Tapper started, and then Iara leaped from the water in a glistening arc, jackknifed over the railing, twisted in midair, and landed like a ballet dancer in Hawk's frantically outflung arms.

"Thank you for catching me," she said, wiping her hair back out of her face with one hand as she put the other arm around his neck. "Without my ride, I am afraid I may need a little assistance."

"Hey, no worries." Hawk grinned. "Superstrength, right?" Tapper snorted, and Hawk realized what that sounded like and added, "Uh, but I mean, not that you're like heavy or—"

"Excuse me," came a call from over by the Lake Foundation building, and Hawk breathed a sigh of relief even as he turned around and saw a security guard coming toward them. He was a big black dude, and his outfit was about as close to *cop* as a security uniform could get. "What's going on?"

"I am very sorry," Iara said, shifting her weight in Hawk's arms in some kind of secret girl way that turned her from *awkward hunched-up cold wet person* into *innocently seductive lounging babe like when Princess Leia is lying on the bed in the white dress right before Luke comes into the cell to rescue her in* A New Hope, *but specifically the white dress, not the gold slave bikini, because that one is sexist.* "I fell over the railing, and this brave man rescued me."

"You fell over the railing?" The security guard frowned. "Into the generator pool? This is a private area. How did you even get in here?"

"We were invited," Iara said, still smiling, and leaned in against Hawk. In a tiny voice, she added, "Get me close to him, please."

"Right," Hawk said, and then, as the security guard looked at him, Hawk said, "Right!" again in a more believable voice. "We were invited." He stepped forward. "Plus if we could get inside, I think she needs a doctor to look at her, uh, ankle."

Iara shifted again in Hawk's arms and did *something* that didn't make a noise Hawk could hear, but kind of made her throat vibrate a little against his chest, and that wasn't distracting *at all*.

"So yeah," Hawk added, "you should have a thing saying we can come in without a badge or a pass or, you know, whatever, one of those things that . . ." Still moving forward, he looked over at Tapper, who was standing there with his arms crossed, looking at Hawk in utter disdain. "Dude, did you wanna . . . no? Nothing?"

"You're the smooth one," Tapper said, and it was still pretty dark, but Hawk thought there might have been the ghost of a smile on his face now.

"Whatever is going on here," the guard said, "none of you are going anywhere."

Iara's throat did its weird thing again, and then she said, *"You were told to let us in with no official record,"* and her voice made Hawk's whole body tingle.

The guard blinked. "Oh, you're the ones I was told about! I'm so sorry, miss, are you all right?"

Iara shifted again in Hawk's arms, and he couldn't see whether she was smiling, but he guessed it was pretty good, whatever it was. *"The instructions were for five of us in total."*

The guard blinked again. "If I remember right, there should be another two of you, shouldn't . . ." He broke off, looking past Iara. "What's happening to the pool?"

Hawk turned around and looked at the pool, which had begun bubbling. The light coming from the glowing miracoral on the bottom had been a pretty gold when Hawk had been swimming in there, but now the light was an angry red, and it was definitely an *angry* red, hitting Hawk's eyes in a way that made him want to pull back with the same instinctual fear gripping his muscles as he'd have gotten from seeing a bright-colored spider crawling toward him on the table.

A moment later, Lori and Maya uncoiled from empty air and collapsed onto the pavement in a boneless wet heap.

"What is that?" the guard shouted.

"You gonna make him think *this* is normal?" Tapper asked Iara.

"Ahhh . . ."

"Didn't think so." In a flash Tapper was beside the guard, fist extended, and the guard was on the ground unconscious.

"What happened?" Hawk demanded.

"Cold and big, cold and big," Maya was saying over and over again, which Hawk thought was probably a bad sign.

Lori was already back on her feet, and while there was water on the ground around her, she seemed entirely dry. "Something went wrong with the miracoral. We had to change the plan." She looked at the guard. Her face didn't have any expression in it. "Tapper, drag him someplace less obvious."

"Like where?" Tapper asked, but Lori was already walking briskly toward the door.

Hawk hurried after her, shifting his grip so that Iara would be more comfortable. It would have been easier to do a fireman's carry, but Hawk figured that would be rude.

"What happened to the miracoral? Did it zap you?" he asked Lori.

"When we got close, it moved to defend itself," Lori said. Then she paused, winced, and shook her head, the first real expression she'd had. "Listen, Maya is a little shaken up. Can you . . ." She looked over at Hawk and seemed to realize for the first time that he was carrying Iara. "Okay. I'll see if she's all right."

"I've got her," Tapper growled, and Hawk saw that Maya was back on her feet, holding his hand as they came to join Hawk and Iara and Lori. "She doesn't need you doing anything else weird to her right now."

Lori opened her mouth, but whatever super-rude thing she would have said was cut off as Iara said, "Another guard."

This guard was a heavyset white guy with a big mustache. Hawk turned to him and cleared his throat as the guard pushed the door open and looked their way.

"Everything okay?" he called over in a casual relaxed voice that was not at all the voice Hawk had been expecting. He was looking past Hawk, and Hawk glanced back over his shoulder.

The big security guard, the black guy that Tapper had just knocked unconscious, was somehow standing next to Tapper where Maya had been. He nodded and gave the heavyset guard in the doorway a jerk of the head that conveyed *all good, bro*, in universal dude language, and the guard in the doorway nodded and stepped back inside, letting the door close behind him.

"Tapper, did you by any chance get the guard's security card?" the big guy said in Maya's voice. Tapper held up a thin slip of white plastic between two fingers.

"Dude, Maya, that is *awesome*," Hawk said. "Also, you speak dude really well for a girl."

"Yes, nicely done," Iara said. "How do you make your clothing change its appearance?"

"Oh, I can't," Maya said.

"Wait." Lori blinked. "So what are you *actually* wearing right now?"

"Umm, we should get moving. Thanks." Maya took the security card from Tapper.

"*Alemã*, I bought you clothes!" Iara said.

"You did, and it was supernice of you, and it gave me a lot of great ideas!" Maya said brightly.

"Good to know," Hawk said, and felt Iara laughing silently against his chest as they headed inside.

05

MAYA

The lights inside the Lake Foundation building were glaringly bright after the darkness outside. Maya kept herself looking like the guard as she used the key card to open the door, and then waved them inside with what she *hoped* was a normal hand-wavy motion a normal guard would make. "So we're in," she said as the door closed behind them, and looked at a small kitchenette with doors leading off to either side. "Did we have a plan for after, which I wasn't paying attention to, or . . . ?"

"They went to a great deal of trouble to get us. Hopefully in a building with so many computers, there will be some record of why," Iara said. She still looked comfortable in Hawk's arms, which, good for her, Maya figured, even if Hawk looked a little less like a burly fireman than someone trying to carry too much laundry so as not to have to make a second trip. "If we locate a mainframe, I may be able to find out why they came after us."

"Hang on," Lori said, and fiddled with her phone. A moment later, it began playing an audio stream.

"We're here this morning with Tia Lake of the Lake Foundation. Thank you so much for joining us."

"It was my pleasure, dear. The miracoral is a vital part of our lives today, and the Lake Foundation is committed to developing our new resources to the fullest."

"All right," Lori said, and dropped the volume. "We're clear as long as she's doing the interview."

Everyone went quiet while they thought about that. At least Maya assumed that was what everyone else was thinking about.

Maya was thinking about the miracoral seeming so happy and friendly and warm around her, and then turning red all of a sudden and all the little lobster things swarming out of the coral and coming at them. Maya was thinking about flailing to get away while the swarm closed on them, a cloud of claws and bubbles, and then how Lori's hand, still linked with Maya's, had tightened, and then—

"I think we should split up," Maya said, breaking the silence. "We're a big group right now. If we split up, we'll attract less attention, right? Lori and, and, and"—she thought about who else would like hitting things—"*Tapper* can go look in Tia Lake's office for like special information? And the rest of us can find a computer so Iara can do her thing?"

"That's actually not stupid," Tapper said. Maya flashed him a thumbs-up.

"Sweet." Hawk nodded, or at least Maya thought he nodded, since he still had an armful of Iara. "So, which way is which?"

"The executive offices are on the top floor," Iara said. "We will search for the central servers here on the main floor." She smiled at Tapper and Lori. "Hunt well."

"Always do." Lori nodded to them and took off with Tapper in tow.

"So yeah," Maya said as soon as they were around a corner, "wherever Lori goes when she teleports or whatever is super-bad."

Iara and Hawk looked at her in confusion. "What was it like?" Iara asked.

"Superbad. I just said!"

"Okay, so what does that mean?" Hawk asked. "Was it like . . . space?"

It had been dark and cold. Maya hadn't been able to see anything at all, or even tell which way was up or down as she floated dizzily in that other place, but even with all that, she had somehow known three things: First, even though she couldn't tell which way *down* was, there had been *something* below her, something that called that other place home; second, whatever that thing below her had been, it had been *really really big*; and third, *it had seen her.*

"It means we shouldn't make her do that very often." She looked at them indignantly. "And now we find the server room, right?"

"Correct, *alemã*." Iara's lips curved into a sweet smile. "Let us go."

The main floor had a big open space with a lot of cubicles, and the hallways were marked with meeting rooms. Hardly anyone was in yet. Once they passed another guard, and Maya, still in Big Security Guard shape, nodded to her as they went by.

Finally, up on their right, Maya saw a door labeled SERVER ROOM. She walked up to it confidently, since that was what the guard would have done, and turned the handle . . . or tried to. The door was locked.

"Can either of you pick locks?" she asked.

Iara shook her head. Hawk shrugged and said, "Uh, kinda. Hang on." He eased Iara to the ground gently, so that she was sitting against the wall with her legs folded beneath her. "You okay?"

"I believe I know how to sit," she said, smiling up from under her bright green bangs.

"Oh, yeah. Right." Hawk turned back to the door. He reached out and brought the handle down without any particular effort. Maya heard the sound of metal snapping inside the door, and then it swung open.

A trio of guards stared out at them from a room filled with big rows of computer equipment.

"Uh, hey," Hawk said. "So this guard here said that I was supposed to come here and check . . . something."

Maya stepped into the doorway behind Hawk and waved wordlessly, hoping she wouldn't have to say anything.

Then, as yellow-green eels slithered from the guards' mouths instead of staying inside like they were supposed to or, even better, *not having been there at all*, Maya decided that she had other problems.

LORI

Lori's phone had started buzzing almost as soon as she headed down the hallway with Tapper in tow. She was ignoring it.

"You gonna check that?" Tapper asked.

"Nope." Lori kept walking. If Handler wanted to talk, it could wait.

"Whatever. You worried about security cameras as we go up?"

Her phone buzzed again. That was likely Handler telling her it had the cameras covered. "My power should knock out the security cameras."

"If you say so."

Her power. The monster that let her be human enough to feel things, but not human enough to fool the miracoral.

They reached an elevator. Lori punched the up button. Her phone buzzed again. "I don't care," she muttered.

"Yeah, I can tell by the way you're refusing to answer your phone and gritting your teeth and all," Tapper said, glaring. "Definitely not caring."

"You know, there's a reason nobody likes you," Lori said.

"No kidding."

It wasn't what Lori had expected, and she looked over at him in surprise. He was totally dry now, his dreads pulled back, and his red sweater giving his skinny frame a little more bulk. His eyes glittered as they caught the overhead lights.

"You *know* you get on people's nerves?" Lori asked, looking at him in confusion.

"I'm not stupid," Tapper muttered.

"Then why do you act like such a jerk?"

"This is the best I can do." Tapper glared. "How come Maya was scared when she teleported with you?"

Because it's not teleportation, Lori didn't say. *It's getting pulled out of this world and into Handler's, and for just a minute before you're dropped back into this world, you can see everything, and you know the truth, so* Maya *now knows the truth, and so much for her smiling at me and asking to be water-breathing buddies.*

The miracoral had known the truth. It had been friendly and nice to Maya, but as soon as Lori got close . . .

The elevator dinged, and the doors slid open. "Come on." Lori stepped in and hit the button for the top floor.

Tapper followed as the doors started closing, shoulders hunched. He stood on the other side of the elevator cabin. A moment later the elevator lurched into motion.

"You kill monsters," he said as the elevator climbed.

"That's the job."

"Why?"

"Somebody has to."

"How, then?" Tapper's eyes jerked over to her, then back away.

"You'll see." Lori's phone buzzed again. "Fine," she muttered, and looked down at it. All the texts were some variation of the last few.

Handler: You need to be careful.

Handler: Be angry at the miracoral if you want.

Handler: But the thing in the water was BIG. There could be feeders here.

Lori: This is how we learn more.

Handler: And yes, I got the cameras, thx for asking.

Handler: I don't want you getting hurt.

Lori: If I die, you'll grow another me.

Handler: Hey.

Lori: Don't. I saw the miracoral turn.

Lori: Stop complaining. At least you'll get to eat.

The elevator lurched to a stop, and Lori slipped her phone back into her pocket as the doors slid open. "You ready?" Lori asked Tapper as they walked out.

"Depends on how you kill the monsters," Tapper muttered.

I don't, Lori didn't say. *I have this monster, and it kills them, and I used to hope that I was real and just stuck with it like*

*some horrible fairy godmother, but the miracoral loves you guys
and hates me, so I guess that answers that.*

And now Maya knows.

She wiped her eyes. It didn't change anything. She had Ben,
and Ben was real, and she was going to protect him. Right now
the easiest way to do that was to kill another monster.

The hallway was nicer up here on the top floor. The carpet
was forest green, and the walls were bright white and covered
with art. Lori led the way.

They passed expensive-looking offices, all of them empty and
dark. At the end of the hallway, a large double door was flanked
by a panel that read TIA LAKE, CEO.

Lori turned up the volume on the phone.

"—*responsible for bioengineering the miracoral in the first
place,*" the radio guy was saying.

"*Of course,*" Lake replied with that assured confidence, "*but
even so, there's so much about it that we don't understand.
That's why we're taking steps to take our knowledge of the
miracoral to the next level and better all of humanity.*"

Lori clenched her hands into fists. "We should be safe, but just
in case, stay out of my way."

"Done." Tapper looked at the last door before Lake's room.
It was unlabeled, and Lori thought she heard something coming
from inside. Someone moving furniture. "Should we care about
that?"

"Later."

Lori turned the handle on Lake's door and flung it open.

The office was unoccupied, and everything in it looked
expensive. The desk was mahogany, and the chair was sleek
and made from black leather. The art on the wall was all dark
blues and purples. Most of it was abstract stuff, but it somehow
reminded Lori of being underwater. The window looked out

over the ocean, which was still gray with predawn light. The bookshelves had sculptures that were all curvy and spiky and generally weird.

She looked back at the desk, trying to figure out what was wrong. After a moment it clicked.

Tapper walked in slowly, taking stock of the room. "Rich."

"Rich and fake," Lori said. "No pictures of a family. No sticky notes, no pens, no coffee mug."

"None of those desk-toy things for people like me to fidget with," Tapper added. "She knows she needs a desk to act like a person, so she gets one. But she doesn't get any of the stuff that goes with it."

"Fake," Lori said again. The desk had an office phone and two large flat-screen monitors lined up with perfect precision, with cables leading down through a hole in the desk to a computer below. The glossy black keyboard and mouse on the desk were wireless. "Let's look at the computer."

"Better than nothing." Tapper zipped closer. "Doubt a feeder stores all the good stuff on its personal desktop machine, though."

"She's doing a radio interview," Lori muttered. "If a monster can do a radio interview, it probably uses a computer."

"You throw around 'monster' real easy," Tapper said, still looking around. "Am I a monster?"

"I . . ." She looked at him. He was slouched, hair already pulling free from where he'd tried to tame it.

Her phone buzzed twice for *no*, and for a moment Lori was irrationally angry that Handler was telling her what to say.

"No," Lori said anyway. "I don't know what you are, or what happened to you, but I don't think you're a monster. But *she is*, all right?"

"Why, because you couldn't lie to her?"

"Because she wanted to kill me, and that means she's a danger to my brother, too," Lori said, ticking off the points on her fingers. "And she tried to do *something* to all of you. Experiments or torture or something."

"So you care about us?" Tapper looked over. "Hunh. Then maybe you're not a monster either."

Lori shut her mouth and kept walking around the room. She pulled out the chair and brought Lake's computer out of sleep mode, but it was locked. "Do you know anything about hacking computers?"

"No." Tapper looked down under the desk. "The cables aren't even tangled. Even I don't set up my computer without getting the cables tangled."

Lori sighed and, out of a mild sense of anxiety and the thought that it might help her guess the password, turned up the phone again.

"*The miracoral isn't just an energy source or a new alternative polymer that can replace our dependence on oil,*" Lake was saying. "*The applications to medicine are astounding as well. In fact, we are very close to some exciting breakthroughs in the field of treating diseases using miracoral augmentation.*"

"Or you *were*," Tapper muttered, "until we busted out of that black cargo container."

Lori tried typing in "miracoral" as the password, and then "MIRACORAL," "Miracoral," "m1r@c0r@l," and a few other combinations. Nothing worked.

"*So, Ms. Lake, can you give us a picture of what these advances might look li—I'm sorry, are you all right?*"

"*Fine, fine. Just a phone notification. The Lake Foundation is busy at all hours, sometimes busier than others.*"

"Nothing." Lori glared at the password field. "We've got nothing." She glanced back at her phone, then picked it up and typed quickly.

Lori: Can you get us in?

Handler: No. Security here's more than normal.
Handler: Hard to keep the security cams down, even.
Handler: And just got harder. Like something's pushing.

"We've got more than nothing. There's something there on the floor." Tapper pointed to a spot by the desk. "Something happened last night. Those eels were here. They fed or killed or . . . something."

"Okay, that's . . ." Lori broke off. "How can you tell?"

"Because I can *see* it," Tapper said, his voice harsh as he looked away. "You get to kill stuff, the blonde is Mystique, Pint-Size is bulletproof, and even Ipanema can mess with people's heads. I can see stuff."

"You also get superspeed," Lori added.

"Come on. Nothing else here." Tapper left the office. "Let's see what—" He broke off as Lori's phone rang. "Seriously?"

"Sorry!" Lori glared at the phone. It said "J Vickers Cell," and she picked it up. "Hi, Jenn!"

"It is way too early for *Hi, Jenn*," her friend deadpanned. "Anyway, sorry to bug you on the job, but Ben's up, and he's concerned about how you weren't there when he got up." Jenn was using the careful language that indicated she was trying to be a Responsible Babysitter.

"Oh, for . . ." Lori sighed. "I *did* tell him before he went to sleep last night that you'd be there when he woke up."

"Yeah, that's what I told him," Jenn said agreeably, "but he said that just because I was going to be here, it didn't mean you were going to be gone, and you never said that you were going to be gone, and—"

"Yeah, yeah, I get it." Lori pinched the bridge of her nose.

"You mind putting him on?"

"Sure thing."

There was the sound of the phone on the other end of the line jostling, and then a tiny "Hi, Lori." Her phone buzzed, and she looked at it.

Handler: Remember, he's seven.

"Hey, little guy." Lori found a smile from somewhere deep inside her. "How are you doing?"

"I was worried when I woke up and you weren't there," Ben said.

"I'm sorry that I didn't make it clear that I'd be off at work this morning," Lori said, rolling her eyes. "But Jenn is staying with you, and since you're already up, you'll have time to play with her before you go to day care."

"Um," said Ben, and Lori winced, because she had *really* been hoping that one was gonna slide by smoothly, "if Jenn is here, can she stay with me until you come home instead of going to day care?"

"Well, I think that Jenn may have other plans for today," Lori said.

"Jenn said she's free as long as we need, so she can stay all day until you come home, okay?" Ben asked, although "asked" was stretching it.

Jenn, you traitor, Lori thought, and said, "Sure thing, little guy. But only if you eat your breakfast, okay?"

"Okay!"

"I love you. Put Jenn back on."

"I love you too."

The phone made more crazy jostling noises, and then Jenn said, "It's really okay."

"I shouldn't be too late," Lori said. "Thanks. Also, tell him that breakfast includes a banana."

"Don't worry, Lori. We'll be fine. And when you get back, you can try on the outfit I got you."

"See you!" Lori hung up the phone and looked over at Tapper, who was actually kind of smiling. "What?"

"Weird to see another side," Tapper said, still almost smiling.

"If it helps, I can gripe at you to eat your fruit at breakfast too," Lori muttered.

"I'm good." Tapper moved around the room, still looking, and Lori followed. The phone kept playing the interview.

"And you really think it's possible to make advances like that, to augment humanity?"

"I absolutely do, dear. We already wear glasses to improve our vision. We take vitamins to strengthen our bones. While enhancing ourselves with what we learn from the miracoral might sound absurd right now, imagine a world in which we solved world hunger with sea farms and genetically grown superfoods. Imagine life without disease, without war over natural resources, perhaps even without aging. If the miracoral has that potential stored in it, I intend to see it unleashed."

"And how close would you say you were, ma'am?"

"While I can't get into specifics," Tia Lake said with a smile Lori could hear over the radio, *"I think I may have some of the answers in my office right now."*

Lori winced right as her phone buzzed.

"Tapper," she said, "that sounds like she knows we're here."

"How would she know that?" he said, glaring over at her.

Handler: So hey

Handler: Maybe possible those password attempts tripped an alarm

Handler: And that the alarm pinged Tia Lake's phone.

"Um, no idea," Lori said. "But we should probably get moving." She stalked out of the office. The room next door still had something going on behind the door, someone moving a desk or a chair. "Come on. We check this, then we grab the others." Her phone buzzed.

Handler: Or leave now.
Handler: Or that.
Handler: Instead of being dumb.

Tapper glanced back. "Ready?"

"If there's a feeder inside, just stay out of my way," Lori said.

Tapper nodded and tried the handle. It was locked, and he sighed, rolled out his shoulders, and then *blurred*. One moment he was standing in front of the door, and then next the door was swinging crazily from its hinges with small pieces of metal and sawdust puffing out in a cloud around Tapper's extended fist.

There *was* a feeder inside, a strange thing that—

an old woman in a shawl—maybe the pattern had been bright once, but now it was faded—and she was hunched over and harmless, nothing to trouble yourself with if you passed her washing her clothes by the stream

—could have passed for human if seen at a distance in bad light, but in the light of the bright and sterile room, it was clearly a leathery thing covered in plates, all colorless claws and twitching mandibles.

And it was strapped to a long gurney on what passed for its back, with a bulbous mass of yellow pulsating at its abdomen. It turned to Tapper and Lori with a shelled and antenna-eyed face as they stared at it in shock.

"Please help me," it said.

Tapper turned to Lori. "I'm out of your way."

IARA

Iara was sitting against the wall, huddled in the light blue sun-dress she had worn before she had known their adventures today would include swimming. She had no problem with swimming—even before the change, it had been lovely to slip through the water feeling weightless and relaxed—but it called for a different outfit.

Snuggling with Hawk had been quite enjoyable, though.

Now Hawk was standing as tall as he could to block the door-way from the guards and their guns. "Hey, guys, chill," he said as the eels slithered toward him. "You don't wanna shoot me. Like seriously."

"No," said one of the guards Iara had seen before Hawk had blocked her view. "She said bullets would not hurt you. She said we had to share, but that we'd get them back."

"Wait, what do you mean the *eeyarrrrrrgh*!" Hawk stumbled back, clutching at the eels coiled around him. One of them had already snaked its way up his leg and around his torso and was trying to force its way into Hawk's mouth.

Using the wall as leverage, Iara pushed herself up to an awk-ward crouch, the best she could do with her limited mobility. "Maya, are you strong enough to throw me at them?"

"These are just fake muscles!" Maya said, and then, "Wait! Maybe!"

As Hawk dropped to one knee, still vainly grabbing for the eels, Maya lunged at Iara—without moving her feet. Her arms stretched out unnaturally far and caught Iara's hands, and then Maya *pulled*, her arms snapping back as she did.

It was not as graceful as the superhero team-up move Iara had hoped for, but it worked nevertheless. Iara sailed through the doorway.

The guards had been standing and watching their eels, and they raised their guns but did not have time to aim as Iara smashed into them. She struck down one, pushed off him, and caught the second with a punch to the temple that sent him sprawling.

She was faster in the water, but a hero fought with whatever tools she possessed.

Then she landed hard on her side and lay gasping and scrabbling as the third guard turned to her. She got her legs under her and lunged as best she could, knocking his gun away before he could aim, and he stumbled back, grabbed the gun another guard had dropped from by the doorway, and stepped back out of reach into the hallway. Behind him, Hawk was still flailing and grunting on the floor.

The guard did not look cruel or villainous, or even blank like the men on the boat who had tried to kill them yesterday. He looked desperate, his eyes pleading and his face waxy even as he brought the gun to bear on her.

Then Maya fell down onto the guard from, apparently, the ceiling, tangling him up with her long limbs. The guard flailed, and Maya's long fingers slid around the wrist of his gun hand as he spun.

The gun went off, and then again, and Iara rolled away before she realized that the gun had not been aimed at her.

It was aimed at Hawk. Again and again it fired. Hawk, of course, was fine.

The eels coiled *around* Hawk, however, exploded messily.

The guard began screaming as the last eel fell from Hawk, dead and slimy. Maya rolled off the guard, arms still around him, and slid through his legs before twisting. The guard somersaulted over her and slammed into the doorframe.

"Impressive!" Iara called over.

"I hated wrestling," Maya said, her skin shimmering as she slid back to her natural state, complete with skinny jeans and the same lime-green T-shirt with a smiley face on it, "but being superflexible helps a lot."

"*Grrrrraaah!*" Hawk yelled, pulling one last eel out of his mouth. It was long, and he gagged as he did it, then flung the creature to the ground and crushed it beneath his heel. "Thanks, both of you," he said between breaths as he pushed himself back to his feet. "I can still taste that thing."

Iara opened her mouth to reply, and then from behind her came a wretched wail. She turned awkwardly and looked over her shoulder.

It was the guard she'd knocked down. He was looking at the remains of the eels lying in the hallway, his mouth hanging open, one muscle in his cheek twitching.

"No, no-no-no-no!" he cried, and lunged forward, knocking Iara down.

She rolled over and got her hands up, ready for an attack, but he was already past her and out in the hallway. He clutched one of the dead eels in his shaking hands.

Then he opened his mouth and tried to shove the eel inside.

"Dude!" Hawk shouted, and knocked the guard down.

"Let her back in!" the guard shouted, crawling toward another dead eel. Hawk blocked him, and the guard tried frantically to reach past him. "I need her, *I need her!*"

"What is he doing?" Iara asked, feeling sick to her stomach as she looked at him.

"She needs to eat," the guard muttered, still trying to reach past Hawk. "She eats and it takes the pain and you don't have to be here anymore and *I need her.*" He lunged again, and when he bounced off Hawk's immovable frame, he fell back, tears starting to stream down his face. "I need her."

"You're saying the eels kill you," Maya said to him. "Is there one still in you? Is it making you do this?"

"What," said the guard. "No! I'm, I'm, I'm . . . I'm starting to remember, and I don't have to remember when they're there! You do what she asks, and they stay, and you don't remember the things that hurt you!" He looked at Maya, and Iara saw him try to compose himself. "Please. I don't want it to come back. I want to be fine. Let me be fine. Feeling nothing is better than feeling pain!"

Maya gave the guard a sad little smile. "I know it feels better to take the pain away, but this won't help you get better. And you need to get better, okay? There are people who—"

"No!" The guard lunged—not at Hawk this time, but at Iara, and Iara flinched before realizing he sought the gun beside her. He grabbed it, brought it up under his own chin, and fired.

Iara looked away. When she opened her eyes, her sensitive ears ringing from the echoes of the gunshot, the guard was on the ground. There was blood on the wall behind him. Out in the hall, Hawk and Maya stared at the dead man in horror.

Iara took a breath. Another. Even the heroes could not save everyone.

Then she swallowed and made her voice strong. "We know the eels affect their victims. An addiction, even as they consume them from the inside out. It is good to know this. It is better than not knowing."

Hawk looked over at her, his breath still uneven. "I don't know."

If he was looking at her, though, he wasn't looking at the dead man on the ground. "Pick me back up, please," Iara said, and he came forward and gently lifted her in his arms. "Maya, come in and close the door."

"What do we do?" Maya asked, her voice tiny.

Iara pointed at the computer servers behind them. "We find what we came here to find. We find out what we are and why Tia Lake wants us."

LORI

As she stood there in the stark white room looking at the feeder strapped down, her phone buzzed.

Handler: Okay. This is new.

"Superhelpful," Lori muttered, and then looked at the feeder. "What are you?"

"I was doing my wash, and she took me," said the feeder. It pulled against the straps holding it down to no effect. "I was washing the clothes."

"It's doing something that makes it look like an old lady," Tapper said, voice tight. "But it's not. Are they all like this?"

"Yes. You can see what it really is?"

"I see everything, remember?" Tapper grimaced.

"What are you?" Lori asked again. "The truth."

"I wash the clothes of the ones that will die," the thing said. It cocked what was probably its head at her. "The smell changes in the parts that aren't here yet." Lori's phone buzzed.

Handler: bean nighe
Handler: Scottish relative of the banshee
Handler: No idea how you pronounce it

"You mean you kill them," Lori said. "You . . . what do you do? Tracking pheromones? You catch the scent of people who have illnesses, and you eat them."

"I wash the clothes," the feeder snapped back at her. "The smell needs to change so it matches the parts that aren't here yet."

"It can sense the future," Tapper said. "Parts of it are . . . I don't know, shiny. Blurry. It's like how things look when I go fast. It smells when people are going to die, and then it kills them and . . . I don't know." He pointed at its belly, distended and covered with the bulbous mass of yellow. "That's not part of it. It's something else, another one or—"

"A parasite," Lori finished, and Tapper blinked, then nodded.

"She can't grow more of her here except in others like us," the feeder said. "We make them from the little bits, and once they are big enough, she puts them in the prey here to grow." It looked at Tapper, mandibles on its face clicking. The almost-human face crackled and jolted into an expression that could have been pity. "She wants you. She told me. She wants the touched." Her eyes clicked over to Lori, and the look of pity fell away like two gears with half of a face on each, turning from humanity into alien angles. "Not you. You are just prey. You are not going to die soon, little dear. I could smell if you were. That is my gift to you." Its mandibles clacked. "In return, will you free me? A poor thing that only washes the clothes of the ones who will die. Will you show kindness?"

Lori walked over to the bed where the feeder lay strapped down. The mass of yellow pulsated, not regularly like a heartbeat but as though something inside wanted to get out. "Take my hand," she said, and reached out.

The feeder's little claw clasped Lori's hand, pinching sharp enough to hurt, and the feeder said, "Yes, I have many clothes to wash, little dear, and I—"

The fangs came out of an impossible space and closed down upon the feeder on the table, spearing through it in a dozen different places. The feeder shrieked and thrashed, limbs flailing under the restraints, and then, as the great curving fangs closed, the feeder went still.

One of the fangs had pierced the yellow blob at the thing's abdomen, and Lori watched with sick fascination as it popped open. Dozens of tiny snakelike forms slid out and splatted limply on the white floor. She realized they were tiny eels, lying dead in the slime that had held them.

A moment later the fangs withdrew, still locked around their prey, seeming to fall away into the distance even though there was no distance for them to fall into. A moment after that the bed was empty, the straps loosely holding nothing.

"Guess I've got the *second*-worst power," Tapper said.

The laugh bubbled up inside Lori, a stupid little chuckle that found its way out as she turned to him. "Thanks," she said, and shook her head. "I needed that."

"Yes," said a voice from the doorway behind them, "I needed that *too*, which makes you *eating* it a bit of a problem."

06

IARA

Iara settled into the seat by the server. She rolled out her shoulders, pulled the keyboard and mouse toward her, and squinted at the screen.

"It requires a password," she said.

"Well," said Hawk, "I guess we could wait until one of the other guys wakes up." He nudged one of the guards Iara had knocked out.

"I don't know how to hack computers," Maya said, shoving her hands into her pockets. "I mostly just played lesbian dating sims."

"I do not believe this will be a problem," Iara said, smiling over at her. Then she looked at the computer tower beside the desk and *clicked* at it.

"You can hack computers with your voice?" Maya asked.

"I knew a few tricks before I changed," Iara said, and rolled the chair over to one side. She was glad that Tapper was not present. He would have said something about Oracle again, the computer hacker in a wheelchair, and she would have been annoyed with him. She looked at the computer tower again and *clicked*. "It was slow and boring most of the time. This made it much faster."

"That is supercool!"

Iara shut her eyes and let out a breath. With her two triangulating clicks, she had an image of the processor, and somewhere between feeling and hearing, she could sense the electric currents, the hum of the current through the room and countless little ones and zeroes carrying all the information she wanted.

"What *kind* of lesbian dating sims?" Hawk asked casually.

Boys, Iara thought, and *clicked* a third time.

When she opened her eyes, the password field was filled with a bunch of dots. She hit enter, and the desktop flashed into place.

"We are in," she said, and flipped her hair back over her shoulder. "Unless you have anything more pressing to discuss." Hawk blushed and looked down. "So. Let us hunt."

She did a search for her own name and found a massive collection of files, all encrypted. A few *clicks* cut through that, and then she was at something she couldn't just click her way past: an exceedingly large group of Word documents.

"Aw, man, you didn't tell me we were gonna have to study," Hawk muttered.

"We seem to be part of something the Lake Foundation cares very much about." Iara frowned, biting her lip as she scrolled through the list. "The company makes most of its money harnessing the power of the miracoral, and this is . . . we are . . ." She sighed. "This is a great deal of data."

"There," Maya said, and pointed, and Iara looked at Maya with one eyebrow raised until Maya blushed and added, "Um, there's a doc with a name different from the others. All the others look like dates or versions or something, right, but that one that says 'Nix Vector' is different."

Iara smiled. "Well hunted." She opened the document.

Executive Summary:

The mutation of the Nix strongly correlates to the miracoral incursion. While it is not conclusive that the Nix are intended as an agent of the miracoral, or indeed that the miracoral is a causative agent in their creation at all, further study is warranted.

All Nix located so far appeared human before the miracoral incursion, and all have birth dates within the same year. There is no common ethnicity or location associated with the Nix mutation, although all Nix either lived near water or participated in aquatic sports (swimming, water polo, etc.). Whether the mutation is a by-product of the incursion or a response to it remains unknown. Regardless of cause, all Nix have undergone physical mutation evidencing new abilities, most tied to increased aptitude for aquatic survival. Physical testing and dissection will yield more data on specific ability sets and known levels of mutation from human norm. Because of the results of early experimentation on Subject Campbell (see below), the eel symbiote will not be introduced to the Nix upon capture of the subjects.

Targeted Candidates:

Bautista, Joshua: Mutation includes significant physical augmentation and resistance to physical injury, along with the ability to last up to an hour on a single breath.

Campbell, Sarah: UPDATE: Upon capture, Campbell was exposed to an eel symbiote. The subject immediately suffered seizures and was dead within minutes. It is unclear at this time whether this was a matter of incompatibility between Nix biology and the eel symbiote, or if it was a deliberate decision by the element responsible for the creation of the Nix to terminate the subject rather than let it become compromised by the eel. Prior to death, mutation included bioluminescence in nonliving tissue (hair, fingernails) and the ability to generate electric fields.

Costa, Iara: Mutation includes moderate physical augmentation and hearing, as well as possible electrochemical reception. Note that Costa suffered an incomplete L2 spinal cord injury in childhood. This has not been corrected by the mutation, but Costa's abilities are strongest in water.

Daniels, Shawn: Mutation includes dermal adaptation, the ability to consciously reconfigure the properties of skin cells, which he uses to increase the effective sharpness and density of his limbs.

Fin—

"We can't read this all now," Maya cut in, and slid Iara aside. "Let me copy it to the USB drive I got." She pulled out the keychain that Iara had bought her yesterday and popped open the drive. "We can read it later together, all right?"

"All right, *alemã*." Iara scooted out of the way, a little taken aback, as Maya slid the drive in. "I suppose you are correct. Do we have a plan for meeting the others?"

"Um . . ." Hawk thought for a moment. "No. You want me to call Tapper?"

"That would be good, thank you . . ." With a little smile, she added, *"Joshua."*

The caught-by-his-mother look on his face was perfect.

LORI

Lori spun, hands balled into fists. The man in the doorway was short, portly, and unassuming, with curly hair that was starting to go bald in the front and a casually annoyed expression.

"Who are you?" she asked.

"Says the intruder who set off the alarm and interrupted Ms. Lake's interview," he said dryly. "I'm someone who is really looking forward to explaining to Ms. Lake how her longest-lasting incubator just got eaten. You can call me Kirk. And *you*"—he cocked his head, then smiled—"would be Angler Consulting." His gaze slid over to Tapper. "And your new friend Latrell Taylor. How are you, Mister Taylor? Still hoping to get that scholarship?"

"Is he human?" Tapper asked Lori without taking his eyes off the man. "He looks human."

"Oh, what kind of question is that?" Kirk asked, rolling his eyes. "Are *you* human? After what's happened, your body constantly on the edge of exploding into motion and your eyes taking in far too much information, are you human anymore? But then, you weren't even sure before, were you?" Kirk's voice was soft, pattering along without worry as he smiled at Tapper. "And after all, the first thing you thought when you got our little information packet was that this had to be a mistake, because you weren't good enough, weren't smart enough, that you were just a disappointment to your mother . . . and your second was wondering if maybe, just maybe, *we could fix you.*"

There was a whoosh beside Lori, and then Tapper was in front of Kirk, and Kirk's head rocked back where Tapper's fist had landed, and then Tapper was blurring into another punch, and another.

And Kirk still wasn't falling.

Suddenly Kirk's hand was on Tapper's shoulder, and Tapper was on his knees.

"A little overwhelming, isn't it, Mister Taylor?" Kirk asked. "Don't worry. I don't think I *can* fix you, but I can make sure you don't hurt your mother or disappoint your teacher or have any of the kids at school look at you from the corner of their eyes ever again, and isn't that what you really want?" Tapper's head was bowed. He had one arm still up, but Kirk was holding it. "Maybe you'll be on the table, or maybe you'll be in a tank, but you won't be hurting anyone with what you are anymore."

"He'll pass." Lori lunged in, knocked Tapper from Kirk's grip, and grabbed Kirk's wrist. "Let's see what you taste like."

She waited for the fangs to come out of nowhere and spear through whatever Kirk was.

Kirk smiled at her. "Oh, honey." And then he twisted his arm so that he was grabbing *her* wrist instead—

the phone was going to ring again, and Mister Barkin was going to tell her that they were taking her brother away because Lori couldn't take care of him, she was a terrible guardian, and her brother deserved better, deserved someone smarter and more organized, and the worst part wasn't that Mister Barkin was going to say it, the worst part was that when it happened, Lori would be relieved, because at least finally now it was done, and there was no more wondering and no more worrying and no more trying and failing and pretending she loved anyone, because how could she, she wasn't even human

—and Lori realized that her phone was buzzing frantically in her pants pocket.

She was on the ground. When had she fallen to the ground?

She scrambled back, yanking her arm out of his grasp. The

tiles on the white floor were cold beneath the palms of her hands as she crab walked away.

"Don't get up," Kirk said, his voice still casual. "In fact, get used to this room, because Ms. Lake really wants to meet you, and I've got a feeling you'll be spending a lot of time here." He came forward, unhurried and smiling. "And when it's over, the world will have one less monster in it. Isn't that what you really want?"

Lori was still scrambling away from him. Her hands slipped on something wet on the floor, and she sprawled out on her back. Kirk didn't change his pace. "What are you?"

"I don't have giant fangs or crushing superstrength or a kung fu grip," Kirk said. He reached down, and Lori kicked at his hand, knocking it away, and then scrambled back out of reach until her head cracked against the wall. "But we all have to eat, don't we? So when I get ahold of something I want, *I tell it the truth*." He smiled again. "That's all I do."

Lori pushed herself back to her feet. Kirk was still coming. "What about Lake? Feeders don't work for each other. You compete for food—killing people."

"Feeders?" Kirk actually did stop now, chuckling. "Isn't that a little prosaic? Why not call us 'breathers' or 'reproducers'? Everything feeds, Miss Angler Consulting. You just disapprove of my dietary choices." He raised an eyebrow. "But if you're going to use a metaphor, then *use* it. You think Ms. Lake is just another *feeder*, like that thing you killed out on the docks or the one you just killed in here?" His eyes narrowed, making his smile turn suddenly nasty. "She's *big*, Miss Angler Consulting. She likes to have someone to clean the bits of her that she can't reach, clear away the extra scraps she doesn't want to hunt down herself."

"You're like one of those birds that cleans the crocodile's mouth," Tapper said. He was back by the other corner, and his voice was a little unsteady, but he was on his feet and glaring.

Kirk rolled his eyes. "The word is 'symbiosis,' Mister Taylor. I'm sure even the public education system probably mentioned it once or twice."

"The word is 'parasite,'" Tapper shot back. "You cling to her flank and eat her leftovers and hope she never notices you."

"Oh, look at you, trying to offend me." Kirk turned to Tapper. "Do you think that little distraction is going to save Miss Angler Consulting? Do you think it's going to make her not think of you as *that creepy jerk* anymore? It must be hard, knowing everyone thinks of you as so rude, so angry, when all the time you're hiding, because if they saw what was underneath, it would be even worse."

"You . . ." Tapper paused. Then he reached into his pocket. "Hang on, got a call."

"Children today," Kirk exclaimed, and looked over at Lori. "You can't even have a decent conversation anymore, with everyone looking at their phones."

"Yeah, we've got trouble," Tapper said into the phone. "They're on us. Yeah."

"Well, then," Kirk said, turning back to Lori, "I guess you get to go first." He stepped forward again.

"No, it's too far," Tapper said. "Can you get the lights?"

Kirk reached out, and Lori ducked under his grab, hammered him in the ribs, grabbed his arm, and punched him in the jaw. It was like punching rubber—it didn't hurt, but it didn't seem to do much either. Kirk spun toward her, and she blocked the sweep of his arm, kicked him in the knee, and yanked on his arm as she kicked his ankle. He was heavier than he looked, though, and his other hand clapped down on her waist—

she couldn't do it, couldn't take care of him on her own, how could she ever think it was possible, she was nothing, just a sad, weak thing pretending to be a real little girl, she didn't even care about him, not really, he'd be better off with someone who really loved him

—and Tapper slammed into her, pulling her free, and she blinked in the sudden darkness and realized that the lights were out.

"Hang on," Tapper muttered, and Lori started to ask why or to what, and then they *blurred*, and it was a crushing rush of force all through her body, Tapper's grip like iron as he held her, and the breath blew out of her lungs as something shattered, and as cold air whipped around her, Lori realized that what had shattered had been the windowed wall looking out over the miracoral pool.

Tapper let go. "Best I could do," he called over as their arc turned into a fall.

Lori had time to get her breath back before they hit the water.

The cold was as much of a shock as the impact itself, and she flailed, inhaling water and then realizing that she was actually *inhaling* water and kicking blindly, frantically, wondering how far under she was, how close to the miracoral that had attacked the last time she'd gotten close to it. The water was grabbing at her clothes, pulling her down, and—

A hand closed around her and pulled her up, and a moment later she broke the surface, still coughing.

"You're really bad at breathing water," Tapper said beside her.

Lori spat out the last of the water, then looked around. They were in the middle of the pool. "I thought there were motion sensors."

Tapper looked back at the Lake Foundation building, which had a broken window up on the top floor. A moment later, Hawk kicked open the door they'd used to get inside, Iara in his arms and Maya close behind them.

"I think we're done with stealth mode," Tapper said. "Come on. Let's swim."

"Hey." Lori started swimming after him. He turned back, treading water at a speed that made it foam around him. "Thanks for the save."

Tapper looked away. "Thanks for not teleporting out and leaving me on my own back there."

"Yeah." *Yeah, it's not really under my control, and now that you say that, I'm not sure why Handler didn't do that,* she didn't add. "Let's just hope the others found more than we did."

HAWK

A few hours later they were back on the rooftop at PortManta, all of them dry and not just Tapper, who apparently used his super-speed to vibrate all the water off him, and man, that sounded kind of dirty. Iara was back in her chair, wearing her leather jacket over a creamy white sundress that made the warm red tones in her skin stand out. She munched on a breakfast burrito and shot him a grin when she caught him looking.

"So we're something called Nix," Hawk said, looking at the late-morning skyline and hoping he wasn't blushing as much as he felt like he was. "What's that, anyway?"

"It's not *angels,*" Tapper shot back. Hawk winced. Apparently Tapper had heard him yesterday. "Maya, send us the file." He popped a hard candy into his mouth and crunched it loudly.

"Okay, hang on." Maya had a smoothie and was fiddling with her phone. "I transferred it over from the USB drive with the cord that came with it—"

"After I showed you how," Tapper added.

"—and I'm just getting it formatted right so it's easy for us all to read on our phones, and also I was really hoping to see something about the fae or—"

"Please, *alemã*," Iara said, smiling, "so we can all read."

"Right! Sorry! Okay, here you go." She pressed a button on her phone. "Check your mail."

"Would've been faster to set up a cloud," Tapper muttered, glaring at his phone, Maya, or the world in general. Then he started scrolling, his fingers moving faster on the screen than Hawk could follow.

"It seems . . ." Iara had her lips pursed, looking at her phone. "It seems Tapper was correct."

"Duh, Ipanema."

Iara sighed. "The document suggests we—all Nix—are mutations. If I understand correctly, they believe we are linked somehow to the miracoral."

"The Lake Foundation is the big corporation responsible for the miracoral," Lori said, frowning at her own phone. She'd grabbed new clothes as well—jeans and a dark blue blouse that was light for the cloudy day—but she didn't seem to mind the cold. Summers in the Pacific Northwest must run cooler than summers in Austin, Hawk decided. "At least, that's the public story. Lake was just saying in the interview that they engineered it to help create renewable energy and replace oil-based plastics."

"They're lying." Tapper didn't look up from his own screen. "They want something from the miracoral. They're studying it—that's how they figured out how to use it for power—but they didn't create it. Looks like it showed up about two years ago—"

"Isn't that around the time the water rose?" Maya asked, and then frowned. "I mean, I think? It's kind of hard to remember when it's not written down anywhere and nobody else will talk with you about it."

"That's right." Lori nodded, smiling over at her. "Or at least, I remember it that way too. The water rose, and then . . ." Her face clouded over, and she blinked away an unhappy thought. "Then the miracoral came, and the Lake Foundation started using it for electricity and making things out of the gray plastic."

"That's all extra," Tapper said, scrolling down fast enough that his fingers blurred. "Stuff they found out while trying to learn its weakness."

"When did you all get your abilities?" Lori asked.

"A year ago," Maya said. "I remember, it was after I switched to swim team, and people were being jerks, and then all of a sudden I could, you know, do weird stuff."

"Same here," Tapper said. "They think the miracoral did something to us. They think we might *be* the weakness they're looking for."

"Their mistake," Hawk said, grinning. "Those eels in the computer room found out the hard way not to mess with us."

Iara didn't grin back. Maya flinched a little. *Girls,* Hawk thought, and rolled his eyes.

"So, uh," Maya said, looking away, "if we're linked to the miracoral, does that make us mermaids?"

"No. Gah. Stop." Tapper glared over. "And they're crayfish. Or crawdads, if you're a Southern hick instead of a Midwestern ditz."

"You could be a mer*man*?" Maya offered. Tapper kept glaring.

"Regardless of who is a mermaid," Iara said, smiling at both of them, "their studies on the miracoral are inconclusive. When they study the coral, it seems completely normal. It has none of the properties that make it useful."

"It's a feeder, then," Lori said in a low voice.

"Like the thing in the white room?" Tapper asked. "Or Kirk, or the eels, or SpongeBob?"

"Like all of it." Lori sounded angry; Hawk saw that the hand not holding the phone was balled into a fist. "Feeders don't show up on camera most of the time. If you ran a test, the instruments would show that nothing was there, or something normal. That's how they work. And Lake had one chained up by her office."

"She was using it," Tapper cut in, voice rough as though daring her to argue. "Like those wasps that lay eggs in the spider, and then the eggs hatch and the larvae eat their way out. Only she was breeding more of those eels."

"Well, that's another thing we did today, then." Hawk grinned over at him. "No more eel makers, right?" He thought for a moment about those things crawling on him, curling around and trying to force their way into his mouth, and then put the thought out of his mind.

"Yes." Lori nodded. "And she had another one working for her. Kirk. My—" She broke off for a second as her phone buzzed, then started again. "My power didn't work on it. It was like . . . I need a place to latch on, to attack. Usually when I touch them, that's all I need, but whatever Kirk is, it couldn't see him. So whoever Lake is, she's big enough that she uses other feeders to breed her pets or do her dirty work." She shook her head. It almost looked like she was going to cry. "We're no further than when we began."

Hawk stood, and in a moment, he was beside her. "Hey."

She glared up at him. "Look, we've got two more days, and then she finds me and comes after my brother, and that *cannot* happen. I will not *let* it happen."

She was scared, Hawk realized. Using sad and angry to cover it.

"You don't do a lot of team sports at school, do you?" Hawk asked.

"Like you do, Pint-Size?" Tapper shot back.

"I did football." Hawk grinned. "Being small makes me harder to tackle. And also, it's good for teaching strategy." He dropped to one knee beside Lori. "Look, you start at your own twenty, you run for four yards and get tackled, it's easy to look at that and see how little you gained. But you've also set up a second-and-six, which means you can pass *or* run. You've put your team closer to a first down, one step closer to the other end zone."

"Ah," Iara said with a little sniff, "*American* football."

"Provided you can convert on third-and-short," Maya added, and then, when everyone looked at her, "Sorry!"

"How do you know so much about football?" Hawk asked with a laugh.

"You don't think they have women's teams at some schools?" Tapper snapped. "Or coed?"

"Whoa, dude, chill." Hawk raised his hands in mock surrender. "I'm just glad to have someone else here who gets it. Anyway, point is, you guys are smart. Keep reading. If they studied the miracoral and wanted to study us, they had to have other stuff about the miracoral and what it does, right? We pulled all their data. Maybe we can find out why we turned into Nix. You figure that out, we're solid."

"It's not just mutation," Tapper said. "It chose us."

"Like changelings?" Maya asked.

"Not like—arrgh!" Tapper glared over at her. "No! Something made us into Nix on purpose!"

"Why?" Lori asked.

"Because it was screwing with us." Tapper put his phone down. "Because it hates us."

Iara gave him a soft smile, hands folded in her lap. "I know it seems hard, the things we must face now, but if we are brave—"

"Because we were all broken," Tapper snapped, cutting her off, "so it thinks we're useless, fair game, the weak kid the bully picks on because nobody else will care."

"Are you like that?" Maya said quietly.

"Shut up!" Tapper blurred to his feet and stalked across the rooftop, his fingers twitching. "Just shut up. I was . . . You think *I don't know*?" He wasn't looking at them. He was blurring in place. "You think I don't know how I sound all the time? I had pills. They were expensive, and my mom's insurance only covered like half of it, but they *worked*. Stuff didn't come at me all at once anymore. I could see one thing instead of seeing everything. I could, I could walk in a crowd and not feel like all the talking was gonna make me crawl out of my skin. And then *this* comes, and all of a sudden, it's all *there* again, and I can't, I can't, the pills don't work anymore, and every time I let everything speed up, it's like it's all there going through me. It's screwing with me, just like it gave Ipanema mermaid powers because she's stuck in the chair, or . . ." He looked back at them, and his mouth worked for a moment like words were fighting to come out. "Or whatever. It did this to all of us." He looked over at Iara. "Sorry."

"Partial paraplegia." Iara sat up straight. "It was a car accident. I had spent years convincing the boys that a pretty girl could like Superman and the Avengers just as they did, that I was not a 'fake geek girl.'"

"Oh, that's a thing in Brazil, too?" Hawk asked.

Iara nodded. "But after the accident, when I am out of the hospital, when I am back with my friends? The store where we would buy our comics is at the top of many stairs." She shook her head. "If anyone thinks my disability makes me weak, that is their mistake. But you are right, Tapper. I was angry. I did not fit."

"And Pint-Size is right too," Tapper muttered, not looking at Hawk. "We got a win. We know more than we did."

"Heck yeah, dude." Hawk forced himself to grin over, since

Tapper was trying, even if he didn't speak universal dude language. "We kicked butt."

"We did." Iara flashed Hawk a smile after Tapper didn't, and really, if only one of those two people was gonna smile at Hawk, he was okay with it being her. "We struck a blow against the monsters and escaped unharmed. We are one step closer to destroying them. Tonight, we celebrate that."

"Wooo!" Maya waved her arms in what was possibly the white-girl-est attempt at . . . something . . . Hawk had ever seen. "Pizza and movies and kissing games!"

"You guys can celebrate," Lori said, pushing herself to her feet. She had one arm wrapped around herself. "If we're done, I think I should probably go home before the sitter starts sending ransom notes." Her phone buzzed, and she glanced down at it.

"Is that her now?" Iara asked. "If you need to go, we can call you when we find something in the files."

Lori looked at her phone for a long moment, and then jerked and looked up. It was weird, Hawk thought. Even though Iara had spoken, Lori looked at Maya for a second.

"Um, if you guys want, maybe you can come to our place," Lori said, and then she wasn't looking at any of them. "There's more room for pizza and movies, and . . . just as long as you're quiet when Ben goes to bed."

"Party at Lori's place," Tapper said, and Hawk saw a tiny smile on the skinny guy's face.

LAKE

Tia Lake stepped into the white room where her breeding host had been staying. Her black stiletto heels clicked on the tile of the floor, the echo the only noise in the room. The chair was empty, as Kirk had said it would be. The dead eels lay in a pool of slime on the floor, the only remaining sign of what had been there.

Tia Lake's mouth was pressed into a thin line of red across her pale white face. She turned to the guard who had shuffled quietly into the room behind her. "And on the main floor."

The guard's eyes were glazed, but there was still something in his face. Not fear. He was too far gone for that. Sadness. "Three of them dead. The men tried to save them, but it was too late. They vanished."

"I'm sure they did." They would have died to save the eels, were it possible. That was how they worked.

She wanted to kill more guards now, but that wouldn't help her plans. She had to focus on that, now more than ever.

"Ask Kirk to come to me," she said, and the guard left at a jog.

Tia Lake knelt down beside the little dead eels, alone in the white room.

While the dead ones slid from the world naturally, these had never been born. They were less than living, not wholly part of her but not wholly distinct. They were still here, hours later.

Her fingernails carved little furrows into the white tile of the floor.

Small as the eels were, they were still enough of her that people would remember them, remember *her*. Still enough to trap her.

She scooped the dead little eels up in her hands and brought them to her mouth.

"You are nothing," she said as she shoveled them in.

IARA

Iara looked over when Maya said, "Ooooooooooooh, page twenty-three, page twenty-three! It says I'm an octopus, I think!"

Tapper, whose fingers blurred faster than Iara could follow, was there a moment later. "It does *not*!" he said with annoyance, and then read aloud. "'Mutations of the Nix suggest that the miracoral recognized advantageous traits of aquatic species and adapted subjects accordingly. Subject Maya Finch displays greatly enhanced flexibility and camouflage, similar to that of several species of octopus.'"

"Right, like I said!"

Iara finally reached the page. "So our abilities are not random." She kept reading. "It says that Shawn is . . ." She stopped herself, sighed. ". . . *was* similar to some type of stingray."

Maya reached over and touched her arm. "I'm sorry."

Iara smiled at her. "We cannot change what occurred, but we can seek justice for him."

"'Physical durability and resistance to toxin consistent with . . .' Dude, I'm a turtle?" Hawk said, frowning. "I never got bitten by a radioactive turtle. I'd remember that."

"I don't *think* I've been bitten by an octopus. Do octopi even bite people?"

"They have beaks." Tapper's fingers blurred on his phone. "Also the plural is 'octopuses,' and *also also*, nobody got bitten by a radioactive anything. You're thinking of Spider-Man."

"Okay." Maya frowned. "What if it's because a turtle was the last thing you touched before the miracoral found us, and like, I don't know, genetic stuff was—"

"Have you ever touched an octopus, Blondie?"

"I had fried calamari a few times," Maya tried. "But I didn't like it as much as onion rings."

Tapper sighed. "So no, the Nix probably didn't mess with us using *Teenage Mutant Ninja Turtles* rules."

Smiling, Iara read her own profile:

Subject Iara Costa's physical ability in water and radically improved hearing and electroreception are consistent with several species of dolphin.

"I actually sometimes swim with the river dolphins," Iara said happily, also noting that nothing in the notes said anything about her trick to change people's memories. So they did not know everything.

"Okay." Maya raised a finger. "So that's a point in favor of the Ninja Turtles theory."

"No, we are not doing this. I know I've never touched . . ." Tapper kept reading. "What is a peacock mantis shrimp?"

Hawk tapped on his phone, then began to laugh. "Oh, dude, I thought the turtle was dumb, but yours is so much worse," he said, and held up his phone for them all to see.

Tapper glared at the brightly colored bug-looking thing on Hawk's phone. "I am not a shrimp!"

"Wow, it's known for being grumpy, punching things so fast that it breaks the sound barrier, and having extra stuff in its eyes that lets it see more colors than anyone else can."

Tapper sighed grimly. "I'm a shrimp."

"Sorry, man." Hawk continued to laugh. "We can't all be cool dolphin-mermaids like Iara." He grinned at Iara, and she returned it. He was very cute when he smiled.

"No, Tapper, use it!" Maya said, leaning in and nodding encouragingly. "Now that you know, maybe you can figure out other stuff you can do?" She closed her eyes and screwed her face up in fierce concentration.

"Do *not*," Tapper said, "squirt ink on the patio."

"Oh. Sorry."

"There is one thing in these notes," Iara said, looking out across the rooftop, "that confuses me."

"I keep waiting for them to talk about what part of space the feeders are from," Hawk said, shaking his head and using his finger to scroll down through the document on his phone.

"It's not space," Tapper said, as he had every time Hawk had said something to this effect. "It's an alternate dimension we can't perceive because it's outside our frame of reference."

"Right," Hawk said. "Like space."

"Still no."

"They speak of all of us, plus Shawn"—Iara sighed, shared a little nod with Tapper, and kept going—"as well as a Sarah woman who died when they tried to make her into a puppet."

"Wait, if they knew that we died if they put an eel in us, why'd they try to put one in Pint-Size?" Tapper asked. "You said it was on him like bad anime."

Iara snorted, Maya blushed, and Hawk looked confused. "Yes," Iara said finally. "But it could have just been trying to choke him. There were many."

"Plus, eels are pretty stupid," Hawk added, grinning.

"My point," Iara said, since she kept getting interrupted, "is that there is nothing here about Lori."

With hearing as good as hers, it was easy to notice when the rooftop went quiet. She looked up. "What? We are certain she is not a Nix?"

"The miracoral is," Maya said quietly.

Iara frowned. "Even so, I assumed that Lake would list concerns about someone who hunts monsters, like Lori does."

"If that's the truth," Tapper said, grimacing.

"When she teleported us," Maya said, wrapping her arms around herself as though suddenly cold, "we went into this place that even you would have found weird. Uh, no offense."

Tapper waved it away. "What was it like?"

"It was wrong," Maya said, "and it was cold, and big, and something there was looking at me."

Tapper nodded. "She didn't kill the other feeder, the way she said she did. Something *else* killed it. She grabbed it, and that let the big thing sense it, and then it came out of *shut up not space*," he said rapidly, glaring at Hawk, who had his mouth open. "The point is, she has something bad tied to her. She's not like us at all."

Hawk shrugged. "So she's got some kind of superweird guardian angel?"

Tapper rolled his eyes. "I like it better when you keep trying to make it about space."

"So what does this mean?" Iara asked. "She helped us against Lake. She is continuing to help us. If you are saying she is an enemy—"

"No!" Maya said, and then looked over at Tapper, hurt. "You were supposed to say it with me."

Tapper looked at her for a long moment. "She cares about her brother," he said finally.

"And she cares about other people," Maya added. "She cares about us."

"Right," Hawk said, "so we could twist ourselves up in knots worrying about it, or we could just go with it, and if it turns out she's a monster—"

"She's not!" Maya insisted.

"But she took you into a place that creeped you out," Tapper said.

"Yeah, but—"

"And she's got a monster looking over her shoulder, and she breathes water even though she isn't like us," Tapper went on. "So think about it."

Maya glared. "She's on our side!"

"Guys, chill," Hawk said. "We've got enough *real* stuff to worry about, right? It's like you're looking for ways to feel sad about stuff instead of letting it go. Can't we just have a pizza party and hang?"

"Yes," Maya said firmly, and looked over at Iara. "Now, if you guys will excuse us, Iara is going to take me shopping . . . ?"

LORI

Lori got off the afternoon ferry and stalked down the sidewalk toward home before she could lose her nerve.

She *could* just tell them Ben needed routine, which was *true*, and she'd meet them tomorrow. It wouldn't be unfriendly, just practical. None of them had someone they had to take care of. Maybe that was the smarter thing to do. Maybe—

Handler: Celebrating is a thing normal humans do, kid. FYI.
Handler: Ben will be fine.
Handler: Pizza and movies and kissing games.

Lori shoved her phone into her pocket. Those texts had arrived at PortManta, right as she'd been ready to leave again.

What did Handler even mean by that? Was that a reminder that she was supposed to impersonate a normal human? Was she supposed to lie to everyone and pretend the miracoral hadn't turned an angry red and sent crayfish after her because it had recognized her as a nonhuman threat? Was she supposed to forget every thought that had raced through her head while Kirk had held her arm? Was she supposed to act like Maya had forgotten what it was like when Handler had taken her into the other place?

It didn't matter. She dashed up the stairs and opened the apartment door. "Ben? Jenn? It's me!"

"Hey, Lori!" Ben called from the living room. A moment later Jenn came out into the hallway, a curvy girl with a smile full of dimples and bangs dyed bright pink, tugging a sweater over her T-shirt.

She appeared alive and mostly conscious after a day with Ben, and she smiled a bit wearily at Lori. "He's been great. He didn't want to eat apple slices at lunch, so we did applesauce instead, which I hope was okay."

Lori smiled. "It's fruit of some sort. Thank you so much."

"You can thank me by trying on what I got you," Jenn said, flashing a grin that brought out the dimples in her cheeks, and held up a long-sleeved ruffled black top with a sassy red lightning-bolt pattern.

"Oh, that's pretty," Lori said happily, and then, as she figured out how it would look on her, added, "Like with an undershirt?"

"Ha-ha, nope!" Jenn tossed it to her. "Maybe a cute bra if you want to show off the straps, but otherwise, you wear this, *like with courage*." As Lori stared helplessly at the top in her hands, Jenn's voice softened. "Lori, come on, I'm not gonna make you look bad. It shows off your collarbones, which are really cute, and the crop top only does a little bit of midriff, so you tie a sweater around your waist or something if you don't like it."

"It's . . ." At least it had a back. Jenn had a much stronger opinion of Lori's body than Lori did.

"Look, trust me on this," Jenn said. "It's not a clubbing outfit. You wear it with jeans or those nice capris you got back in the spring, and as soon as you walk into the room, it'll be like, *bam, boobs*, but like in a classy way!"

Lori laughed. "I will try it. I promise. Once I'm not exhausted from work."

Jenn shook her head. "We're gonna get you a man, Fisher. I swear it." She gave Lori a hug, then called back into the living room, "See you later, Ben-to-box!"

"See you, Jenn-and-the-Ho'grams!" Ben called back happily, and as Jenn left, Lori shut the door behind her.

The kitchen had dirty plates on the counter and the twist tie from a rice-cake bag by the stove, ready to catch fire next time Lori tried to make dinner. She shoved the former into the dishwasher, shoved the latter into the utensil drawer, and called out, "Ben, would it be okay with you if I had friends come over?"

"Who are they?" Ben called back.

Lori headed into the living room, which had Legos all over the floor along with Pokémon cards and several sheets of paper with stick figures having brightly colored battles on them. "They're from work. They wanted to come over. They're going to bring pizza."

Ben looked up from where he was building . . . something? Maybe a submarine. Maybe a Pokémon. Something, anyway, out of Legos. His big dark eyes were narrowed suspiciously. "Cheese pizza?"

"No, I thought we might try pizza with fish and asparagus and scrambled eggs on it," Lori said thoughtfully, and as Ben burst into horrified giggles, she added, "Yes, cheese pizza. So is it okay?"

"Sure." Ben went back to his Legos.

Lori considered making him clean up, and then remembered that it was his apartment too, and she'd just sprung the guests on him, and decided to let it be instead.

"Thanks, little guy. I appreciate you being good with the change in plans."

"'Our family might get there late . . .'" Ben called back from the living room.

"'But we'll get there together,'" Lori finished, glancing over at the dumb sign above the sink and shaking her head. She cleared several weeks of mail and notes from day care off the kitchen table, closed the door to the office, and got out glasses and plates. Iara had insisted that she would take care of everything else.

She took the crop top back into her room and looked at it skeptically.

Well, she *had* promised.

She put it on with the nice capris that Jenn had mentioned

(and insisted Lori buy in the first place), fiddled with the neckline a bit, and checked herself in the mirror.

"Bam," she whispered, and tried to settle the nervous giggle trying to escape. *But like in a classy way.*

And that was when the knock on the door came, of course. Lori headed back out into the kitchen, paused, darted back into her room, pulled a long-sleeved flannel top around her waist, and called, "Okay, remember, Ben, guests mean what?"

"Close the door when I pee," Ben called back without looking up.

"Thank you." *Boys,* Lori thought, and opened the door.

The gang was there. Hawk was wearing a new Hawaiian shirt and had his hair slicked back. He was putting down Iara's wheelchair—with Iara, now wearing a pale green sundress the same color as her hair, still in it—as the door opened. "Oh no. Stairs. I forgot about the stairs."

"It is nothing," Iara said, grinning and patting Hawk on the arm. "Hawk was happy to show off his muscles." Hawk grinned and looked down, embarrassed. "You look lovely."

"Got pizza," said Tapper, coming forward with large steaming boxes in his arms as though prepared to run Lori over if she didn't get out of the way. "Where do I put them?"

"Kitchen table's great," Lori said as she moved aside, and Tapper stalked past her and into the kitchen, which faced out over the living room, so of *course* the first one Ben had to meet was Tapper.

"Hi, what's your name?" Ben said from the living room.

"Tapper. You're Ben?"

"Yeah, hey, Tapper, what's your favorite Pokémon?"

Tapper frowned. "It depends on the generation. By the numbers, Squirtle clearly has the best stats, but if you can evolve fast enough, Charmander eventually—"

"I like Dedenne," Ben said brightly, "because he does electricity to communicate, and sometimes he makes a squeaky noise when Team Rocket shows up!"

"Wait," Tapper said, "that totally disregards Dedenne's stats, and Discharge isn't even that good an ability . . ." He took a breath. "Okay, yeah, Dedenne's cool."

Lori breathed a silent thank-you to whoever made most boys fundamentally similar and headed back to the front door. Iara had just gotten her chair up over the little ledge and inside, and she wheeled past Lori, giving Lori a smile that Lori didn't quite get. Hawk followed her, holding the door open for Maya.

"Thanks for having us over, Lori!" Maya said as she came in, the last one inside. She wore a bright pink blouse open over a lacy satin undershirt. A short pleated black skirt danced around her waist, showing off long legs that ended with strappy black sandals.

"I, um," said Lori, and realized she was still looking at Maya's legs, forced herself *not* to look at Maya's legs, and looked up instead to see that Maya had done something with her hair so that instead of the simple pixie cut it had been before, it bounced out in excited little waves like it was saying hi to Lori. Maya smiled. Lori's face was hot, and she was pretty sure she was blushing. "You're welcome," she finally blurted.

She was saved mercifully by hearing Ben asking Iara if she was Professor X.

"Oh no, I have to make sure he doesn't say anything," Lori said, and hurried back to the kitchen in time to hear Iara laugh and Hawk say something about her being She-Hulk instead, because of her hair.

Lori's phone buzzed, and she yanked it from her pocket.

Handler: Lori. Chill.

Lori: What is this? What is going on?

Handler: You're celebrating.
Handler: Like a person.

Lori: Why is Maya wearing all that?

Handler: She's probably not wearing anything.
Handler: You know, shape-shifter.
Handler: So if it helps, just think about her being naked.

Lori shoved the phone back into her pocket, smiled at Hawk and Iara, watched Tapper hunt through the Lego pieces, and decided to grab a piece of pizza.

Her heart was hammering and she was still pretty sure something was going to go terribly wrong at any second, but tonight, the monster was telling her not to worry. It wanted her to celebrate.

Like a person.

TAPPER

The floor had rough ragged carpet that stretched and scratched and snagged his forearms when he moved. The Legos were scattered across it. They should have been on something flat. They would have been right angles then. Instead they were bright and shiny in all the colors and glittered everywhere at him. Red and green and blue and yellow and other red and too many to track. Some of the reds were supposed to be the same color but weren't. Different batches maybe. Different chemical mixtures. The mix of chemicals put too much blue into one of them so that it was a tiny bit darker.

"Ash's Pikachu is so cute." That was Ben. Ben was Lori's brother. He talked a lot. It had been confusing at first. Now it didn't bother Tapper. Sound didn't get to be too much for him the way that colors and light did. He just had to say something when Ben was done. "She's the most famous Pokémon."

Ben was building a dragon robot. He didn't care about the colors being wrong. Even the ones that were very different. One wing was blue and another was green. One of the dragon's legs was a half-made leg from another Lego set. All the pieces were perfect and crisp. The rest of the dragon robot was all thrown together from pieces that had been in Ben's box.

He was done talking.

"Pikachu is male."

Was that mean? Would that hurt Ben's feelings? Looking would tell Tapper. It would also mean looking at Ben and seeing all the muscles in his face move when he talked. Flesh tone changing in the cheeks and even under the hair from blood flow. The little old coffee table had fake wood paneling with one corner chipped off in the shape of a triangle to show plywood underneath. He had to say something else.

"He's an it in the games." That was better. Ben liked Pokémon. He wasn't scared when Tapper knew things. That had been too harsh. He still needed more. "Though." He put it on the end. People did that to show they were done talking. It connected the words. "Though" and "through" and "rough." They looked like they should sound the same. Ugh ugh ugh.

Tapper moved the more-red-blue pieces into a pile. They fit together nicely when he organized them. The red-red pieces went into another pile. The glitter from the different angles made it still look like different colors. But he knew they were the same. They were just in different places.

"Oh." Ben paused. "Cool."

"You appear to be enjoying yourself." That was Iara. Tapper looked up. She wasn't talking to him. She was talking to Hawk. Hawk's head and shoulders and knees were all pointed toward her. He was smiling. It looked natural. Tapper wondered how he did it.

The light from the kitchen was bright and glittery. The glass bowl around the lamp hadn't been cleaned in a long time. It was frosted but uneven. There were eight dead flies stuck inside. Seven were upside down. One was on its side. Lori had a dish in her hand. It didn't match the other dishes. The pattern on the inside of the dish was a spiral instead of a plain white with blue edges. The dish was old. It had tiny little scrapes from forks and knives and little discolorations from cracks deep inside that weren't on the surface yet.

"I'm taking the win." That was Hawk. He was talking to Iara. Tapper knew because that was where Hawk was looking. "There's always room for pain." His smile was bright white against his dark skin. "And that'll kill you if you let it." One of his teeth was more yellow than the others. It might be a cavity. The smile still made Hawk look handsome. "So you've gotta relax and be happy." He said "gotta" and not "got to." There was no space between the words.

Lori put the plate away. Tapper wondered if he should tell her that it was going to break someday. Maybe not. All plates did that. The cupboard door had one new hinge and one old hinge. The new hinge was shinier and caught the light as she opened the door. Above the sink next to the cupboard was a sign:

OUR FAMILY MIGHT GET THERE LATE

Then a picture of a car with too many things.

BUT WE'LL GET THERE TOGETHER

Tapper's mom would like that sign. Even though whoever

loaded the car was stupid for putting so much stuff into it.

Even his eyes could barely see the thing behind Lori. It was always behind her. It was big. Too big to see. And Tapper saw everything. But it wasn't all here. A cord of colors that were too shiny to be real normal colors in this world came from Lori's back and went someplace else. The refraction was thicker than water. All Tapper could see was the size and the cord.

"Do you think Lori needs help?" That was Maya. Maya was on the other couch by herself.

What Maya was asking wasn't the real question. It was hard. Tapper didn't always know what the real question was. Sometimes he thought he did. Sometimes he said the answer to the real question and made people angry. Weird boy creep god why does he even talk to us I bet he smells.

Lori didn't need help. It was her house. She knew where everything went. Her heart rate was lower than normal. Her skin was flushed because of it. She bounced a little when she took steps. Her glossy dark hair bounced with the steps.

A light came from the thing in the other place. It came down the cord too fast for anyone but Tapper to see. At the end of the cord it reached Lori. Lori stopped and looked down at her phone.

"You didn't dress up like that to sit on the couch." Tapper tried to say it in a way that made it okay for Maya. It needed more. It needed what a normal person would say. "And she can't complete simple sentences whenever she looks at you." That was better. Maya would know that it was good to go. Maybe. No. Maybe not. Maya's hair was three yellows darker than wheat. It had been only two yellows darker before. Maya's clothes were darker too. They were closer to the color of the couch now. "So go get her." Better. That made sense. But it didn't sound nice. "Blondie."

Maya smiled at Tapper and then looked down. Maya's skin

went darker. But it was a blush and not because Tapper had made Maya sad. Maya's clothes slid brighter too. The saturation turned up.

"I'll think about it."

Tapper turned back to Ben and the Legos.

Being a person was hard.

LAKE

"Heck of a mess," Tia Lake's aide, a round and unassuming man with a constant little smile, said cheerfully as he walked into the white room. "The people who do the windows say the version the rest of the building has was technically discontinued, and they can get us a replacement from a similar line, but there's a chance that the light will hit it slightly differently, and in the late afternoon, you'll be able to—"

"Stop. Karkinos." Tia Lake turned to him. She used his older name, his first name, when they were alone. He had gone silent but still stared at her with an agreeable unworried smile. "My best incubator is dead, and the Nix escaped. Tell me why I do not use you as the new host."

"You could." Karkinos shrugged, his jowls twisting with his smile. "It's been a good run, Mistress, but if you think I can help you more by popping out little eel babies than I can finding the Nix and Miss Angler Consulting, it's not like I could stop you. I have *always* been yours to kill at your whim. And also, it's been *Kirk* for the last few centuries."

Tia looked at him more closely. Something bothered her. "You speak the truth. You are not afraid of me."

"I know what I am, Mistress." Karkinos's voice was even. "I am useful, and I am hard to kill, and I eat better following in your wake. When you are gone, I will either mourn you or"—his eyes wrinkled with his smile this time—"I will never remember you at all. And if you kill me, it'll have been after a long stretch of good eating."

It had been so long. She was so close. She wanted to rend and tear and finish everything.

But if she destroyed her servant, she would lose what help she had. She needed the Nix. The Nix were the key to unlocking the miracoral, and the miracoral was the key to bringing the Leviathan.

And the Leviathan was the key to oblivion, and without oblivion, she could never be forgotten.

Tia Lake let out a long breath and adjusted her black blouse. "Tell me how close we are to getting the financial data on Angler Consulting."

"Two or three days at most," Karkinos said, and raised a finger. "But. Would you care for another lead?" He held up his personal tablet, which had an image on it.

It was grainy and blurry. "Our cameras are better than that," Lake said.

"Unless another feeder tries to jam them," Karkinos agreed. "Most of it was garbage, but once you pushed back against it, a few frames came through with enough data for me to clean up into still images. This one in particular is useful."

The image was from Tia Lake's office. Her security camera, she thought.

A woman—no, a girl, with long dark hair and lightly sun-kissed skin—was standing in her office. In one hand she held her phone.

Karkinos used his finger and thumb to zoom in on the girl's phone. Tia Lake could clearly read, "J Vickers Cell."

She gave Karkinos the faintest fraction of a smile. "You are tracking it?"

"As we speak," he said, tugging on his suit with a proud little sniff. "And when I encountered our little interlopers, I did get ahold of one other little thing . . ."

LORI

Ben had gone to bed a little after nine, after hugging everyone, promising to show Tapper the *rest* of his Pokémon cards tomorrow, and getting thoroughly distracted on every step of the brushing-teeth-and-using-mouthwash-and-taking-melatonin-and-multivitamins process.

It was now ten thirty. In the living room, a dumb action movie was playing. Iara had moved onto the couch and was sitting next to Hawk.

"Hey, is the bathroom the second on the right, or the third?" Tapper asked, heading down the hall.

"It's the second," Lori said, and shot Tapper a confused look. "There *is* no third door on the right."

Tapper shrugged. "Got it." He headed in quietly, so as not to wake up Ben, whose bedroom was right across the hall.

Lori had dealt with dishes and was now sitting in a kitchen chair at the edge of the living room. She kept thinking there was something else she was supposed to do. Drinks? Iara had brought soda—Ben had gotten *one* glass, enough for him to bounce around for an hour but not enough for him to be up all night—and everyone was topped off. Dessert? She'd grabbed a box of cookies from the pantry and put them on a plate, which was kind of a waste of a good plate but was what polite people did instead of just dropping the box on the table and calling it close enough.

Normally when she thought about things like this, she got a buzz from her pocket and looked to see what Handler wanted her to do, even if that was just "Chill." Her phone was suspiciously silent, however.

Maybe she should run the dishwasher, she thought, and was about to get up when Maya slipped onto Lori's lap and put one arm on Lori's shoulder to steady herself.

"Hey!" she said, smiling superclose while right there in Lori's lap, not very heavy since she was slender but also very warm and wearing some kind of light perfume. "You doing okay? You've been kind of running around working all night, and it is super-lame of us to make you do all the work just because it's your place." She looked at Lori in concern, biting on her lower lip.

"Um, I, no, it's okay," Lori stammered. "I just—"

"Oh no, I said superlame." Maya put a hand on her mouth. "I used to say that all the time, but now I'm friends with Iara, and it's like a *thing*, and I need to stop saying it, right? I don't think Iara cares, mostly because I asked her and she said no, but still, I *do* need to stop saying it. Right. Okay. That was it. Last time using 'lame.'"

"I hadn't really thought about it," Lori said, and didn't add, *because I was remembering what Handler said about what you were wearing, and now I'm terrified to move my legs.*

"I think Hawk is worried," Maya said softly, looking out at the living room and the dumb action movie and Hawk and Iara on the couch. Lori saw the green-haired girl's hand curl around Hawk's, and Hawk jumped a little, and then his fingers twined together with hers.

"He looks okay to me," Lori said, and Maya turned back, and her face was closer now than it had been before, and her eyes were a really light blue, the only color in her pale face besides the pink of her lips. "He, um, I think—"

"He likes her," Maya said, her voice even softer, and she leaned in even closer to make sure Lori heard the words, "but he's, like, afraid, probably because of the wheelchair, right? He's probably never done anything with a girl in a wheelchair, and he doesn't want to mess it up, but he's nervous and ashamed because he's not sure he deserves to be happy, and it's making him wonder whether he shouldn't do anything." She smiled a crooked little smile. "I hope he works up the nerve to do something. Life is too short to be ashamed of who you are. They are both supercute and would be supercute together, and he shouldn't be afraid of doing something because of stuff that nobody really cares about." The hand that was hanging over Lori's shoulder was tracing a little circle on Lori's upper back. "Right?"

This is it, Lori thought. *Handler, if you're going to tell me this is a bad idea, this is when you do it. Maybe I'm a person and maybe I'm not, but if I were, this would be when I did something, and if you don't stop me, it's going to be your fault . . .*

Her phone didn't buzz.

"Right," Lori said, and leaned in and kissed her.

BARKIN

Jonathan Barkin glared at his front door as the bell rang. After a day of screaming children, he needed his quiet.

He put down his book and his fork, shoved his dinner away from his place as he stood up from the table, and stomped over. If this were another door-to-door kid gathering money for school, he was going to tear them a new one. The public school system might be going down the drain, but "No Solicitors" was a phrase everyone needed to learn.

He opened the door. "Yes?"

"Mister Barkin?" asked a short, fat man in a gray suit. "Mister Jonathan Barkin from"—he looked down at a tablet in his hands—"Sandee Day Care?"

"Did you see the sign?" Barkin asked with some annoyance, gesturing at the NO SOLICITORS sign over his mailbox.

"I did, I absolutely did, and I am absolutely devastatedly sorry about having to disturb you," said the man, "but I had a few questions I needed to ask you."

He clapped Barkin on the shoulder—

she was gone, she was gone, she had left him and it didn't matter what she said, it was about him, she said he had changed, and she was right, and the job took everything he had and there was nothing left when he came home, they were sucking the life out of him, and now he'd lost her and the truth was he didn't even care about it, because he was better off alone

—and Barkin was on his knees, and the fat man was pulling something from a jar he'd had in his pocket. A slick yellow snake that twisted in the fat man's hands.

"Starting with," said the man as he brought the snake toward Barkin's face, "who have you been calling lately about their little brother?"

WEDNESDAY

07

LORI

"Are you okay?" Lori's brother, Ben, asked the next morning in between spoonfuls of yogurt.

"Yep!" Lori rinsed off the plate from his toast (properly, without butter, this time) and did a little spin to the dishwasher to load the plate. "Why?"

"You're very bouncy today," Ben said. "Is it just that you're happy because your friends came over last night?"

"Mm-hmm," Lori called back, flipping the dishwasher door up with one foot and snapping the light switch with the dish towel. "It was nice having them over, wasn't it?"

"Yeah. I like Tapper." Ben thought for a moment and then added, "He knows a lot about Pokémon. Am I done with my yogurt?"

"If you want to be!" Lori danced to the happy little song playing in her mind and took a probiotic pill that Handler had told her contained good gut flora or something.

"You didn't even look," Ben called over from the table.

Lori deliberately turned and looked at her little brother, who held the yogurt cup out for inspection. It was perhaps half-full.

"Close enough for today, little guy," Lori said, and grinned at him. "Now, do you want to go get Legos for day care today?" She was going to have to come up with a cover story for day care, since she'd kept Ben at home yesterday. She hadn't thought of one yet and was having trouble caring.

Ben frowned at the clock, which read 7:25. "Are you not grumpy about us being late?"

Lori let out a slow breath. "Not today, kiddo. I don't have work in the morning, and you were really nice to my friends last night, so today, we are going to be nice to each other. 'Our family might get there late . . .'"

"'But we'll get there together.'" Ben gave her a little smile. "Okay. If I get my Pokémon and Legos superfast, can you come with me on the late ferry?"

Lori checked her phone. Iara had said she would text Lori when she had a new lead, and so far there was nothing. "You've got it." She headed to her room and pulled on a sweatshirt that was warm enough for what promised to be a breezy day.

She had one more day to find Tia Lake and stop her. One more day to destroy the Lake Foundation and Kirk, whatever he was, and all those eels. Part of her wanted to panic about it, but she'd panicked about it yesterday, and that hadn't much helped, had it? At least they had a file.

And Lori had friends. Not friends like Jenn, who just thought she had a job that kept her busy after school, friends who would turn blank when Lori asked if they remembered anything about the water rising. Friends who were like her.

Maybe even friends who *did* like her.

She thought of Maya and the one kiss, which had ended with

Hawk making a "D'awwwww" noise until Iara whacked him, and her own face hot and Maya blushing but still grinning as she shot Hawk a dirty gesture. She thought of Maya's hand pulling against hers when they said good night, like Maya wasn't ready to let go even as she started down the stairs with the rest, her fingers warm in Lori's hand, and then Maya pulling away and running her fingers through her bouncy wavy hair and still blushing.

She didn't know *everything* about Lori, but that was okay. Nobody knew everything about someone else. Everyone was allowed to have secrets, and if Lori's secret was that she wasn't a real person, then maybe if Maya liked her enough, it didn't matter. What made someone a person except other people? Maybe if Lori *felt* like she felt something, it didn't matter if it was just Handler doing a good imitation of making a person who felt something. Maybe acting like you were real was what really mattered.

"Lori?" Ben called over from his room.

"Yep?"

"What's nooky?"

Maybe Lori was going to have to kill somebody.

"Have you been watching Let's Play videos without me around again?" Lori called back in sudden desperation, wondering if the world was *actually* going to open up and swallow her here in her bedroom.

"No," Ben said, incredibly helpfully.

"So where did *you* hear about nooky?"

"Hawk asked if Maya was thinking about it last night, and she said yes, a lot."

"Um," Lori called back. The birds and the bees flashed across her mind. So did euphemisms about grown-up kissing. "It's a thing you put on pizza," she said instead, and in a fit of inspiration added, "but only if you're grown-up." Her phone buzzed, and she glanced down at it.

Handler: Redirect, redirect, redirect!

"Hey, have you got all your Legos?" she asked.

"Oh, right!" Ben called back, and Lori heard the merciful sound of plastic bricks clattering all over the room.

"I'm going to brush my teeth, and then we'll go." Lori pulled her hair back into a ponytail, then looked it and thought about Hawk and Maya talking last night, tugged it out of the ponytail, and brushed it a few more times.

Maybe the true test of being a person was mortification. She'd never seen a feeder get embarrassed. That had to count for something.

IARA

On the rooftop of PortManta, Iara took a long slow sip of the berry smoothie Hawk had brought up for her and smiled at him. "Thank you."

"No worries." He was wearing another short-sleeved button-up shirt, this one beige, again left open with a thin white under-shirt beneath that clung to his frame. His dark eyes sparkled as he smiled at her. "No sense in you having to do another elevator trip, right?"

"I suppose." Why could it not be simple politeness, or him finding her pretty? Why did it have to be because of the chair? Iara forced another long sip, ignoring the brain-freeze headache it gave her, and eventually Hawk walked over and flopped back down in his chair next to Maya and Tapper.

Today, Iara wore a long purple sundress with thin straps that left her arms bare. She had pulled her pale green hair back up in a tumbled knot atop her head, so that her neck and shoulders were bare in the breezy morning air.

She *knew* she had attractive shoulders. There were *some* benefits to swimming or pushing a wheelchair for most of one's waking life.

But yesterday Hawk had carried her around the Lake Foundation building, and last night it had been the stairs leading to Lori's home. Now all he could see was a girl who could not do things herself, regardless of how much she had already done for the team.

"You need anything?" Hawk asked, seeing her look. "I could go back down and—"

"No," said Iara, and forced a smile. "I was only thinking. Sorry." She put her eyes back on the screen of the tablet computer she'd had the man at the electronics store *remember* selling her yesterday after their adventure. It was easier to read things there than on her phone.

That could have been why Hawk had asked if she needed anything. It could have been chivalry, an understanding that she was doing more research while the rest of them browsed the Internet and checked their mail.

It wasn't, though.

She had really thought that he was different. Or at least that he *could* have been different. Or that he would stop thinking of her as helpless once they were out of danger. It had seemed that way to her yesterday, before they snuck into the Lake Foundation. Now . . . she sighed to herself and put it aside.

Some of the notes had been made by scientists, and much of it was raw data and jargon that she didn't understand. It took her a while to realize that "subject lost" meant that someone had died, which made the data much more disturbing. Eventually Iara skipped to overviews or executive summaries, since the language was more plain there, and it was easier for her to understand what was meant. It did not help that in many cases, the scientists themselves did not understand what they were studying.

Supposition that external dimension comprises primarily antimayaer belied by positron-emission testing, one of the notes read. *Laws of physics as conventionally understood do not apply in this instance, but the biological testing on living Nix samples may yield means of eliciting pain response from the miracoral incursion.*

"Well, that sounds unpleasant," Iara murmured. "Do any of you know the English word 'antimayaer'?"

She wasn't sure she was pronouncing it right, and the looks that Maya and the boys gave her suggested as much. "Is that like antimatter?" Hawk asked.

"No, or she would have *said* that," Tapper muttered, going back to his phone with a glare. "It's her legs that don't work, not her eyes."

"Dude," Hawk said.

"It is fine," Iara said to Hawk firmly.

"It's probably just a typo." Maya looked down and gulped her chocolate smoothie. "What else does it say?"

Iara sighed. "They want us because Lake wants the miracoral," she said.

"But like, they *have* the miracoral," Hawk said, looking down from the rooftop at the water below. In the late-morning light they could see sporadic glittering flickers that were bits of miracoral-dotted support pillars below. "They use it for electricity, right? And our chairs and stuff?" He tapped the gray-pink plastic of the chair he sat in, working the material with one of his fingernails.

"Lake wishes to . . ." Iara sighed again. "I think that to Lake, it is a key. She can harvest it, but she wants it for something more. It can . . . it may be to get what she desires."

"So we're a way to the miracoral, and the miracoral is a way for her to get what she *really* wants." Tapper glared. "Figures we're just a step for her."

Subject found unsuitable for implantation and gestation of new growth, read another note. *Removed to Deepwater Lab for hybridization potential. Subject restrained and introduced to live coral bloom. Bloom produced red coloration; symbiote defenses destroyed subject. Tia Lake present; destroyed remains of subject as well as miracoral bloom and symbiotes. No sign of transdimensional alarm detected from miracoral. No interest from Leviathan detected. Formayaing of possible distress signal may be outside parameters of this universe; further results difficult to measure.*

"I do not understand this all," Iara said, "but there is another laboratory. Deepwater, they call it. They do more tests there. Lake does some of the tests herself. She wants something called Leviathan."

"Great!" Maya shot Iara a thumbs-up. "Does anything in the document say where it might be?"

"Let me see," Iara said, and began scanning the document again. "Oh, what is the word 'formayaing'?"

"Just science garbage," Tapper said, waving it away. "Forget that, and get us an address. Then we can go find out what Lake is and kick her slimy butt back to wherever it came from." He jerked to his feet and rattled his empty cup. "I'm getting more. Anybody want something?"

Maya smiled at him. "If I could get a four-pump mocha double-blended mint-chocolate frapp—"

"Ugh, just give me your cup, it has the old order on it." Tapper held out his hand without looking, then glared at the cup Maya passed him. "Amount of sugar in this, it's no wonder you can barely do sentences. Least I'm self-medicating when I hit the caffeine. Pint-Size, Ipanema?"

"I am fine, thank you," Iara said. Hawk shook his head.

Tapper stalked off, muttering to himself.

"Jerk," Hawk muttered in a voice Iara wasn't supposed to hear, except that as a Nix, whatever that meant, she had very good ears. Then, in a voice she *was* supposed to hear, he said, "Don't let him get to you, Iara. You're part of the team, just like the rest of us."

Iara smiled at him. He had pretty skin the color of wet earth, and his body was warm and his smile infectious.

"And don't worry if it's a pain getting you into this Deepwater Lab. I've got no problem carrying you around when we get there," he added with a grin.

Iara tried not to sigh. She had green hair and a pretty smile, and her skin was like a summer sunset on a day that had seen storms, and yes, the chair, of course. And while boys who offered to help when necessary were lovely, boys who could only see the chair were usually bad kissers.

"I will see what I can find," she said, and looked down so that she would not have to look at him.

LORI

They didn't catch the on-time ferry, or even the one after that. It was close to ten when Lori got Ben onto the ferry. While she was fine letting him go on the morning ferry, whose driver knew Ben and had a lot of other kids on the boat as well, the late-morning ferry was filled with adults in suits. Lori hopped on the ferry along with Ben to ride with him.

She flashed her pass at the driver, who nodded, and found a spot for her and Ben to sit near the back. Ben was kicking his legs in the air under the seat, making a little Lego ninja on his backpack rattle each time he hit it. "Can you pick me up early today?"

"I think so." Lori smiled over at him. "And you remember today is Wednesday, so you've got swimming in the afternoon?"

"Awww." Ben said it more out of habit than real feeling. "Do I have to go today, even if I'm tired from your friends coming over yesterday?"

"Uh-huh." Lori managed to not roll her eyes.

"But I don't really like going to swimming."

"Nobody *likes* going to swimming," Lori said, and then winced, because being relaxed was probably making her a little too honest, "but you need to do it to stay healthy, and also so that you're okay if you ever fall into the canal."

"I can swim *fine*," Ben said, and *did* roll his eyes.

"Then maybe when these lessons are done, the teacher will say that you're done with Starfish level and can move up to Turtle level, so I *know* you're fine."

"If I get to Turtle level, can I get the new Lego dragon-bot that turns from a robot into a dragon and has flick missiles?"

"Absolutely," Lori said without missing a beat. Her phone buzzed.

Handler: That set is $149.

"Or at least *a* Lego set," she amended, which Ben pretended not to hear.

They arrived at the Sandee Day Care stop a few minutes later, and Ben leaped from the boat with boundless energy, backpack trailing behind him by one arm.

Lori followed him down the sidewalk. On the left was the middle school where she'd gone a few years back, still closed for the summer, although a group of students was running out front in gym clothes, probably doing summer training for one of the sports teams. On the right was the elementary school where

Ben went, vacant except for the playground area, where kids ran around the swing set and monkey bars while their parents sat at benches nearby. In a canal city like Santa Dymphna, open room for kids to run around was a precious commodity.

Past the elementary school was Sandee Day Care, a small brick building whose imposing features were softened by paintings of sun and rainbows and animals running around in fields. The day care shared its fenced-in playground with the elementary school, and the children were outside running. A number of harried-looking day care teachers watched them run and play and generally tried to keep anyone from bleeding.

Ben dropped his backpack by the fence. "Hi, Josh!" he yelled into one of the packs of kids. "Guess what! My sister said I could get the Lego RoboDragon Rampage!" He turned back to Lori and gave her a hug. "Bye, Lori."

"Bye, little guy. Have a good day."

"Are you dropping him off?" came a man's voice, and Lori winced, covered it, and looked up at Mister Barkin, who was coming over with his usual disapproving expression.

"Yes," Lori said brightly. "We had a bit of a slow morning, since I didn't have to get to work early."

"You know that normal drop-off hours are between six thirty and ten," Mister Barkin said severely, giving her a tired glare. It looked like he'd had a rough night.

"Yes, I know," said Lori, and looked at her phone, which read 9:56. "Which is why I tried to get him here around ten, and here we are!"

"It's very important that the children arrive on time," Mister Barkin added. "If he gets here much past ten, I may not always have teachers available to take him. You also didn't send Ben in yesterday, and it's important that we know when children aren't coming in, so we know how many teachers we'll need."

"I know," Lori said again, keeping her polite smile stapled to her face, "and I'm so sorry that I forgot to call. I kept Ben home yesterday because he wasn't feeling well." Her phone buzzed, and she glanced down at it.

Handler: Stomach bug. They always back down when you say "stomach bug."

"What's wrong with him?" Barkin asked sharply.

"Oh, he had a little stomach bug," Lori said, still smiling, "and he *seemed* to be better yesterday, but I didn't want to risk getting anyone else at day care sick—"

"Oh, no, no no no," Barkin said quickly, "you should definitely do what's right for Ben."

"And we came in late today because I wanted to make absolutely sure he was feeling better," Lori added.

Barkin glanced at Ben a little nervously. "Well, we appreciate that." Then he recovered and turned back to her. "Also, you haven't given us the money for the pizza party on Friday."

"Oh, I didn't know there was going to be one," Lori said, now comfortably back on the defensive. Seeing Ben coming back from his group of friends to grab his backpack, Lori called over, "Ben, were you supposed to give me a flyer for a pizza party on Friday?"

"Oh," Ben called back, still rooting through his backpack. "Yeah. You need to give money to day care." He looked up at Lori and Mister Barkin. "Also, I don't want to have any nooky on my pizza, please."

Lori closed her eyes and let out a breath through her nose. "I will make sure to order you a cheese pizza." She turned to Mister Barkin, who had his mouth open, and, since the world had failed to open up and swallow her whole as she'd been hoping right then, said, "I'm not sure where my little brother picked up this new language. I'm hoping it wasn't from the older children here."

She had been trying for a redirect, but Barkin's face seemed to go blank instead. "Little brother," he mumbled.

Lori shoved a few bills into Barkin's hand. "Now, if you'll excuse me, I have to go to work. Bye, little guy!" she called to him, and dashed away before Barkin could think of a comeback, her phone buzzing in her hand as she did.

Handler: Good save.

Lori: I am going to kill Hawk and Maya.

Handler: Fair. Maybe use the RoboDragon Rampage.
Handler: I hear it has flick missiles.
Handler: Which it better, for what we'll be spending on it.

Lori was interrupted by the phone ringing. The caller ID said "Tapper," and she brought the phone up to her ear. "What have you found?"

"Find a suit you're good to wear in front of Blondie," he said. "We're going swimming again."

HAWK

They met at the spot Iara had picked, a large dock not far from Reef Square. The shopping plaza was busy with afternoon shoppers, and little vanilla-scented ferries puttered by, dropping people off and picking them up. Looking up from street level, Hawk watched people cross the broad canal on the same gray plastic bridge they had used on Monday, when Lori had shown them the train car. The day had turned cloudy and windy, and he thought he could see the bridge sway overhead. The idea of crossing a bridge made of the stuff still creeped him out, so he let it go.

Iara had gotten them money using her "you remember this" trick and sent them off to get something they could swim in. Hawk had gone for dark gray board shorts that were like the ones he had back home. He was wearing those and flip-flops and a swim shirt with a sea turtle on it. He didn't actually need a swim shirt, since the water wasn't particularly cold, but if they were going to be exploring another laboratory, he didn't want to be walking around shirtless.

Tapper and Maya were waiting by a bench, doing something on their phones. Hawk wasn't sure if they were playing together or arguing. Possibly both. "Like I see how he *could* mean it like that," Maya was saying, "but maybe he just honestly thinks you haven't seen the show in a while and should watch it again to like *enjoy* it!"

"He's saying I haven't watched the show, and my opinion is invalid," Tapper said, his phone clenched in a white-knuckle grip, "so now I destroy him." Tapper wore black wetsuit shorts with a deep red stripe down the side and a short-sleeved top of the same material. Hawk guessed he hadn't been the only one who didn't wanna run around shirtless.

"Or," Maya said, "*or* you could like maybe just post a gif back to him—"

"Of *course* you say it with a soft G," Tapper muttered.

"—with a cat doing something cute, and *that* could be your comeback, and then your account doesn't get locked again, but he still like *knows* that you don't agree with him . . . ?" Maya trailed off hopefully. She was wearing a bright pink two-piece swimsuit with a tied-off T-shirt over the top and a little matching wrap around her waist. Hawk wasn't sure how much of it was real and how much of it was, well, Maya, but it was a cute look for her either way.

Tapper glared at her sullenly. "It'd have to be a really good cat pic."

"Hey, guys." Hawk waved, and they looked up at him. "Any sign of the others?"

"Yes," came Lori's voice, and Hawk looked over to see the girl coming their way. She wore a dark blue wetsuit that covered her from neck to ankles, plus swim shoes. Her hair was pulled back in a tight ponytail. She looked more like a ninja than a girl about to go swimming.

Then Maya said, "Hey, Lori!" and because Hawk was looking at Lori, he saw a little color come to Lori's cheeks.

"Hey. Um, what have we got?" Lori asked. "Tapper said it was a lab?"

"Ipanema found it," Tapper said, springing from the bench and glaring at a passing jogger until he was safely out of earshot. He ran his hands through his hair. "Someplace she does the nasty stuff, where she doesn't have to pretend to be people."

"Iara said that it was in an old place that was a gym or something before the water rose," Maya added. "She saw that the Lake Foundation had bought the building and done a bunch of repair work, but the part of the building above the water is just part of Reef Square now." She pointed over at the plaza. "Like I think it's either the frozen yogurt place or the place with the overpriced shoes, but I didn't really—"

"Nobody cares, Blondie," Tapper said.

"Okay."

"Well, I care." Lori said it quietly, like she had to get the words out before she thought about them, and when Maya blinked and grinned and blushed, Lori added, "We might want frozen yogurt after all this."

"Right." Maya smiled shyly, then looked over at Hawk. "So we're just waiting for Iara. Do you have any idea where she is?"

"She said she'd meet us. Guess she's running a little behind." He shrugged. "I'm sure she's doing the best she can."

"Here she comes," Lori said, pointing, and Hawk looked over.

Iara's hair was *not* pulled back in a ponytail. It tumbled down behind her in curly green waves that matched both the bikini top she wore and the frames of her dark sunglasses. A blue-and-purple wrap clung to her hips, and little seashell charms on the fringes jangled with every step she took.

Every step she took was actually a kind of hop, as Iara came toward them using a pair of stainless-steel forearm crutches. She planted the crutches in front of her, then hopped forward with both legs together. *Plant-hop, plant-hop,* Hawk thought.

"I can carry these along with me as I swim," she said, pausing and holding up one of the crutches. "I persuaded someone at our old hotel to get them for me."

"If you want," Hawk said, and then, "I mean, yeah, if that's what works for you, and if you need somebody to carry them—"

"She wouldn't bring them if she couldn't bring them," Tapper cut in. "We good to go? We're drawing attention out here."

"I really love your top!" Maya said to Iara. "Would you super-mind if I made mine a pink version of it?"

"We spent time picking out an *actual* swimsuit," Iara said, smiling at her. "I gave you money!"

"Yeah, but then I got hungry and bought some frozen yogurt, and they had a thing where you got an extra topping if you gave a donation to a wildlife fund, so I added some for that, and also I'm a tiny bit scared of swimsuit dressing rooms, no offense," Maya said, mumbling at the end.

"When this is over," Iara said firmly, "we will shop."

"When this is over," Tapper cut in, "we can all go back home and not have to get in each other's business anymore."

"Where are we trying to get to?" Lori asked, looking around. "Tapper's right. If this place belongs to Lake, she may have people up here watching."

"It should be below the dock," Iara said, gesturing with a tilt of her head. "We can enter the water right here, then swim underwater to reach it. Hopefully no one will think to look down into the water."

"Wait, isn't that where we threw the old man into the water?" Maya asked. "We threw the old man into the water right over an evil underwater lab?"

"We saved his life," Iara said firmly. "He is fine."

"Are you sure you're okay to get over the railing with those?" Hawk asked Iara, looking at the waist-high railing between the sidewalk and the canal. "If you want, I could—"

"If I need assistance," Iara said politely, "I will ask. Until then, you may assume I am fine."

"Okay," Hawk said, "but—"

"Dude," Tapper said, "stop."

For a moment Hawk remembered being back at school—which one, he couldn't even remember now, he'd moved so often—and offering to help a girl. One of the guys had said something like, "Look at the new guy trying too hard," and it had sucked.

Then the feeling whisked away, leaving a pleasant emptiness behind it, and Hawk shrugged. "Whatever, dude, be a jerk if you want. Just because you don't care what she's going through doesn't mean that the rest of us can't show a little consideration—"

"Excuse me," came Iara's voice, and Hawk looked over to see that she had already crossed the sidewalk to the railing and was undoing the wrap at her waist. A man in a suit looked at her in concern as she turned the wrap into a kind of makeshift bundle and tossed her sunglasses into it.

"Um, miss, you can't swim in the canals," the man in the suit said. "It's illegal, and the miracoral is actually dangerous. You don't want to get hit by a boat, either—"

"Why did the water rise?" Iara asked, cutting him off and holding both crutches in one hand.

The man in the suit went blank. "Guess it was just one of those things," he said flatly, and as he said it, staring at nothing, Iara dove smoothly into the canal.

The man in the suit stared blankly at the spot where Iara had been. After a moment he looked around as if trying to remember what he'd been doing. Then he walked off.

"Nice." Hawk chuckled. "Probably could've just waited a minute, though."

Tapper snorted and shook his head. "I know you're invulnerable, but somebody still needs to smack you upside the head." He looked over at Maya and Lori. "Come on. Ipanema's showing us up."

The three headed for the railing, and Hawk, angry for a moment and not sure why, let the feeling go away and headed after them.

08

LORI

Lori walked quickly to the railing, vaulted over cleanly, and then sank beneath the water of the canal before any boats came by.

She was a decent swimmer. Anyone who lived in Santa Dymphna had to be. It wasn't as though people swam to school, but the simple likelihood of accidentally ending up in the water after slipping while getting off the ferry made sure that while kids on the mainland were learning to ride a bicycle, the children of Santa Dymphna were treading water or swimming laps.

Lori had done a few perfunctory years of swim team when she'd been Ben's age. She and Jenn had even done distance swimming during the school year, when some of the popular kids at school had gotten excited about it, and she'd spent far too much money on a good wetsuit. She hadn't worn it since the start of summer, though.

Then, as she thought about it, she wondered how much of that was true. What had Santa Dymphna been before the water rose? It hadn't always been a canal city, so why would she have been focused on swimming as a child? Maybe it was a false memory.

Maybe all of me is a false memory, she thought, and then decided that wouldn't get her anywhere. *Or maybe I should just focus on stopping Lake and keeping Ben safe.* She looked up at the sunlight flickering brightly above her, and then she sank down beside the scum-slick green canal wall and sucked in a lungful of water.

It didn't *hurt* to have the water fill her lungs, but just as before, there was a quick moment of flailing panic, of having to fight the feeling that she was drowning until her lungs were completely full and decided that they could handle water just fine. Then it was eerily peaceful. Breathing in the thick water made time seem to move in slow motion, and she could taste the salt water more than smell it.

All around her the canal was a cool rippling field of gray-green, the old features of the buildings that made up the canal wall ominously murky in the distance. Scattered here and there on the bottom, she saw the telltale golden glow of the miracoral, usually near buildings that would use it for power. *You stay down there,* Lori thought, glaring at the nearest patch, *and I'll stay up here.*

A moment later a puttering engine noise sounded behind her, and Lori turned to see the foamy chaos of the boat coming her way. She dove a bit lower for safety—though still well away from the miracoral—and watched as the boat sped by, leaving a trace of the vanilla scent of the miracoral fuel in the water behind it. She had to stop herself from plugging her nose as she looked up at it. The surface overhead split into the white foam of a wake, and a moment later three dull splashes marked the others jumping in as well.

Tapper sank like a stone, and then blurred in the water and evened out. Hawk did the breaststroke, movements slow but controlled as he cut through the water. Maya flapped wildly, as far as Lori could tell, kind of pulling herself through the water like she was holding on to bits of it, but somehow it still seemed to work for her.

She'd also taken off her T-shirt and wrap, and her bikini was *very* bright even in the murky gray-green water. She smiled and waved to Lori, and Lori felt herself blushing and waved back.

"Are you coming?" came Iara's voice suddenly through the water, as clear as if she were speaking normally.

Lori looked around in the murky water. "Where are you?" she said, or tried to say. What she actually said was more like, "*Whrblbrblbrbloo?*"

"If you swim toward the shopping plaza, I am at the corner, where it opens up to the docks," said Iara, who had apparently heard her just fine.

"*Obrbl, webrblbrblbrrr!*" Maya called back, and Lori was glad that it wasn't just her who couldn't talk underwater. At least that wasn't something all the Nix could do that she couldn't, another little sign that she wasn't really one of them. Lori glared down at the miracoral, then started swimming.

She didn't have any swimming powers. Handler hadn't neglected to tell her *that*, anyway. While Tapper blurred through the water in a frenzy of bubbles and Hawk coasted with slow graceful strokes, Lori just swam like a normal person, albeit one who stayed below the surface and didn't come up to breathe. Maya kept pace beside her, or rather flopped ahead with her uncanny flexibility and then waited for Lori to catch up, looking over from time to time with a cheery smile to offer encouragement and a friendly "*Yurblbrblbreat!*"

The building on their right was uneven. Back before the water rose, it had probably been a bank or a museum, someplace with big fake pillars to impress everyone who walked by. Now it was home to a lot of seaweed, as well as tiny little fish who stayed close to the weeds and darted away when one of the Nix got too close. A cluster of miracoral grew by the base of the building near the corner. As they got as close to it as Lori was willing to get—still several meters away—she had to close her eyes against the harsh glare of the brain-shaped cluster. The light didn't seem to bother Maya, and Lori tried to ignore it.

By the time they reached the corner, Hawk and Tapper were already there, treading water next to Iara, who had her crutches tucked under her arm. With the other arm, she was gesturing ahead. "There. You see it? This is where the Deepwater Laboratory is, but . . ."

Lori reached the corner and looked at the docks at Reef Square. Or at least where the docks should be.

It couldn't be right. The docks were where the boats tied off when people came to the shopping plaza. Reef Square had no direct access to the ocean—you could get here only from the canals—so it wasn't like the little man-made bay needed to be deep enough to allow for oceangoing freighters. It shouldn't have been any deeper than the canals themselves, fifteen or twenty feet at most.

Instead a dark chasm yawned out ahead of them, the water deepening to an inky black.

Up at the surface, the pale light of the cloudy day was broken by the silhouettes of boats, their wakes tailing behind them as slowly splitting curls of white. Looking at where they were clustering, Lori could make out the docks themselves, and the water there at least seemed shallow. The little bay, really no more than a wide intersection where several canals joined to give access to the docks, somehow had a massive hole in it.

"I do not know," Iara said. "It is real, or real enough that it did not return echoes when I sounded."

"*It'sbrbeal,*" Tapper said sharply, and Lori caught that, at least.

"I do not know whether this was made by normal means," Iara said, "or if it is something tied to Lake or created by her. Or something else. No one would make a dock next to such a thing back in Brasil, but here, perhaps they do not even notice it."

Guess it was just one of those things, Lori thought, and shuddered.

Then, because someone had to, and because Handler had said that she only had until Thursday morning, she started swimming.

The others made all kinds of bubbly excited noises behind her, but she ignored them, and after a moment Iara said, "She is right. We have no choice. Stay close. I can guide us to where Deepwater should be."

A moment later she darted past Lori. Even with crutches tucked under her arm, she sped through the water with impossible grace, one arm knifing back and forth to pull her through the water in an effortless glide. She went a little ahead of Lori, then turned and looked back at them, her hair rippling around her like brilliant green seaweed.

Maya and the others were there a moment later, all of them moving slowly enough that they could stay together, and all as one, they swam down into the darkness.

The first thing that struck Lori was the cold. It wasn't the normal cold of deeper water. It was cold with a mind of its own; cold soaked in around her like fog and then stabbed at her armpits and feet, completely ignoring the wetsuit and swim shoes that should have provided more protection. Lori looked up at the surface and saw that it was dim and distant, the boats little black dots against a wan gray sky, though she didn't think they had dived down that far.

The ground fell away below them. One moment it was the normal canal floor, old concrete and asphalt overlaid with silt and sand, and the next it was a yawning abyss. Lori had been looking to see whether it sloped down or ended in a jagged cliff, but still somehow she had missed it. Or it had *made* her miss it, she thought.

She wished she could use her phone underwater. She wanted Handler, and not just the buzz she could feel through the protective pouch, but a real message, where Handler would say something practical, or even something silly, and that would let her know what to do, what to feel.

Stupid, she told herself. *Stupid. I'm not even a real girl. I don't need Handler to tell me what to feel. I feel whatever Handler wants me to feel, and right now, it wants me to feel cold dread and a creepy sensation of being watched, because that's a valuable survival mechanism that will make me be careful and not get myself damaged.*

So she kept swimming.

Her fingers kept making little phantom movements, like they'd be checking her phone for messages if they were holding it, but that wasn't too bad.

Iara was still ahead of them, darting forward and then waiting. Even in the darkness, Lori could see the others. They were all a little lighter than the darkness, like they were at one of those glow-in-the-dark mini-golf or laser-tag places and wearing clothes with a little white thread in them, only the glow was faintly gold instead of UV purple.

After a little bit, Lori realized that all the Nix were glowing with the same light as the miracoral.

Down and forward they swam, still going. Lori looked up, and the surface was just a vague gray suggestion far overhead. Her friends were dim golden silhouettes, and Lori was part of the darkness, cold and alone.

Iara paused up ahead and made a clicking noise—

From below, the cold changed in rippling waves, and Lori heard the shifting rumble of something moving, something *very large.*

In the protective pouch on her upper arm, Lori's phone buzzed twice.

Lori kicked forward desperately and slapped Iara's shoulder.

"What—" Iara started, and Lori clapped a hand over Iara's mouth, shaking her head frantically. Could Iara even see her in the darkness? Should she say something? Would that be as bad as Iara's click? Would whatever it was hear them? Would it *see* them?

Then Tapper was there, patting Iara's arm and then pointing down. He spread his hands apart, miming something large, and then he put the palms together, like he was praying . . . then tucked his head to the side and put his praying hands under it, resting his head on them like a pillow. Not praying, sleeping.

Something large down there, sleeping.

Iara swallowed and nodded slowly, eyes wide.

She pointed at Tapper, then, and Tapper blinked, then nodded and took the lead.

His eyes shone like tiny little rainbows in the darkness.

They all followed behind Tapper as he went down, down into the darkness. Lori felt something slip into her hand and glanced over to see Maya looking at her, forcing a worried smile. Lori didn't know if Maya was worried about losing track of Lori, the only one who didn't have the little miracoral glow, in the darkness, or if Maya was just worried, period.

Either way, Lori didn't pull her hand from Maya's grasp. It made swimming a little harder, but no one was trying to go fast anymore.

Up ahead Tapper slowed, and the darkness slid slowly back

to gray. Lori realized she was looking at a wall. Some of it was old metal, overgrown with seaweed. Other parts might have been glass once. They'd been replaced with the pink-gray plastic that came from the miracoral.

Below the building, where there should have been sidewalk, there was nothing. Not concrete, not the ocean floor, not ground and old sewer pipes or anything that *should* have been here. Lori tried to look closer, but her eyes slid off the darkness, like she was trying to grab hold of half a bar of wet soap.

There was a door, reinforced with the plastic but still functional. Tapper pulled on it, then grunted a little and pulled harder, but it didn't budge.

It clanked, though.

Below them, more movement, and this time everyone heard it, felt it, the sudden dread of the small rodent who freezes at the scent of the wolf.

Maya pulled her hand from Lori's grasp and went to the door. She traced the doorframe with her fingers, looking for catches or hinges or *something*, Lori thought. Lori kept treading water and trying not to think about what was down there below them, as though thinking about it might draw its attention to her. Nothing to see here, just a tiny fish not worth anyone's time.

Maya found something beside the door and worked at it, a small lever. Hawk drifted over and helped, and a moment later the door opened ever so slightly, a crack no wider than Lori's palm.

Maya went to the door and pushed against it. She wriggled, like she was trying to squeeze into tight pants, and then she went still and very slowly slid one hand through the crack. Then went her arm, up to the elbow, then up to the shoulder, and Maya leaned forward and grimaced, like she was listening for something, and slowly, carefully, slid her head through the tiny opening.

Below them came a sudden rush of bubbles, and the bubbles

glowed with their own green light, and the water around them was hot as it rushed up past them, and tasted like blood.

Maya had both arms in now and was stretching slowly as she pulled herself through.

Lori pressed against the wall of the building as the others did the same. The bubbles foamed up in greater numbers, and below them, something moved, something enormous, waking up, breath hot with hunger. The others were still glowing, and Lori had the sudden wild thought that it would *see* them, that she had to get away from their damning light into the safety of the darkness, where she could disappear.

Had she been able to move, she might have done it, but even as the thought came to her, something roared up, and Lori's muscles locked her in place, frozen with instinctive terror.

The shape was impossible to get fully, but it was long and so huge that it covered her field of vision. It was not so much lighter than the darkness as dismissive of it. In the light cast by the green glowing bubbles, its hide was slick and shiny and the same sickly shade as the eels.

It roared past them, so huge that hot water tore at them with its passage, and then it was gone, and Lori was spinning, tumbling helplessly as the great thing's wake tore her free from where she had been pressed against the wall, and she choked and flailed as green bubbles swirled around her, thinking only, *I can't make noise, I can't, it will come back.*

A hand grabbed hers.

Lori focused on the glowing golden form of Tapper, who hauled her back to the building. She was upside down, and she kicked herself back around. Maya was gone—or no, not gone, Lori realized, as the door opened a moment later, all the way this time, and Maya leaned out and waved, and they all rushed in, floundering and jostling.

The door slammed shut behind them a moment later, and a moment after that there was a whirring, clunking mechanical noise, and blinking in the darkness, Lori felt the water swirl and swish around them . . . and then her head broke the surface, and she coughed out the little bit of water that was still in her lungs and blinked at the dim but normal lights in the ceiling.

It was an air lock, she realized, looking around the small, featureless gray room. The water was rushing out through grates in the floor, leaving them safe and breathing air again.

"Hey, are you okay?" Maya asked, and Lori looked up at her, and only then realized that she was looking up at her because she was on the ground, somewhere between crawling and curled up into a ball, shaking.

"S-super." It came out with a little stammer. Her teeth were chattering. "J-just really looking forward to swimming out past whatever that was."

"It was like those eel things," Tapper said, "only bigger." He was already dry, his hair sprouting everywhere.

"Kind of a lot bigger," Maya added. *She* was back to looking like she was in a pretty pink T-shirt and jeans.

"That's what killed Shawn, I think," Lori said, and her phone gave one long buzz for "yes." "You said Lake was trying to attract something called Leviathan?"

"That thing is big enough to be Leviathan," Hawk said, rubbing his arms.

"No, it's the same as the eels," Tapper said impatiently, "and they work for her. If *that* was Leviathan, she'd've found it by now, no problem. I think that's what Lake works for, or uses, or . . . something."

"Whatever it is, I apologize for waking it," Iara said. She'd slicked her hair back behind her ears and had pushed herself to her feet, crutches cuffed over each wrist. Her red-brown skin glistened in the pale fluorescent lights, and she had goose bumps. "I did not know."

Lori wanted to remain curled up like that. If she just lay there, she wouldn't have to learn more about what that enormous thing was and what it meant and how she was much more like it than she was like Maya and Iara and the boys. She could have stayed there on the floor forever.

But she didn't have forever. She had until tomorrow. After that Tia Lake found Ben.

If she were a real person, like she was pretending to be, she wouldn't let that happen.

"What matters is that we made it." Lori pushed herself to her knees, then took the hand Maya offered and pulled herself to her feet. "Come on. Let's see what was worth coming down here for."

IARA

Hawk wouldn't stop looking at her as she made her way down the hallway attached to the air lock. It made her want to beat him to death with the crutches.

She knew that walking with the crutches was slower, and she knew it did not look dignified to someone who had no idea how long she had spent in therapy learning the step-to gait, how much strength and coordination it took, or how much her back would ache for the rest of the day as a result.

She also knew that she would *not* be letting Hawk carry her around like a baby anymore if there were any way to avoid it, and a little backache was a small price to pay.

"Hey," Hawk said as she swung her legs forward, "if you want—"

"I *want* for you to stop staring," she snapped, and Hawk flushed and looked away.

Plant crutches, swing legs, plant crutches, swing legs. Iara sighed and looked at the others.

Lori was still pale and shaken, and she walked with her hands curled into fists, her weight light on her feet, as though she were ready for an attack from any quarter. Maya, who really ought to have gotten a real swimsuit, was walking close beside Lori, and good for the two of them. Tapper was in the lead, blurring ahead down the hall and then pausing to look around and wait for the others to catch up. It struck Iara as a little annoying until she realized that it was just what she had been doing back in the water, when *she* was the fast one.

The hallway had been sculpted from the gray miracoral plastic and was lit by white ceiling panels that flickered and buzzed annoyingly. They passed a changing room that contained only old towels and forgotten diving equipment, as well as a closet with cleaning supplies.

At the end of the hallway, a large double door awaited them. It had once had a window in the top, but the window had been covered with plastic, giving Iara no clue what was on the other side. There were little holes in the floor before it, where something had once been bolted to the ground. Iara looked at the little holes as they approached, and then at the slick tiles on the floor, with part of a little swooping pattern with a grain like sandpaper that caught roughly on her feet. The gray miracoral plastic was new, but the rest of it . . .

"I believe this was an exercise facility before the water rose," she said. "There would have been . . . I do not know the word in English. When you enter with a ticket, and you push the bar, and it allows you to go forward but not back?"

"A turnstile," Maya said. "Lots of gyms have those by the front desk. I guess if it got turned into a lab, the juice bar and the little table with all the free towels are probably gone too."

"The towels aren't free," Tapper muttered, glaring at all of them. "You pay for them as part of membership."

"I don't know," said Maya, "they always got angry when I took the towels home—"

"Stop." Lori looked at all of them. "I'm scared too, but we need to keep moving."

Everyone looked guiltily away.

"*I* wasn't saying anything," Hawk said, sounding amused.

Lori pushed the door open, and Iara followed her through.

She had been expecting computers or laboratory equipment, lots of tiny offices. Instead there was a vast dark chamber on the other side of the door, and it took Iara's eyes a moment to adjust. It was more like a cave than a laboratory, she thought. A lair.

There *was* electronic equipment, but it was plugged into the floor or stacked haphazardly on flimsy card tables, leaving little LED lights to blink here and there as the main source of light. Rather than walls, the impression she got was of sloping curves. Support pillars around the massive room were dim silhouettes in the faint light. They seemed to curve and branch out near the walls and ceiling, but it was an illusion caused by the vines that twined around them, sickly yellow and . . .

Not vines, Iara realized. Eels. The walls, the support pillars, all of the room was covered with the creatures. While the eels that worked people like puppets were less than a meter long, some of the ones here were enormous, fat and glossy and longer than she could track, as she tried to determine where one ended and another began.

"This is her lair," she whispered.

"Okay, so I am superinvested in figuring out who Tia Lake is and everything," Maya said, looking into the room, "but I am *also* kind of not going into that room full of things that crawl down your throat and enslave you."

"They're asleep, Blondie," Tapper said quietly. "We don't make noise, they'll stay that way."

"Do you promise that if they wake up, you will superspeed me out of there before they get me?" Maya asked, shifting her weight anxiously from one foot to the other.

"That depends." Tapper gave her a sour smile. "I only rescue people who can correctly answer what the best Studio Ghibli movie is."

Maya considered. *"How to Train Your Dragon?"*

"I swear, you do it on purpose."

"Come on." Lori walked in, steps light and quiet. The others followed, and for a moment, Iara was there in the doorway alone.

Then Hawk looked back, and before he could ask, Iara glared and shuffled forward. The hard rubber tips of the crutches scuffed the ground, but no more than a heavy footstep, as she made her way into the lair.

The darkness was deliberate, she realized as she left the safe fluorescent light of the hallway. The overhead lights had been removed, and there were floor lamps scattered here and there, usually near the electronic equipment. The buzzing noise must have bothered Tia Lake, Iara thought.

There were eels on the floor here and there, twining around each other like braided ropes to connect the different groups around the pillars. Iara could hear them breathing, or whatever it was they did instead of breathing—a slow raspy rustle that made it sound like the whole room was whispering. She wondered if everyone could hear it or if it was audible only to her.

The others stepped over the eels carefully. Iara tried to go around, until she saw that there was nowhere to go. Then she took a slow breath, let it out, steadied her crutches, and carefully hopped over them.

One crutch slid on the slick tile, and she landed with a little thump, just saving herself from a fall with a grunt as the other crutch jolted its way up her arm with the effort of taking her weight.

The eels stirred, a few centimeters from her feet, and the raspy whisper paused for a moment. Iara froze, swaying. She wanted to take a step to balance herself, but knew that if she did, it would be an ugly, ungainly step that made more noise. She balanced, suddenly sweating in the cold stale air, holding the crutch that had slipped off the ground so that it could make no more noise.

After a long and breathless moment, the slick, ropy mass of the eels seemed to settle, and the raspy whisper began again. Iara let out a breath and looked up at the others.

Maya and Tapper were both looking back at her. Maya shot her a thumbs-up, while Tapper had his arms half-out, ready to leap forward if she fell.

She returned the thumbs-up and nodded her thanks. "I am fine," she mouthed, and Tapper gave her a quick nod and moved ahead.

She started moving again, looking around at what else was on the floor, now that her eyes had adjusted to the dim light. Electronics of all sorts—computers, of course, but also speakers, as well as large power tools that she thought would be more at home in an auto shop. Off by itself, a large doughnut-shaped device stood upright, with a low table on wheels ready to roll the patient into the tube. Iara had undergone many spinal scans in the MRI machine after the accident, and she looked away from it with a grimace.

Other things were not electronic. A great stone slab etched with forms that might have been Egyptian—or Incan, for that matter. Piles of books scattered on the floor, some left open, others with pages torn free. A great curved sword, its hilt beaten gold and shaped like coiling snakes. An old stone statue of a woman with snakes wrapped around her arms and legs. And bloodstains, so many bloodstains.

Iara saw that the others had stopped up ahead, and she hurried to catch up, thankful that she had no more lines of the eel creatures to hop over. On the floor rested an aquarium as long as Iara was tall, and half as wide. Sitting in the water, glowing a warm and inviting gold, was a cluster of the miracoral.

The floor around the aquarium was etched with writing. It was in dozens, maybe hundreds of languages, some using the Latin alphabet, others using Cyrillic letters, or Greek, or Hebrew, or something that might have been Arabic. There were pictograms as well, carved into the tile with painstaking precision, a little cloud of words all around the miracoral.

Iara found it in Portuguese first. *Venha aqui e comer.* She kept searching, and a moment later saw what looked like old Tupinamba. She knew only a few words and the bedtime song her mother always sang, but it looked like the same message, even if she wasn't sure the grammar was right: *Ur iké u.* Then again in English: *Come here and eat.*

"It's the same in both English and Tagalog," Hawk whispered. "*Halika't kumain.* Like a really formal invitation."

"And Mandarin Chinese," Lori added quietly. "*Lái zhèlǐ chī.*" Everyone looked at her in surprise. "I did an immersion school as a kid."

"I just thought you were kinda tan," Hawk said.

"What about you, Tapper?" Maya asked. "Do they have it in, um . . . ?"

"Ebonics? No. I only speak English," Tapper said. "What about you?"

"Maybe they have it in lolcat?"

While they went on, Iara looked at a computer printout of an old stone tablet. This one had a woman on it, lying on her back, and her dress turned into the waves of the ocean. Monsters crawled out of the ocean, things that looked like snakes or lizards or men with scorpion bodies . . .

"The Lake Foundation," Iara whispered, and turned to the others. "In English, what does 'foundation' mean?"

"It's like a company," Maya said, "only sometimes it does non-profit work, and on some shows, it's the people who give the good guys secret robot cars."

"Yes," Iara said, "but it can also mean the, the . . ." She waved a hand in irritation. "The *base*, the *bottom*, yes?"

Tapper nodded. "The part everything else sits on."

"Lake is not just a name, I think," Iara said, and pointed at the woman. "I think she *is* the Lake Foundation. She is the source of it, where it all comes from."

"So the statues and stuff all around here . . ." Maya gestured. "That's *her*? I thought it was Medusa. Or *a* medusa, since in some shows it's a type of monster instead of a person."

"Could we *not* base plans on how to beat the evil monster lady on TV lore, Blondie?" Tapper made a quiet but very emphatic noise. "And if you're thinking Greek, think of Echidna. Mother of monsters, including the hydra." He gestured at the eels hanging from the support pillars around them. "Lots of snaky heads, cut off one and another appears. Sound familiar?"

"I watched a lot of *Xena* reruns growing up," Maya said hopefully. "My dad was confused about how I always drew Xena and Gabrielle holding hands."

"Tia Lake," Lori murmured. "Of the Lake Foundation." She pulled out her phone and started typing.

Iara checked her own phone, which had no signal. "Your phone works?"

"It always works." Lori frowned. "I'm doing a search. Let's see what we get for 'water monster goddess tia . . .'"

She finished typing, and then her eyes widened.

"I think I know who she is."

"Who? Not what?" Tapper reached over for her phone, and Lori jerked it away from him with a sudden flinch, then recovered and held it out so they all could see.

In religions native to the Mesopotamian region, Tiamat is a primordial goddess of the ocean, who mates with Abzû (the god of freshwater) to produce younger gods, and later with Kingu to produce monsters. She is presented as both a beautiful woman, symbolizing creation and fertility, and also as a sea serpent or dragon later defeated by Marduk (or in earlier versions, Anu) in an early example of Chaoskampf, the struggle of a cultural hero against a chaos monster that is usually draconic or serpentine in appearance.

See also: Tiamat (disambiguation)

"Okay," said Maya after a moment, "I feel like there's a geeky thing here that the guys who played the dice games used to talk about, where the red dragon head breathes fire, and the black one breathes lightning—"

"Please don't," Tapper growled. "And the black dragon head breathes acid."

"She is a Sumerian goddess," Iara said. "She is thousands of years old."

"She's a monster," Tapper said. "She *is* that giant eel thing we swam past to get here. The human shape is just a disguise."

"That's sick," Hawk said. "So it's like a feeder making everyone think it's a real person, and its real body is hiding down in the dark . . ."

"None of that matters," Lori said, her voice quick and clipped. Her phone buzzed in her hand, and she jerked it away to read it.

Then she looked at all of them and grimaced. "What matters is that we only have until tomorrow to kill her."

"So how does this help us?" Hawk asked. "We maybe know what she is. We don't know what she wants, except that it has to do with the miracoral." He pointed at the words etched into the ground around the cluster. "Maybe if we figure out what she needs, we'll figure out a weakness, and then we can hit her there."

Stepping carefully, as though the words on the floor might hurt him, he moved toward the aquarium on the floor. The glow of the miracoral intensified as he drew closer, its warm golden color inviting him to keep coming. Iara could hear the color in some part of her mind, her special gift letting her process the growing light as a song as pure as the chime of a bell.

Then, from behind them, a woman's deep voice echoed across the chamber.

"It seems I was a fool for trying to capture you," said Tia Lake as she entered the room, her stiletto heels clacking on the floor, "when you were willing to come here yourselves the whole time."

09

LORI

Lori's phone had begun buzzing almost immediately, but she couldn't look away from the woman coming toward them.

Tia Lake—Tiamat?—was tall and perfect. Her hair was black and silky and tumbled down past her shoulders, her lips were blood red, and her skin was alabaster. She looked ready to order the death of a stepdaughter or negotiate a major business deal, and as she walked into the room, lights came on, tracking her position to put her in a spotlight.

"You are the Nix I captured, yes?" she asked, and her voice *pulled* at Lori, just like before. It was worse in person. Her voice was the most important thing in the world, it was Lori's whole brain, and the question got inside her head and expanded until the pressure threatened to make it explode.

"No," came bursting from her mouth, even as all of the others said, "Yes."

Lake looked at her with a curious smile, one immaculate

eyebrow arching. "You must be Angler Consulting, then."

It wasn't a question, and it let the pressure off of her mind. Lori opened her mouth to lie and found that the words wouldn't come out.

"You are Tiamat, ancient goddess of oceans and creation," Iara said while Lori stammered.

Lake turned to Iara, her little smile disappearing. "One of many names. Too many. You are linked to the coral, as you all must see. Can you communicate with it?"

"I do not believe so," said Iara. Lori saw that her eyes were glassy.

Then she did look at her phone as it buzzed again.

Handler: Kk, we need to get out of here.

Handler: We don't have a weakness for her yet.

Handler: & if she can wear heels while deep-sea diving, she's pretty powerful.

Handler: Iara has superhearing. Weak vs Lake's voice.

"Have you touched it?" Lake asked.

"No," Iara answered.

"Do, please." Lake smiled gently as Iara turned and lifted her crutches to move toward the aquarium.

"Stop her!" Lori shouted. "You have to block out the voice! Music or shouting or—"

"Got it," Tapper said, and boxed Iara's ears hard. Iara shouted and fell to the floor, clutching at her head.

Lake circled them, her face neutral, and stopped before the little aquarium tank with the piece of miracoral in it. It went red as she approached, and when she tapped on the glass, a dozen of the crayfish sprang out from it, pincers flashing with crackling arcs of energy. "It will not answer me. Not yet. Will it speak to you?" she asked Lori, stepping away from the tank.

"No. It hates me too." Lori stepped between Lake and the others. As the woman's attention fell upon her, Lori felt every tiny imperfection hit her with crushing force. One leg of her wetsuit had ridden up ever so slightly and was starting to itch. Her hair was drying in a tangled mess from the salt water. She looked lumpy and frail and weak and pathetic, and she was slouching, but she couldn't make herself stand up straight. "You've been here for thousands of years, feeding and killing. Why do you need the miracoral?"

Lake's eyes narrowed. "Who are you?" Then she smiled and stepped forward, her heels clacking. Around her the eels started to slither. "No, *what* are you?"

"I . . ." Her phone buzzed. She dropped it to her side and squeezed her eyes shut against the hot sting. The others were going to hear.

Maya was going to hear.

"I think I'm a feeder," came the words, lunging out like vomit, "like you. I'm not real."

Lake was perhaps ten feet away. "You're nothing like me, child," she said easily, "and now that I can really see you, I understand." She reached out.

Then wind rushed past Lori, and Lake staggered backward as Tapper blurred into her, fist extended. "Back off!"

Hawk was there a moment later, carrying a marble statue of a snake coiling around a woman. He yelled as he threw it, and Lake staggered again as the marble shattered against her.

Lori looked at them in confusion.

Maybe they hadn't heard what she was.

Her phone kept buzzing. It was heating up from doing it so much, and she glanced down.

Handler: KEEP HER TALKING WE NEED INTEL

"What are you?" she shouted as Lake recovered. "What are you, *really*? What do you want?"

Lake's face twisted into a snarl of disdain that sent Lori cringing back. "You cannot grasp what I am. I come from a place beyond your comprehension."

"What, like space?" Hawk asked, and stepped in with a solid punch. Her head snapped back, but she didn't fall. Her hands closed on Hawk, long fingernails perfectly manicured and painted the same red as her lips, and she hurled him into a pillar. The eels hissed and creaked and twisted around him.

"The coral mutated you," Lake called out. "It must want you for something."

Tapper flashed toward her, but this time she caught him and slammed him to the floor, and eels slithered around him as he shouted and fought, a blur of panicked motion. "How do I make it scream?"

"I don't know," Lori said, and heard the others echo the words.

Lake's face twisted in rage, then went still. "Useless, all of you. Perhaps it will respond to your pain."

"Why?" Lori yelled at her again. "Why do you need it?" As Lake's attention focused on her, she shifted over to the side, away from the others. Under the great mass of oily, dark yellow skin in the shadows, Hawk was still struggling. So was Tapper, at the edge of Lake's spotlight. "Why do you need the coral?"

Lake started toward her, her lips pressed into a thin line. "Because you are right, children. I *am* the goddess Tiamat. I came to this world thousands of years ago, *and I am trapped here*." Her gaze pinned Lori in place. "I want out of this pitiful tide pool. I want to return to the deep water."

"So leave." The words tumbled from Lori's mouth of their own volition. "Just go home."

Lake's hands curled into fists, and the eels nearby hissed and began to slither toward Lori. "I *can't*, you idiot child. I am something greater than you can ever know."

"You are the giant eel monster we passed in the water on the way down," Lori said. This time, the words were her choice. "That's the real you, isn't it? The eels, your human body here . . . those are just extensions of you."

Lake sneered at her. "Correct, little girl, but not what I meant. My body may be powerful, yes, but my mind, my *self* . . . You cannot lie to me, and you cannot deny me answers when I seek them, because your mind has *taken* part of me *inside you*. I am seared into the consciousness of all who behold me. Even the imperfect knowledge passed down in legends contains some of me." She stopped and gestured sharply at something Lori couldn't see.

A moment later, lights came on around it—a bronze bust of Medusa.

"And as *tiny*, as *insignificant*, as you are, your minds pin me to this world. As long as I am *remembered*, I am captive. Can you imagine what it is like to be trapped," Lake hissed, "locked into a prison of existence by the flawed and imperfect image of you that others hold in their head?"

Lori thought of Mister Barkin glaring at her, of Hawk offering to carry Iara, of Tapper glaring at everyone as he sat alone, and the words came out all by themselves. "I think I can."

It wasn't the answer Lake had expected. She paused for a moment, head cocked thoughtfully as she observed Lori. "Then you understand why I need to be free of it."

The eels slithered into a circle around Lori. Most were normal size. One was as long as Lori was tall, though, thick and glossy.

They weren't touching her yet. Behind Lake, Hawk and Tapper still struggled under the coiling piles upon them. "How?" Lori asked, hoping Handler was ready with something.

"For thousands of years, I pulled against my bonds," Lake snarled, "hoping to no avail that the world would forget me. But then the miracoral came, another visitor from the deep water, and its cry of pain attracted something even greater."

"The Leviathan," Lori guessed, and Lake nodded.

"I sear myself into this world," Lake said, slashing her hand through the air in irritation, "but the Leviathan is even larger than I am. Its presence *erases*, leaving only gaps imperfectly filled, with no memory or understanding."

Like the water rising, Lori thought. Out loud she said, "So everything you're doing to the miracoral . . . You're trying to get it to cry out. You're trying to summon the Leviathan?"

"It will erase this world," Lake said with a hard smile, "and then I can return to the deep water. But first let us look at *you* . . ." She stepped toward Lori, and the ring of eels surrounding Lori began to tighten.

Then a keening wail cut through the air. It started loud, and then turned shrill and painful, and then turned into a buzzing heat in Lori's ears, and then was a tiny sound Lori wasn't even sure she could hear anymore . . . and the eels shrieked and fell to thrashing at the sound.

Iara knelt on the floor, her mouth open wide, glaring at Lake as she finished her wail. "The only freedom to be gained is *ours*, monster!" Iara shouted, and Lori saw Hawk and Tapper clamber free from the still-thrashing eels.

Lake let out a slow breath through her nose. "In a moment, little Nix." She turned back to Lori. "If they cannot help me, perhaps you are the difference I need."

She reached out for Lori.

The great eel that had circled around Lori snapped up, coiled around Lake's wrist, twisted, and threw her to the floor. "Okay, hi, sorry, I'm not really a good hitter!" the eel shouted as its colors swam back from sickly yellow to blond hair and pale skin and pink swimsuit.

Lori looked at Maya and swallowed. She'd put herself between Lake and Lori.

Hawk was there a moment later, his swimsuit covered with ichor, and Tapper was beside him, grimacing. They all stepped beside Lori, fists raised, glaring at Lake as she got back to her feet. Back by the aquarium, Iara whooped a battle cry.

Lake made a noise. They'd injured her, Lori thought. *We have a chance.*

Then she realized it was laughter.

"I believe I know who you are, Angler Consulting," Lake said, straightening and flipping her hair back into place. "You hunt things like me, and you fear that you are one, don't you? You fear letting the others find out."

Lori fought it, and her phone buzzed, trying to help, but before she could look down at it, the word popped out. "Yes."

The others couldn't have missed it this time. They were right beside her. She looked away.

"We knew that," Tapper snapped. "Quit trying to make it a thing, Dragon Lady."

Lori blinked the sting from her eyes and looked over. "You knew?"

"I see everything, remember?" Tapper looked over at her, his eyes glittering.

"It doesn't matter what you think Lori is," Maya called back to Lake, her voice quavering even as she raised her fists. "What matters is what she wants to be and how she treats people."

"She tries hard to be a good person, doesn't she?" Lake asked, still smiling. She ignored the little chorus of "yes." "Taking care of her little brother all by herself, making money killing things like me to pay for food and rent. But you, who would deny me the gift of being forgotten, I wonder if you have thought about that, really."

It wasn't a question, and the silence stood for a moment.

The phone buzzed. Lori looked down at it.

Handler: Lori, I'm so sorry.

Confused, she looked back up at Lake.

"Lori," the tall woman said, smiling as the name struck like a blow, "it doesn't really make sense for a girl your age to be raising her brother all alone. What happened to your parents?"

And from Lori's mouth, all by themselves, came the words, "Guess it was just one of those things."

For a moment she just stood there. All at once the world felt heavy, as though the air itself were congealing around her. She could feel, with the itchy pressure at the back of her neck, every eye in the room on her, but she couldn't move, couldn't breathe, couldn't do anything.

"What did you say?" Maya asked, her eyes wide.

"I . . . I . . ." The words wouldn't come.

Lake's smile showed shiny white teeth now. "Where are they? Where are your parents?"

"Guess it was just one of *stop*!" Lori shouted. Her pulse pounded in her ears. "Stop making me say it!"

"The only way for me to escape this *living hell* is to be forgotten," Lake said, and now she was coming back toward Lori. "But I am bound in this wretched world. I can force the truth from your mouths, I can take your minds, but I cannot make you forget. You, Angler Consulting, can tamper with minds somewhat. My assistant could not recall how she got your contact information to hire you for the little thing at the docks. These adjustments, they leave a gap, a little hole that the world fills in and tries not to let its people remember. Like the rising of the waters." She smiled. "Or your parents."

"Guess it was . . ." Lori bit her lip, forced the words back. Every time she tried to think, something slipped away.

"Maybe your connection will help," Lake said. "If the miracoral refuses to scream for me and lure the Leviathan back, perhaps *you* will help me escape the shallows of this world . . . especially since you are as false as I am."

Lori couldn't think. It was falling away, all of it. The room spun around her. She was a monster who thought she was a girl who thought she was a monster, a monster real enough to cry. Guess it was just one of those things.

She lunged forward and grabbed Lake by the wrist.

Look at the microbe on the plate.

Pretend that as it oozed forward in its own primitive way, you bit down into the plate, crunching the glass beneath your jaws as you heard the screams of the little microbe who could not see you coming and had no frame of reference for your very existence.

Pretend that as you lean in to get that little microbe on the shattered remains of the plate, you have just a moment to realize how far you have extended yourself, and then, from the darkness where you could not see, something grabs ahold of you, and there are teeth and jaws and where did it come from and you should thrash free but you can't as something

  spears

    into

      your

        side

Lori stumbled with a wrenching jerk that felt like pain in a part of the body she didn't have. The jaws—*Handler's jaws*—speared through Tia Lake, and then just as quickly, Tia Lake slid around them, a mass of snakes imitating a person, and the jaws thrashed in pain and—

HAWK

"What did you do to her?" Hawk yelled as Lori screamed and disappeared. It was like when she usually did her teleportation thing—or when the thing Tapper had said was driving her pulled her out of the world and into . . . space, Hawk kind of thought . . . but Lori had never screamed before.

Tia Lake, whose shape had been running like a watercolor painting held up before it was dry, slid back into her hot-lady form. Hawk could kind of see the eels or snakes that made her, now.

She was still smiling, however. "Nothing that matters to you." She reached into a pocket— how did she still have pockets when she was made out of snakes?—and drew out her phone. "Karkinos," she snapped, punching buttons on the screen. "The Nix are here. I am attending to the creature that freed them. Collect the Nix from the Deepwater Laboratory after I leave, please."

Then she turned on her heel and started to leave the room, the spotlight following her as she stalked away.

Hawk wasn't sure what he'd been expecting, but it wasn't that.

"Hey!" he shouted, and ran after her. "We're not done with you y—"

He tripped in the darkness over one of the big eels on the floor, and it coiled around his foot. Others snapped around his arms, twisting and twining. He clenched his teeth just in case any of them tried to crawl into his mouth again.

Tia Lake paused and looked back over her shoulder.

"What do you intend to do?" she asked in a calm voice that was somehow worse than her yelling, like she had seen this show already and was just reading along with the script.

"Fight you," Hawk said, since he didn't have a reason not to.

"How?" Half her face was shadowed by the spotlight. The one eye he could see was disinterested.

He pulled free from the eels coiling around him with brute force. It wasn't pretty, and it left him stumbling a little, but he did it. "I don't know."

"No, you don't." She smiled, a slow and sultry smile that made Hawk flush even as his skin crawled. "I am Tiamat. I am the Hydra. I am Jörmungandr. I have fought Anu and Heracles and *Thor*, and none of them could kill me, child. I grow back. I *always* grow back. And you are *mine* now." As the eels twined around Hawk again, he tried to fight them off, but this time, they lifted him off the floor, and he found himself flailing against empty air, dangling by eels that held him like ropes twisting around all four limbs. "I will use you later. Perhaps *you* will be what makes the miracoral scream and summon the Leviathan. How do you feel about that?"

"Fine," Hawk said, and he *did* feel fine. It wasn't going to happen, and worrying about it would just stress him out and cause him pain. Feeling fine was better than feeling pain.

She smiled at that. "Interesting. Karkinos will see if you still feel that way when he gets here. But for now, I have other business." She sniffed. "You made it down here, and that is impressive, because my form twists this part of your world apart, a little. If you try to flee, I will be there in that darkness, and I will be very unhappy with you."

"Leave him alone!" shouted Maya, rushing forward and then pausing as eels hissed out of the darkness toward her.

"When I return," Lake went on, ignoring Maya, "I will take

pieces of you away until it makes the miracoral scream. I will keep taking as long as you have anything to give," she went on, her voice rising, and now the one eye Hawk could see as she looked back over her shoulder glittered in the darkness with anger, "because all of you *keep* me here, trapping who I am with your eyes, and if the only way for me to escape is to erase every shred of life from this little world, I will do that. Do you understand me, child?"

Hawk twisted in the eels. "No."

She shook her head. "Unsurprising."

She turned away again, and when she reached the doorway, the eels released Hawk. He fell to the ground, which would have hurt if he hadn't been invulnerable, and as he shook his head and got back to his feet, he saw that all the eels in the room were slithering across the floor after Lake. They coiled around her, hundreds, thousands of them, and disappeared.

Lake didn't get any bigger or turn into a super-Tiamat or anything. She looked the same as she had before.

She walked out without a backward glance, and the door shut behind her, leaving them in darkness.

"Finally," Iara said, scoffing in the darkness. "The snake woman talks far too much."

"You guys could have helped," Hawk called back to the others. It wasn't worth getting mad about, but it seemed like the kind of thing he should say.

"I was there!" Maya protested.

"Think, Pint-Size," Tapper shot back. "We couldn't hurt her. She said she was leaving. You're the idiot who couldn't let her go. The only one who did *anything* to her was Ipanema over here," Tapper said. "Her scream messed with the eels."

"Momentarily," Iara said. "I wish I could do more."

"What do we do now?" Maya asked. "We need to find out what happened to Lori."

"We need to get out of here, Blondie," Tapper muttered.

"Okay, yes, that too."

"Would've been nice to get more," Hawk said, and shrugged. "Guess this trip was a bust."

"Not quite." Iara made a little grunt, probably getting herself back on her feet with the crutches. "We know more than we knew, and we know what this Tia Lake wants."

"She wants everyone to forget her," Maya said, her voice quiet in the darkness. "People remembering who she is, what she is, has her trapped. She thinks the Leviathan can take her out of people's minds, so they all forget her, like they forgot about the water rising."

"And to summon the Leviathan," Iara added, "she wants to experiment on us with the miracoral."

The miracoral, the only source of light in the room, was glowing with the same warm golden light it had held before. Hawk had thought his eyes were adjusting, but then he realized it was growing brighter.

One of them was moving toward it.

"I think," Iara said, "as we have no other plan, we should see what happens."

Hawk saw her silhouette, black against the warm golden light, come between him and the miracoral.

"Iara, wait!" He stumbled forward in the darkness. "You can't—"

"Joshua Bautista," she said without looking back, "I am very tired of you telling me what I cannot do."

She reached into the aquarium and took the miracoral in her hands.

LORI

—Lori choked on salt water, splashed blindly in green emptiness frothing with white bubbles, spun with a rushing dizziness that had her fighting to find out which way was up, and then felt air on her face as she broke the surface.

She coughed and sputtered, blinking stinging salt from her eyes, and saw the sidewalk just out of her reach. The canals, she was in the canals.

She splashed over and grabbed hold of the side. Her hand was trembling. She coughed some more, trying to clear water that had gone up her nose.

Everything hurt. Or more, it didn't, but it felt like it should. Something was wrong, something inside her or about her or . . .

She'd been down below with her friends. They'd been fighting Lake. And then . . .

She was still hanging from the side. She pulled herself up onto the rough edge of the sidewalk, or tried to, anyway. Her arms gave out as she pulled, and she flopped into the water, swaying gently in the current.

She'd gotten her wisdom teeth out a couple years ago. They'd knocked her out for the surgery, and then she'd been home for a few days, recovering. At first it had hurt, like the doctor had told her, and she'd had to rest a lot. (Who had taken care of Ben then? Was it her *guess it was just one of those*—no, don't think about it.) After that the pain had been mostly gone, and she could forget about the whole thing most of the time. But every now and then, either by accident or curiosity, she'd twist her tongue to the back of her mouth and slide it over the strange, rough-edged holes where the teeth had once been. They didn't hurt, but they didn't feel like part of her. They felt like an absence.

That was how all of Lori felt right now.

She pulled again. This time she succeeded in getting her upper body up onto the sidewalk, though her arms trembled as though she'd been swimming for hours. She flopped onto the ground and rolled over, pulling her legs the rest of the way. The sky overhead seemed dazzlingly bright, bright enough that the sidewalk was a hot blinding white beneath her.

"Handler." She coughed it more than said it. Being on her back got more water down her throat. She rolled onto her side and coughed again. She had choked on the water. Could she not breathe underwater anymore? How was she going to get back to the others? "Handler."

She didn't feel the buzz at her thigh. She'd had her phone in her hand when she'd grabbed Tia Lake. Maybe it had gotten lost. "Handler?"

"Excuse me, are you all right?" came a voice from overhead. Lori looked up, squinting, and the silhouette resolved into a woman in a tank top and yoga pants, standing over her with earbuds in her ears and a concerned expression.

"I . . ." Lori blinked. It wasn't as bright as it had seemed, now that her eyes were getting used to the light again. She shaded her eyes, like she did when she came out of the movie theater on a sunny day. "Sorry, I think I fell in."

"You weren't swimming in there on purpose," the woman said, or maybe asked. "The canal isn't safe for swimming." She looked disapproving now.

Lori tried to get to her feet and found that she could. Looking down, she saw the swim shoes and the wetsuit. "No," she said. "I was getting ready to go to swim class with my little brother. I got dizzy all of a sudden and fell in, I think."

"Do you need a doctor?" The woman looked concerned again. Lori watched her face change shape, the lines around the eyes soften and the neck relax. It was like she was watching someone talking to someone else. *This is how people work. When they're angry, they make this face.*

"No." Lori realized she'd been waiting for too long. "I'm just going to sit for a moment. Thank you."

"Okay. Be careful." The woman looked concerned still, but she nodded and jogged off.

"Handler, what happened?" There was still no answer. Lori squinted, keeping her head down as her eyes adjusted. Bright sidewalk, no, just normal brightness, green grass on the other side of the sidewalk, growing up around a chain-link fence. Blinking, Lori looked up to see a swing set and jungle gym, with kids running around, laughing and shouting. Over to the left a brick building blurred into view.

She was outside Ben's day care.

"Lori! Hey, Lori!" The voice caught her as she leaned against the fence, and she tracked it to her brother. He was running toward her, waving good-bye to one of his friends. "Hi, Lori, I missed you! I like your wetsuit!"

She stepped around the edge of the chain-link fence and into his hug. "I missed you, too." She felt ready to cry for reasons she still didn't know, like she was on the edge of something, tongue flicking to the back of her mouth and looking for the gap where something was missing. "Let's go home." Ben was smiling and warm and *real*, and it felt like her vision was finally sliding back to normal after holding his little hand.

"Miss Fisher." Mister Barkin's cold disapproval caught her from the side. "You need to come in and sign him out, please."

"Of course." Lori nodded. Her ponytail, still wet, slapped the back of her neck, and the cold made her flinch. "I'm coming." She turned to Ben. "Do you need anything inside?"

He shook his head. "I have my Legos out here in my backpack. We were having a Lego Pokémon robot race, and I was winning, but then Josh used a set that had flick missiles—"

"Okay, just go get your backpack." Lori smiled as he jogged off, then turned to Mister Barkin and headed inside.

Mister Barkin didn't look very good. His eyes were sunken

and a little bloodshot, and his hair was out of place. He gestured impatiently as she approached. "The sign-out sheet is there, inside."

It was dark in the main day care room. They must have turned out the lights because all the children were outside. She stepped past Mister Barkin to the table where the sign-out sheets were kept. He smelled rank too, she noticed as he got out of her way. Maybe he hadn't showered last night.

He would *never* come to work in that condition.

She realized that having her back to him was making her uncomfortable, and she turned, ready to make up a question about Ben's day, and that was when his hand clamped down over her mouth.

"I'm sorry," he rasped in her ear. His other arm was around her neck, and she froze as he pulled her back against him. "I'm sorry. The eel won't come back until I give you to them. I need the eel to come back, I'm sorry. I didn't give them Ben. I could have, but I didn't—" Blood pounded in her ears, drowning out whatever else he said.

She slammed an elbow back blindly. It hit him somewhere, and his grip loosened. She tensed her fingers into claws and speared them back past her face and over her shoulder, and clipped his face. He gave a little cry, and Lori twisted out of his grip.

"You have to," he said plaintively, looking at her with blood-shot desperation. "They'll just get you and I'll get the eel back and nobody will take Ben, and I care about him, I do, I'm doing this to save him, and I need the eel!"

He lunged and slammed Lori back into the sign-out table, and Lori gasped and jabbed a fist into his throat. He staggered, choking and sobbing, and she slammed the heel of her palm into his face. He stumbled back, tripped over a low shelf filled with children's books, and sprawled across a play mat.

"They'll keep coming," he said from the floor, and Lori leaped over the shelf, came down on top of him, and punched him once, twice, three times, until he stopped talking. Her arms trembled, and she was dizzy again, gasping as she stood over him.

Ben was outside.

She dashed outside, saw him coming toward her with his backpack. "Come on," she called over. "We have to go."

He looked confused, and she grabbed his hand and pulled him out of the yard. She didn't look back into the building. They were all out playing. In a few minutes they'd go back inside and find him. What would Barkin say when he woke up?

"Are you wearing your wetsuit because we are going swimming?" Ben asked. "I don't have mine."

"I don't know." Barkin would either call the police or call Lake. He had Lori's phone number.

He had her home address.

"We might be going out for the night, okay?" she said, and forced a smile as she looked down at Ben. "Like a camping trip, but at a hotel?"

"Why?" Ben asked.

"We just have to, for a day or two." She kept the smile going. "We'll have lots of pizza."

"I don't have my pajamas," Ben said thoughtfully, "or my toothbrush."

The day care teachers began yelling for kids to come inside. Lori walked a little faster, pulling Ben along to keep up. "That's what will make it fun, kiddo. It'll be an adventure."

"Lori, we missed the ferry stop." Ben pointed with his free hand.

"I think we're going to get a taxi." Behind her, kids were starting to head inside. "I just have to get someplace I can call for one."

"Why not just use your phone?" Ben asked, and Lori blinked away sudden tears that could have been from exhaustion or the fight with Barkin or the sudden feeling of her tongue finding the hole where something was missing.

"I don't have my phone," she said. "I lost it."

"No you didn't." Ben tapped her waist. "It's in your pocket."

Lori looked down and saw the familiar bulge in her wetsuit's zippered hip pocket. She unzipped it and fished the phone out. Maybe she'd missed the buzzes or maybe the fight had knocked it from vibrate to noise.

Her phone had a long crack running the length of the screen, splitting into a little spiderweb down at the bottom. It turned on at her touch, and she flipped over to Messages and selected Handler.

Handler: KEEP HER TALKING WE NEED INTEL
Handler: Wait no nonono. You're not like her. You're not a monster.
Handler: Lori, I'm so sorry.

That was all.

Lori: Handler?
<Message could not be delivered.>

THURSDAY

10

HAWK

Come on, come on, come on, Hawk thought, and said absolutely nothing out loud, treading water in the cold darkness. It would succeed this time. It had to.

Tapper worked at a door that was a dull gray in the darkness, his hands blurring and making little bubbles. There was some kind of lock, and he was trying to break it while Maya hovered over him, looking worriedly back over her shoulder into the darkness where *it* slept.

Hawk didn't look back. He didn't have special eyes or ears. All he could do was worry.

Then he remembered that worry was pain, and he didn't need pain, and he let it go away, and he was fine again.

Behind him Iara's voice rang out through the water. "Get inside!"

He looked off into the darkness, and far in the distance overhead, he saw a tiny golden star. It grew steadily as he watched, and then he could make out Iara's body swimming, silhouetted against the light from the miracoral she held. A moment later she was darting past them, eyes wide with panic. "Get inside, get inside! She is coming!"

The water was growing warm around Hawk, and as he turned back to look down into that horrible darkness, he saw sickly green bubbles billowing up toward them.

Close enough, he decided, and moved past Tapper. With a quick jerk, he snapped the lock holding the door closed and wrenched the door open.

Everyone swam inside, just as a great rushing mass of bubbles lit Tiamat, her *true* form, as she rose from the darkness and sent frothing water surging all around them. The impact rattled the door in Hawk's grasp, and he slammed it shut.

Had she seen them? She was too big, and he didn't see any eyes, didn't see any of her, really, just the enormous mass and the impression that she was like the eels.

With a slow bubbling flushing noise, the water began to drain out of the room. Watching it always made Hawk realize that it had been almost half an hour since he had breathed air, and he always started to panic, as though the water wouldn't drain out fast enough. He was fine, though, same as always. The fear whisked away, leaving calm behind.

Iara was lying on the floor, cradling the miracoral in her arms. "I thought it would work."

"What happened?" Hawk asked, coming over to kneel down beside her. "Did the coral do anything to the darkness?"

"No. It was brighter, but when I tried to reach the surface . . ." She shook her head.

They had been trying since yesterday, always with the same results. They would leave one of the underwater buildings and try for the surface, and each time, as the cold crept into their bodies, clammy and slick around them, they would stop.

Hawk could *want* his arms to move, but at a certain point, his body just ignored him. None of the others could get past it either.

"I told you," Tapper muttered. "It's not just dark. It's a hole. Like the world is flat ground, and you're trying to walk from point A to point B, only someone carved out a big ugly chasm in your way."

"But we're already in the chasm," Maya said, for probably the fifth or sixth time since yesterday, "aren't we?"

"No, Blondie, this is all real." Tapper rapped the wall, his hand a blur. "This is point A. Point B is the surface. The chasm is wherever Tiamat comes from. Someplace where this world's rules don't apply."

"Like space," Hawk added helpfully.

"It's not space!" Tapper yelled. "It's another dimension or . . . I don't know. Wherever Lori ended up."

Maya turned to him sharply. "She's coming back!"

Tapper made a little grimace and said to Iara, "Come on, let's see what this one is."

Maya held out Iara's crutches, and Iara took them gratefully, passing the miracoral over to Maya in return. The coral still glowed with its warm and friendly light, the only warmth they had been able to find down here. After a night in what would otherwise have been darkness, that was saying a lot.

Hawk wasn't hungry, either, and he hadn't skipped dinner, bedtime snack, breakfast, *and* brunch in years. That had to be the miracoral too. Feeding them, helping them, something.

But it couldn't get them out.

Hawk followed the others out of the air lock and into the building proper. They'd tried other buildings through the night, hoping to find something useful. Most of the buildings were flooded—which didn't mean that they were empty. There were things in them, more of the eels glowing sickly yellow-green in the darkness, coiled around old rotted furniture and support beams, waiting for someone to wake them up. The buildings that had been fitted with air locks had been abandoned, with old dead computers lying scattered on the floor next to bloodstained mattresses and surgical equipment.

This one looked like it had been a shopping mall before the water rose, and on the tiled floors amid old sales counters that had once held perfume or watches, they found more of the same. This time, the mattresses had straps on the sides, and there was clothing next to them, folded neatly. On the nearest pile, Hawk saw that the socks had the edges rolled down over the tops, like his mom always did to keep them together. He swallowed and looked away. Tiamat had experimented on people here—trying to pull herself from their minds or something.

On one of the mattresses lay what was left of Shawn.

He wore the pants he'd been wearing when he died, but they'd taken his shirt off. His body was pale and purple-blue, his skin waxy. His shoulder and arm didn't fit on right anymore— Hawk could see ugly messy stitches where they'd reattached it. Had it been torn off when Tiamat had killed him, or after, when the scientists had experimented on the body?

Iara had turned away and was sobbing, shaking on her crutches. Tapper zipped forward, then back, then over to a wall that suddenly had a spiderweb crack in it radiating out from Tapper's fist.

Maya put down the miracoral and walked forward slowly. Tears streamed down her face, but she didn't look away. "I'm so sorry, Shawn," she said to the body. "We'll never forget you."

She reached out slowly and laid a hand on Shawn's cheek.

An eel slid out of his mouth and coiled around Maya's hand.

Maya screamed, and as she stumbled back, flailing wildly, more eels poured out of Shawn's mouth, dozens of them, tiny little wormlike versions, and more were wriggling through the stitches on his shoulder as well.

Hawk ran forward and smashed the eels in his hands. Tapper was there too, crushing them in a blur of speed, but more eels were coming, and Shawn's body was starting to deflate as they poured from his mouth.

Hawk shrugged, looked at Tapper, and then slammed a fist down on Shawn's face. As eels and dead bone smashed beneath his hand, he drove his other hand into Shawn's torso, where more of them would be hiding.

It took several blows to be sure, and Hawk hammered his fists onto the corpse over and over again, until finally he stepped back and looked, and the body was still.

The others were still, too, looking at him with eyes wide with shock and disgust.

"What?" Hawk asked, looking at them in confusion. "You guys see a better way to stop them?"

"He was our *friend*," Maya said softly.

"Then I'm sure he'd be pretty chill with us mashing up his corpse to stop the eels from getting out," Hawk said, and grinned. She didn't smile back. "Look, I end up with eels inside me, you're all free to do the same, all right?"

"Why would anyone do this?" Maya asked in a sick little voice, clutching the miracoral to her tightly.

"She hates being stuck in this world," Tapper muttered, "and she's trying to use us to summon the Leviathan to escape. She was experimenting. The document said that putting eels into a Nix killed them, so it's useless for her. Maybe she wanted to see what would happen if she put an eel into one of us that was already dead."

"I don't get it," Hawk said.

"No kidding." Tapper shook his head.

"Fine, whatever." Hawk shrugged. "Sorry if I don't have your crazy eyes or whatever messed-up brain lets you think just like the evil *naga* lady. Maybe if you tell me—"

"Tell you what?" Iara cut in, stopping to lean on her crutches. She shook her wet hair out of her face. "That destroying a friend's body, while tactically sound, is not something a hero does? You do not understand."

He glared at her now. "This isn't a comic book, Iara. You can't blame me for doing the smart thing. Tiamat is a monster. You do whatever you have to to stop monsters."

"It is not blame," Iara said, sounding tired, "and no, she is not. Tiamat is . . . she is evil, yes, but I know how she feels."

Hawk stared at her, shocked. "How?" Tapper was nodding, and Hawk shot him a look. "She's a *naga* lady, dude!"

"She wants to leave, but she can't," Tapper said, "because no matter how she tries to pull away, there's always someone there to remind her what she is." He smiled at Hawk, his eyes glittering in the dim light. "A freak with a messed-up brain."

"Or a girl who needs crutches and *help*," Iara added, glaring at Hawk.

"It doesn't make her right," Maya said softly, "but she's hurting. I can feel her pain."

"That's her problem," Hawk said, and shrugged. "And yours, I guess. Holding on to all of that, keeping it in where it hurts you. Pain is a choice. You guys wanna be sad about Shawn, cool, you go, but I only knew him for like an hour or two. I'm not happy he's dead. I'm not any more angry than I was about Tia Lake kidnapping me and putting those eel things in my parents to mess with their minds." Actually, now that he thought about it, at least Lake hadn't killed them. His mom had sounded happy, even.

"I'm not *anything* about Shawn. I'm fine. And feeling nothing is better than feeling pain." They all looked at him, shocked, and he gestured at Tapper and Iara in irritation. "Like you're just mad all the time, and Iara, every time I try to help—"

"I need help *sometimes!*" she shouted. "But now that is all you can see when you look at me! You do not see *me* anymore, just a chance to look strong!"

For a moment Hawk was angry and guilty and ashamed, and then the feeling whisked away, and he shrugged again. "Well, then, maybe you should—" he began.

That was when the horribly messed-up eel-people staggered through the doorway and attacked.

LORI

Lori had worked with Handler long enough to have picked up a few tricks for remaining undetected. Santa Dymphna's city center provided easy access to anywhere, which meant that someone who was tracked there could be coming from anywhere in the city. If anyone was watching her bank activity, this was the one place she could risk using her cards.

She maxed out her daily withdrawal limit at an ATM in the city center and used her credit card to buy everything she thought she might need for an evening in hiding: new clothes, a bunch of chocolate-chip granola bars and chocolate milk for Ben, toothbrushes and toothpaste, a charger for her phone, and a prepaid anonymous ferry pass, in case her old one was being tracked.

Then she got Ben onto a ferry that took them to the edge of the city, a suburban area with a few small shopping plazas and one old hotel, and booked them a room for the night, paid in cash.

She talked Ben into this being a night of adventure, got dinner at a nearby McDonald's, and charged her phone while Ben watched Pokémon on the hotel television.

Lori: Handler.
<Message could not be delivered.>

Lori: Come on, please.
<Message could not be delivered.>

She woke up the next morning groggy and slow. Every movement hurt her head, causing sharp little pinpricks of brightness at the edges of her vision. She had to ask Ben to slow down, because she couldn't understand what he was saying at first.

It was Thursday morning. This was the earliest date by which Tia Lake might have traced Lori's financial records. Of course, with Mister Barkin under the sway of the eels—of Tiamat—that probably no longer mattered.

She had no idea what she was going to do next.

Were Maya and the others okay? What was Tiamat doing to them even now? She had to believe they were all right, but none of her messages to them had gone through either, and with no way to get back down to them . . .

Lori: Handler, I need you.
<Message could not be delivered.>

All right, she thought. She had to assume Tiamat knew her identity. That meant that she and Ben were in danger. She had to assume Tiamat and her minions were after her. She had to assume that her credit card was being tracked, and anything she did could put her and Ben in danger. She had to assume . . .

"Lori, what's wrong?" Ben asked, looking over at her from the bed he'd slept in.

Lori started and realized that her face was hot. Tears were streaming down her cheeks.

"I'm sorry," she said, and the words caught on something in her throat and came out hoarse, and more tears came with them. "I'm sorry, kiddo. I'm having a hard time, and I'm not feeling so good. I . . . I think we might go on a little vacation, okay? We could make this trip a little longer."

Ben considered this. "Can we go home and get the iPad, then? All of my games are on the iPad."

Lori squeezed her eyes shut. Her head was throbbing. "Yeah, I think we can do that."

She couldn't do this.

It was too big, all of it. She was sixteen and trying to care for a seven-year-old, and he was *good*—he deserved better than her. She wasn't even *real*; she was just some monster made by some other monster as a lure, and now the other monster was dead, and what was she even supposed to do? She could barely get him to day care on time, and now she had to take him and run away and never come back.

Because that was the only real solution. Tiamat wouldn't give up if she stayed in Santa Dymphna. If she took Ben to the mainland, she could . . . what, start over? How did you get new identities? Handler had always just made things happen for her. No, no, she could figure that out. She could live off the grid. She could pick up a job waitressing, maybe, just live a quiet life somewhere and, and, and . . .

"Ben, I'm sorry," she whispered, and he looked over at her, and then got up off the bed and came over to her.

"It's okay," he said, and took her hand in his tiny fingers.

"No, it's not." What if she went to the police somewhere? Would they help? Would they think she was crazy? Would they take Ben away? "It's not okay. I don't know what to do. I can't . . ." She let out a shaky breath. "I don't think I'm doing a good job of taking care of you."

"No, that's not true," Ben said indignantly. "You do a good job! You get me Pokémon, and you help me go to sleep, and you even make crackers and cheese special like Mom did."

"I know, but . . ." *Guess it was just one of those things.*

Lori stopped, wiped her eyes, and looked at Ben.

"What did you say?" she asked.

Ben looked down. "Sorry."

"No, no." Lori took *his* hand now. "You talked about . . . Mom."

"I know it makes you grumpy," Ben said, still looking down. "You're already sad."

"I get grumpy?" Lori asked. "I don't . . . I don't remember getting grumpy when you talk about M-Mom and Dad." She had to force the words out. Part of her mind still wanted to slide away from them.

"You always say, guess it was just one of those things," Ben said quietly, "and then you don't want to talk to me."

Lori felt the whole world contract around her, and she could feel her heartbeat in her temples. "I'm so sorry, kiddo," she said. "I didn't mean to hurt your feelings. It . . . just always made me sad to think of them, but I shouldn't try to stop you."

"That's okay," Ben said, and the simple forgiveness in his little voice broke something inside her, and she pulled him into a hug.

"Thanks, kiddo. Thank you." She held him close, and he hugged her back. "Do you remember how they . . . went away?"

"You never said." Ben was sniffling a little bit now as well. "But it was when the water came up and all the roads turned into canals."

Still holding him, Lori blinked back more tears. Her parents were still blank spots in her mind, little holes her consciousness shied away from. But they were real.

She was real.

Something had taken them away from her.

"I have a hard time seeing their faces," she said.

"Me too," Ben said. "Sometimes I sneak into their bedroom and look at the pictures."

They didn't have a bedroom, Lori thought. She'd been raising Ben alone for two years, ever since the water rose, and she had cleaned every inch of the condo. If there was a room, she'd have stumbled across it.

Unless the bedroom has the same little block on your mind, a part of her suggested.

Kitchen, she thought, and pulled an image of the cramped cooking area, the little tiled floor. *Living room,* and there it was, lower than the kitchen by half a foot for some reason, carpeted, with the old couches and the little coffee tables pushed aside so that Ben had room to play with Legos. *Office,* there off the kitchen, with the desktop computer and the filing cabinet where she kept all the important documents. *Hallway,* same ugly old carpet as the living room, and on the left was Ben's room, and on the right was the bathroom, and then down at the end was the door she didn't open and then there was her room, and that was it, that was all of it—

There was a door she never opened.

It was a terrible idea. They could be watching even now.

She didn't care.

Lori was going home.

HAWK

If the line between shells and puppets (which were definitely totally different from Muppets, because Kermit had never had eels eating him up from the inside) was that puppets were controlling a living person, and shells were just driving a dead body, then these things were probably closer to shells. Their skin was waxen, and their eyes were vacant, and they shambled more than walked, lank hair in their faces and clothes hanging from bodies that were skinny except for grossly bloated torsos. They might not die if the eels inside them came out, but Hawk didn't think they'd do much beyond sit and stare at the wall.

He lunged at the first shell as it lurched through the doorway, slamming into it with a punch that knocked its head clean off. An eel slithered out of the body cavity as the body hit the floor, its slick yellow-green skin shimmering as it uncoiled. Before it could go far, Tapper blurred in and squashed it.

"We must run!" Iara yelled.

Through the doorway, Hawk saw more of them. Whoever they had once been, they were just shells for the eels now, their bodies shriveled and covered in an oily sheen. He thought about when the eel had tried to force its way down his throat at the Lake Foundation and clenched his teeth. "No way!" he yelled back. "We can't take Tiamat, but we can take these things!"

"No, you idiot!" Tapper blurred in front of Hawk, but Hawk shoved him aside and plowed into the room. This had been a clothing area—free-standing wheels with clothes on hangers filled the room, some of them tipped over, and the walls were lined with jeans and slacks on shelves and pictures of muscular guys posing with one leg up on something. The shells lay on the ground. As they saw him, they stood and came forward, arms extended. In a zombie movie, they would have moaned, but they just made wet noises as they breathed, like their throats wouldn't open all the way anymore.

They tried to grab him, but he was too strong. He ripped an arm out of its socket, turned, and backhanded another into the wall so hard that it splatted. It felt simple, pure, the impact of him on them. He swatted another, smashed it into the wall, and then crushed the eel that slithered out of the body. He wasn't even breathing hard.

They shuffled toward him, knocking aside the hanger displays and tripping on piles of old dress shirts. Behind him, Maya and Iara were yelling.

"She can feel them!" Tapper snapped, stopping in front of Hawk again with an impact that shattered one of the shells. "Remember? If we kill too many, she'll notice! She'll know where we are!"

"Let her feel this, then!" Hawk called back, and slammed into another one, ripping it apart with the force of his impact.

No judgment, no questions, nothing that made him less or broken, just the field of battle.

He mowed down another, kicked one that had fallen apart to the point where it couldn't even get up anymore, and yelled as he tackled the last one. It went down beneath him, and he felt the bones crunch and thought, *Good*.

Then it was done. Nobody stood in the big room except him and Tapper, both breathing hard in the flickering fluorescent light. He stood there looking at the carnage, sweating but unhurt. None of them had been able to do *anything* to him, not punch or push or hold down or laugh or . . .

Behind them came the metal clank of the air lock door.

"No," Iara said, "no, no, no." She made her way into the big room, looking over her shoulder as she came.

"It could be Lori," Maya said hopefully, even as she moved to a wall. A moment later she seemed to slip away, vanishing against a picture of a pretty blond woman wearing a designer dress.

"It's not Lori." Tapper moved beside Iara, his hands raised and tightened into fists.

Footsteps echoed through the room as whoever it was came toward them. It didn't *sound* like Tiamat's high heels.

"Who's there?" Hawk called out, and was pleased to hear how tough his voice sounded. "You want some of what the shells got?"

A man stepped through the door, a portly man of middling height with balding curly hair. "I would *love* some of what the shells got, Mister Bautista," he said with a sour smile. "You children have been running around quite a bit. I've been looking for you all night."

"Kirk," Tapper whispered. His hands trembled a little.

"Mister Taylor," Kirk said affably, "you're holding up very well, considering. Miss Costa, we have your wheelchair waiting for you back at the foundation office. I'm sure you'd find it more comfortable."

"I do not need it," Iara declared, pushing her hair out of her face with one hand.

"Oh, don't you?" Kirk raised an eyebrow. "You don't get tired of the backaches, the blisters? The annoyance of balancing in that awkward almost-standing position all day?" He smiled and shook his head. "When we offered you the scholarship, we did a little research on Brazil. Not the best record for disabled access, hmm?"

"I survive," Iara said, glaring.

"Of course you do, Miss Costa." Kirk was still smiling. "Your parents let you swim as much as you like. It helps them forget what happened to you. It might even let you forget. And now the miracoral has turned you into the Nix, and everything begins again, just like it did for Mister Taylor here." He looked over at Tapper. "We have a new drug that might help you. Wouldn't you like that?"

Tapper glared. "What do you plan to do? You can't stick one of those eels down our throats."

Kirk chuckled. "Can't we, though?"

"You cannot." Iara's voice was sharp. "You tried on Sarah Campbell, and she died."

"Right, right," Kirk said, nodding, "and so we thought that was a no-go, but do you know what's interesting, Miss Costa? What's interesting is the possibility that that's just because the miracoral is connected to you, so if it senses an obvious threat like that, it pulls the plug on the connection. *But*," he added brightly, "but-but-but, if you got a tiny little *baby* eel put inside you, it's possible that it could grow very slowly and start taking you over without the miracoral even noticing."

"That's garbage." Tapper took a little step backward, bumping into Iara.

"Is it, Mister Taylor?" Kirk smiled at Hawk. "How are you doing, Mister Bautista?"

"Fine," Hawk said, shrugging, and came forward, ready to punch the guy, since none of the others were doing anything except standing there looking horrified.

Kirk grinned broadly. "Fine? *Really?* You've been kidnapped, electrocuted, and trapped, and now we're going to do horrible experiments on you, and you're *fine*? Doesn't that make you sad or scared or . . . anything?"

"Feeling nothing is better than feeling pain," Hawk said, and punched him as hard as he could. It was weird that he had to keep explaining this to people.

Kirk's head turned with the blow, and he took a half step back. Hawk hit him again, this time in the gut, and the man bent over. Hawk stepped in with an uppercut that knocked Kirk into a standing position.

The man was still smiling.

"You know, Mister Bautista, *I'm so glad you feel that way,*" Kirk said, and took hold of Hawk's arm—

it wasn't fair, he'd gotten the ball and he'd tried, but they hadn't blocked for him, and the defense had hit him hard, and now they weren't letting him up, they were sitting on him, laughing, and even the guys on the offense were laughing, and he pushed and squirmed, but he was too small, and then came the sharp slap as one of them spanked him, and then even the coach laughed, and he couldn't get up, they wouldn't let him up, they just kept laughing and laughing at the little boy who thought he could play, and all he could think was what was he going to tell his father

—and Hawk, on his knees, tears streaming down his face, looked up and saw guards in wetsuits, like the ones who had come after them that first day on the docks, come marching into the room with spearguns and Tasers held ready.

He waited for the feeling to whisk away, but it didn't, it wouldn't, and he had to cough or puke or something, and he gagged, and then a tiny little eel slithered out of his mouth and dropped into Kirk's other hand.

"How do you feel *now*?" Kirk asked, and Hawk didn't have the strength to pull away.

LORI

Lori stood outside Splash Zone Play Space with Ben tugging on her arm, both of them waiting for Jenn to come.

"I can wait inside," Ben said for the fourth time.

"Since Jenn is going to be in there with you, she needs to be the one who goes in," Lori said, and looked down at him. "It's for safety. You're important to me, kiddo."

Ben sighed. "I know. And you're important to me, too," he said begrudgingly. "But there's no laser tag out here."

Handler would have said something there, would have buzzed on her phone, Lori thought. But Handler was gone, just like the parents she couldn't even remember.

She was real.

"If I wait in the front part, I can play on the game machines," Ben added.

"I'd like to stay out here, just to make sure that Jenn can find us," Lori said, and didn't add, *and also so we have a clear path of escape if she's got an eel in her like Mister Barkin had.*

"We'll be *fine*," Ben insisted, with a petulant confidence that somehow made Lori feel like things would actually be better.

A ferry stopped at the nearby dock, and Lori watched the people disembark, looking for her friend's face, along with signs of anything that could conceivably be wrong or off or weird, any warning sign. She had hunted feeders for two years . . .

How had that started? She remembered Handler explaining it for the first time—*this is a way for us to make money so you and Ben are okay, and it will also make the world safer for people*—but everything around it was fuzzy. How had she known Handler? It was, like her parents, a thing that just *was* in her mind, an accepted fact.

"Hey, Ben-to-Box!" came a friendly yell, and Ben pulled from Lori's grasp and ran to Jenn, who smiled and hugged him. Lori felt a weight she hadn't known she was carrying lift from her. Jenn looked fine, relaxed and happy and normal. "Hey, Lori! More of this consulting stuff?"

"Yep." Lori forced a smile. "I should just be an hour or two, and then I'll meet you back here, all right?" She looked down at Ben. "Be careful in Splash Zone, okay? Love you."

"Love you, too," Ben said absently, and headed toward the entrance.

"You're not okay," Jenn said. It wasn't a question.

"This one is . . ." Lori broke off, looked down into the canal, where the miracoral gleamed.

"It's not just the job," Jenn said, and stepped closer. "Talk to me, Fisher. Is someone . . ." Her eyes widened. "Who did that to you?" she asked, and darted a hand out to Lori's collar.

Lori pulled back fast, pressing her hand to where Jenn was pointing, and felt soreness. She remembered Barkin's arm around her throat yesterday and said, "It's nothing—"

"Hey!" Jenn moved nose to nose with Lori and raked her pink bangs back from her face to glare. "You are my *friend*. If you're in trouble, *let me help*. We can go to the cops. If it's some guy, you know my boyfriend is on the soccer team, and he and his friends can—"

"Jenn." Lori really wanted to collapse into her friend's arms. But if she did that, she knew she'd start crying, and she couldn't afford that right now. "What I need is what you're doing. Watch Ben for a couple hours. Don't leave here. I'm going to take care of this, okay? And if it doesn't work, then I'll come back and get Ben, and we'll figure out what to do next." *Like get fake IDs and disappear forever, assuming that would even work.* "For now, that's everything you can do, okay?"

Jenn held her glare for a long moment, and then finally sniffed and stepped back. "When you get back, you tell me everything."

Lori wondered how much she'd be able to tell Jenn before Jenn's face went blank and she started saying that it was just one of those things. "Deal. Thank you."

"I love you, dumbass," Jenn said, and pulled her into a hug.

"Love you, too." Lori squeezed everything she could into the hug.

It was interrupted by Ben's voice saying, "Are you coming, Jenn?"

Jenn broke the hug. "Right behind you, Ben-to-Box!" She

looked back at Lori. "I've got him. Be careful, whatever's going on."

"Thanks." Lori watched her friend take her brother back inside. The door squeaked shut behind them, cutting off the sound of loud arcade machines and happily screaming children.

Lori got on the ferry, flashed her pass, and sat, watching the water, as the engine churned.

The miracoral glowed beneath the surface, its bright light painful and foreign. Where its radiance didn't touch, the water of the canals was a dark gray-green, fringed with foam that slid away from the ferry's wake.

Maya was down there somewhere. Iara, Hawk, Tapper, too. Tiamat had them.

But Lori didn't have Handler. She'd choked on the water. There would be no swimming through the darkness, no fighting. There would be a short visit home, to get a few needed essentials. And to see if there was anything there to remember.

Then she and Ben would disappear, just like Handler and her parents.

Like one of those things.

It'd be selfish to keep in touch with Jenn after she left. It would put both of them in danger. No parents, no old friends, no new friends.

No Maya.

That was selfish. The Nix, all of them, were powerful enough to take care of themselves. If she tried to help them, she would probably just get in their way, since Lori didn't have powers anymore.

She blinked as people got up, and realized she was at her stop. She hopped off the ferry, her steps on the walkway unsteady.

Nothing looked out of place on the sidewalk. She saw no strange people loitering, watching her home. She nodded to neighbors as she passed, went up the stairs, strangely out of breath by the time she reached the top.

Her key slid into the lock, and she pushed the door open slowly, alert for anything out of place.

It all seemed normal.

She stepped into the entryway. Her fingers trailed on the rough texture of the wall, curled over the hook where jackets and shopping bags hung. She glanced over into the kitchen, where the remains of Ben's yogurt cup from yesterday still sat on the counter. The dishwasher shone the little green light that meant the dishes were done and needed to be unloaded.

She walked forward, toward the hallway. On the right, the office door was cracked open. The big desk full of financial documents had its rolltop pulled down, same as always. On the left, past the kitchen table, where Maya had sat on her lap and they had kissed, the carpeted living room had Legos scattered across the floor and minifigures and other toys engaged in some kind of battle on the coffee table.

The hallway.

Ben's room on the left, bathroom on the right. Lori's feet didn't want to move anymore. She tried to pretend she was just going to her room. There was the little vent by the floor, there was the outlet where she plugged in the vacuum, there were baby pictures of her and Ben . . .

She was being selfish. She was endangering her brother. If the Lake Foundation had found Mister Barkin, it would find Jenn Vickers, and it would get Ben, and it wouldn't be because the feeders were dangerous or Tiamat was evil, it would be because Lori had been selfish, wanting to get answers enough to endanger her brother. If she were a good sister, a good guardian, if she were even a *real person*, she'd get out of here right now and take Ben and never look back. Who cared about answers? When had answers ever helped anything? Answers hurt you. Answers showed you all the terrible things in the world. Answers told you that you were a monster.

But I'm not. I'm real. I had parents, and something happened. Was it you, Handler? Did you do this to me? Did you kill my parents?

There was no buzzing from her phone. Nobody was there to tell her what not to do.

She forced her feet forward, her brand-new shoes dragging on the ugly old carpet.

There was the linen closet, the sheets never quite managing to fit.

There was her room on the left and another on the right but—

There was a door on the right.

She stumbled forward, thrust her arm out, and shoved it open.

A long bed with a dark headboard sat against one wall, with a dresser off to the side. The covers on the bed were a pretty light blue with little yellow flowers, and the bed had been made perfectly, except for little indentations where someone had sat.

Ben had sat there. Remembering.

And she hadn't been there to help him.

The anger pushed her forward, welling up inside her and giving her the strength to move. There was a small bathroom off to the right, and a tiny little detached part of her head said, *Well, that would have been handy to know about all the times Ben was taking forever in the shower.*

On top of the dresser were the pictures.

Her eyes slid off them, pulled back, skated away again, and finally stuck. Her breath caught, and everything felt heavy, her lungs tight and pulling.

Her father was white and had brown hair and a crooked nose and one of those uncomfortable smiles, at least in the ones where he was posing for the camera. His smile looked better in the ones where he was holding Lori's mother.

In the largest picture, they were holding hands, just getting ready to kiss, outside at a park. They were dressed a little too nicely for a day at the park, but not in formal wear. A party, maybe? Inset in the corner was a smaller picture, one that might get stuck on a fridge, of Lori and Ben and their mother, smiling and sunburned at the beach.

She looks so pretty, Lori thought, and felt tears sting her eyes. Glossy dark hair and tan skin a few shades darker than Ben's, dark eyes. Chinese-American, Lori knew, but couldn't say why she knew. She tried to pull her mother's maiden name to her mind and couldn't.

She took us to the beach. We got sunburned, and there's sand on our legs, and Ben has the remains of an ice cream in one hand, and we look so happy, and what happened after that? Who are you, Mom? Where are you? What did they do?

"Handler," Lori said, and it came out cracked and weak. "Handler, you can always hear me. I *know* you hear this. Answer me."

Nothing.

"What did you do to them, Handler?" She forced herself to walk to the dresser. "What did you do to me?" She looked at the pictures. "You let me think I was a monster, and you took them away from me. Why? You turned me into this . . . *thing* that traps feeders to help you *eat*. You *used* me. Why?"

The anger was breaking over into tears, and she felt the room starting to spin around her. She tried to lean on the bed and found herself stumbling toward the door instead, and right then she knew, she *knew*, that if she went outside, she would shut the door behind her and forget everything she had just seen.

She sank to the floor, digging her fingers into the carpet.

"Answer me." The dizziness was worse, and the floor swam and swayed under her hands. "Answer me!" It was tilting, it felt like, and any moment, she would find herself rolling down the incline, right out of the room. *Answer me!*

She reached for that part of her that had been, the part that could move into places a normal person couldn't understand—

Pretend for a moment that you're looking at a microbe smeared on a microscope plate. The microbe has lived its entire life stuck between those two planes of glass. As far as it's concerned, there's no up or down. Everything in its world is forward, backward, left, or right.

Now pretend that it knows.

Pretend that it strains its primitive sensory organs, reaching for a way to understand up and down, pushing against the plate. Pretend that it shows signs of distress, jerking back and forth as though moving that way will somehow translate into the "up" it only now realizes that it needs.

Pretend that it's screaming at you, that in its own way, it's alive and a person with feelings and cares, and that it wants to know, and you don't know what to tell it without breaking it, or even how to communicate, but it's sliding out from under the plate, because it's just a microbe, tiny and insignificant and small, but you've played the trick with the dropper a few times, and even if it doesn't know exactly what it all means, it understands enough to know that there's a place it can go where you are.

Pretend that you reach up from where you're huddled on the floor, your bleeding hand shaking, and catch the plate in your trembling fingers and say, "Okay, I'll try," as the world dims and darkens around you.

—and then the world swallowed her up.

11

IARA

She had never felt more helpless.

There were half a dozen of the troopers, their wetsuits still dripping, holding spearguns trained on her and Tapper. Hawk, who thought himself so big and strong, knelt before the man called Kirk, trembling and crying.

"Look at you, Mister Bautista," Kirk said, smiling down at him. "Feeling a little uncomfortable now? You were *fine* for a while, and now you're feeling everything that you didn't *have* to feel, and it's a bit much, isn't it?"

"Back." Hawk coughed, still on his knees. "Put it back."

"See how easy it is, kids?" Kirk looked at Iara now. "You're not quite as immune to the eels as you thought, and now you're going to come with us and get all eel'd up, and soon everything will be *fine*."

"You will have to kill us first!" Iara proclaimed with a courage she did not feel, and under the words, added a tiny little *click*. She could not see Kirk with the echo. That had never happened before. She could see the guards, though.

"Then we'll kill you," Kirk said, and shrugged. "It's all the same to me, and it sounds like Hawk will be happy to get his eel back, so he doesn't have to feel like a navy brat who's been a loser at every school he's ever gone to. As for you, well . . . we'll still have the pieces, Miss Costa."

"What are you?" Iara asked, shuffling toward him and adding another *click*. The guards tracked her movement but did not fire, and now she had the triangulation and the picture of the room, and before Kirk could answer, she turned to one of the guards and said, *"Kirk is an imposter, and you have to kill him to serve your mistress, Miss Lake."*

The guard's speargun wavered. "Wait," he said, turning toward Kirk. "I think—"

"Kill him," Kirk said with an absent wave, and the other guards all turned and fired without hesitation. The guard screamed and coughed and fell to the ground, twitching, and a moment later, an eel slithered out from his body. "Congratulations, Miss Costa. You got someone killed."

Iara swallowed. "He was a puppet," she said quietly.

"Just like Mister Bautista," Kirk said with an agreeable smile. "I mean, he didn't have as much left, and who knows how much he'd have recovered, but he was still alive," Kirk said. "That means his death is on you. Just like your parents' divorce is on you." He smiled and let go of Hawk, who collapsed, shuddering. "You see, Miss Costa, that's what I am." He started toward her. "When people forget what they are, when they think they've got a clean slate, I'm the one who reminds them." Tapper stepped between Iara and Kirk, and Kirk clapped a hand on his shoulder. As Tapper swayed and trembled, Kirk gently pushed him out of the way. "I'm the one who drags them back down *where they belong.*"

"Don't listen to him, Ipanema," Tapper said weakly.

"Ipanema?" Kirk smiled. "Because of 'The Girl from Ipanema,' who was Brazilian. You know, she was a blonde. Not like Miss Costa here, who has some indigenous blood, enough that all the pretty blond people would look at her strangely even without the wheelchair." He cocked his head at her. "The green hair is about the only part of people looking at you that you can control, isn't it, Miss Costa?"

"My parents did not divorce because of me," Iara said, refusing to break eye contact with the terrifying man.

"No, it was your father's drinking, according to our reports," Kirk said casually, "and I think you know why his drinking became such a problem. He couldn't stand looking at his little girl anymore. Do you ever wonder if it might have been easier for him if you'd just *died* in that accident?" He smiled. "I mean, he'd still be sad, but he wouldn't have to *look* at you."

Iara broke eye contact. More than anything in the world, she wanted to sit down. Instead she quietly said, "You say nothing I have not said to myself."

"But you forget sometimes," Kirk said, and stepped in, hand raised. "That's what I'm—"

He broke off as a sudden roaring rumble shook the room, then looked over at the guards. "What is that?"

"Hi, yeah, so!" Maya said from behind the guards. "You'll never guess what happened to the air lock!"

A waist-high wall of water swept into the room, sending clothing racks flying everywhere and sweeping the guards off their feet.

Iara dropped her crutches and dove into the water as the waves hit. For a moment there was the chaos of the water, throwing her everywhere, with clothes slapping her face like branches.

Then she was back in her element, the girl who had swum the fast rivers even before she had become the Nix. The roar of the water was a message, a signal of direction and power and speed, and she heard the sloshing of clothing racks and the gurgling of the guards, and she knew where everyone was.

Skimming along the floor, she pushed cleanly through the current to where Tapper clung to a shelf, huddled. She grabbed his arm, and for a moment he seemed like he would swing at her, but then he realized it was her, and he let her pull him away.

She shoved away again, darting across the room, weaving through white water and clothing racks like they were rocks in the stream, Tapper's hand clutching her own. She heard Hawk as he tumbled along the floor, still curled up tightly, and she went to him, took his arm, and pulled him into a tight embrace.

"We need your strength!" she called, pitching her voice to cut through the roar of the waves. "Please!"

As the water spread across the large room, its force lessened. She heard one of the guards, now back on his feet, coming toward them, and she pulled away from Tapper, dove down, pushed off the bottom with both hands, and leaped from the water with a punch that sent the guard toppling back into the water.

By the doorway, Kirk stood unmoving, glaring in her direction. She sent him a dirty gesture as she splashed back into the water.

Hawk was up now, clinging to a shelf with Tapper beside him. His eyes were haunted. "I want . . . I want . . ."

"Hey!" Iara swam to him and grabbed his shoulders. "There is much pain in life, but it is *not* better to feel nothing." Then she pulled him in and kissed him hard on the lips.

"Are we doing friend kisses?" Maya shouted, suddenly beside them, her clothing in disarray from the waves and her blond hair slicked back. "Or is that a Brazilian thing that I am totally willing to be okay with? No offense."

"I didn't know if you were coming back, Blondie," Tapper called over the rushing water. "Took you long enough."

"You saw me leave?" Maya asked, and then, "Oh, right, your eyes. Yeah, sorry, I couldn't think of a good way to help, so I broke the air lock instead!"

"Nah," Tapper said, "that was good."

Hawk was flushed from the kiss, but he still couldn't look at them. "The things I said . . . Guys, I'm so sorry."

"It was the eel," Tapper said.

Hawk shook his head. "No. It was me, but me if I'd never had a bad day." His voice was hoarse, but he was holding on to Iara now. "I'm such a tool."

"Yeah," Tapper said. "But you're our tool."

"It's okay," Maya said. "It hurts, but that's life. Life is about hurting and getting better. You're you, and you know who you are, and it's okay. *You're* okay." She looked back to where the guards were pushing aside the clothes racks and getting back to their feet. Kirk was coming toward them as well. "And we should probably run."

Iara looked to the far end of the store, where the waist-high water rushed through a doorway leading into darkness. "Follow me," she called.

With a strong push, she dove back into her element and swam.

LORI

She came out somewhere else.

It was dark, but it wasn't the darkness of a room with the lights shut off. It was the darkness of someplace that didn't *have* light, that didn't understand what light even was . . . or maybe a place that light couldn't understand itself. It smothered her, enveloping her completely as she spun and swam and kicked, and there was no up, no down, nothing, and she couldn't breathe, there was no air, there was—

Her phone buzzed, and the light of the text on her notification screen was a beacon, blazing bright in the endless void. She clutched at her phone, pulled it from her pocket with trembling fingers.

Handler: lori

She unlocked her phone, and her cracked screen glowed even brighter, pushing back the dark. At the edge of the light, she could see shapes like the ones she saw if she closed her eyes and pushed hard on her eyelids, forms that twisted, whose edges never met cleanly. Where the light shone brightly, she saw that she floated in gently rippling liquid—not water, because the way it bent the light was different, but liquid nevertheless, glowing a deep and peaceful royal blue in the light before it faded to the otherworldly blackness at the edges.

She realized that she had forgotten that she couldn't breathe, but still wasn't straining.

And she wasn't alone.

Floating before her was a massive form, a rounded mountain of midnight blue with glittering pinpricks of shining silver trailing along the side. Above, or what seemed like above to Lori from where she floated, was a curving plane that stretched away from the mountain into the darkness, ridged with corded rivulets that broke the regularity of its surface.

She felt a pull, and the strange world lurched around her. It came from between her shoulder blades, and Lori turned even as the world flew, and saw, curling overhead, a cable of ghostly white as thick as her torso. It pulled her around the enormous form, and by the light of her phone, Lori saw the rounded edges turn into something she could understand. The great mountain of midnight blue was the flank, and the curving plane was a fin.

And as the ghostly white cord pulled her around, she saw the great fangs she had seen so many times before, five times her height in this world and jutting out of a gaping maw whose underbite sent them spiraling upward and bristling in all directions. Above those jaws, a tiny pair of eyes met Lori's gaze.

Handler: i tried

Lori stared into Handler's face for the first time, her legs dangling, moved slowly by gentle waves that flowed wrongly, curling in all directions.

When she opened her mouth, the liquid felt hollow, moving away from her lips as though it were afraid of her. That gave her the courage to speak.

"What are you?" she asked, the words leaving her mouth with little bubbles that weren't quite round.

Handler: sorry

She read it, the words small and feeble on the cracked screen, then turned back to the great fanged maw.

"You let me think I was a monster," she yelled, "like you! All this time, you knew! You *knew*!" The words came out raw, ripping her throat with her fury.

Handler: would u have believed me

"You could have tried!" Lori screamed. "Instead you *used* me as your lure! You let feeders attack me, and you let me think I was one of them!"

The great face with its huge maw and tiny eyes didn't change expression, or if it did, there was nothing there that Lori could see.

Handler: tried. u didnt want 2 hear
Handler: had to learn 4 yourself

"Oh, right," she shot back, "like I had to learn about my parents?" The anger didn't stop the tears, and they hissed on her face and twisted against the liquid that wasn't water. "Because you didn't tell me about them, either! What did you do to them? *What did you do to my parents?*"

The ghostly white cord holding her twitched, and she dangled, arms and legs flailing for a moment, as the great maw loomed closer.

Handler: mourned them

One eye focused on her. Even tiny for Handler, it was as large as Lori herself, and the pupil wasn't a circle in the same way that the air bubbles weren't round, the same way that the shapes at the edge of the phone's light didn't come together at angles that made sense.

Handler: your world is the shallows
Handler: tiamat got trapped there
Handler: the coral, me, we fled there

"Fled what?" Lori asked. She was losing the anger, and she grasped at it desperately. "What were you running from?"

Handler: i fled a big feeder, im small out here
Handler: coral hid from leviathan, what tiamat wants

The thing Tiamat wanted. Lori tried to remember what she'd said. "She wanted to make the coral scream. To summon the Leviathan, so it could . . . erase her from this world?"

Handler: lev is 2 big, doesn't fit in ur world
Handler: strains the world through its jaws to catch little bits
Handler: changes things but no 1 remembers

"Like the water rising," Lori said. "The thing Tiamat wants did that?"
The enormous eye blinked.

Handler: like parents

Lori's chest tightened.

Handler: it came after miracoral
Handler: world changed, like waves from fin
Handler: water higher
Handler: ur parents gone
Handler: i saw u, ben alone
Handler: no 1 remembered ur parents, no 1 helped u
Handler: so i tried

It broke across her like a wave then, and she coughed out a sob that bubbled away into the darkness. Another followed, and her shoulders were shaking, heaving with sobs that came from a place deep inside her she had forgotten for years. She squeezed her eyes shut and let the sobs pour out, wrenching her, shaking her free from everything.

She couldn't say how long it went on, only that when the darkness receded again, she was pressed against something, a vast form that was stronger than she could imagine, but yielded ever so slightly under her touch. Her phone was buzzing, words glowing on the cracked screen.

Handler: is ok
Handler: im here
Handler: ur ok

"I'm not," she whispered. She felt it . . . felt Handler beneath her hand. "How come Ben gets to remember them?"

Handler: im tied to him like 2 u

"What?" Lori felt a panicked lurch in her stomach. "Does he . . . do you use him to hunt—" She broke off as her phone buzzed twice sharply.

Handler: no
Handler: hes 7

"So Ben remembers them because he's connected to you." She took a shaky breath. "Why can't I?"

Handler: ben wanted 2 remember

"And I didn't?" she said, and balled her fist against Handler's side. "I wanted to forget my own parents?"

Handler: if it let u not hurt

Handler: guess just 1 of those things

"It didn't work." Lori sniffled and closed her eyes again, her breath still shaky but coming back, and let her head rest on Handler's flank. "I was still hurting. I just couldn't remember why."

After a long moment, her phone buzzed, and she opened her eyes and looked down.

Handler: yes. ur right
Handler: should have tried more 2 tell u
Handler: not good protector

The white cord pulled her away from Handler, and now, as she drew back, she could see Handler's other flank. Terrible rents marred the midnight-blue skin, ragged wounds from which flecks of silver glittered as they drifted into the water. Jaws, Lori realized, jaws large enough to have speared Handler the way Handler speared most normal feeders.

Handler: tiamat
Handler: she'll keep looking 4 u
Handler: thinks u can help bring it
Handler: she's wrong tho, im 2 small
Handler: u get ben & be safe

"What do you mean?" Lori asked. "You can . . . you're not . . ."

Handler: new name 4 u both
Handler: will be on phone
Handler: stay away from coral,
Handler: it can lure leviathan
Handler: so that's what tiamat will want

"What?" Lori flailed against the cord, trying to pull herself through the liquid that wasn't water back toward Handler, but it was no use. She drew back farther, until most of Handler's massive form disappeared into the darkness.

Handler: u r smart and brave and good, lori
Handler: live good life
Handler: sorry couldn't do more

Then the darkness was complete, and it swam around her and pushed until there was no her left, and she slid and fell, the ghostly white cord pushing her out and away.

She landed in her parents' bedroom, the carpet rough on her hands, just in time to watch her phone's battery die.

BEN

Splash Zone Play Space was fun, even if Jenn didn't like going in the play area.

Lori didn't like going in the play area either. She usually sat at the tables and drank a soda and looked at her phone while Ben ran through the obstacle course or went down the slide into the ball pit. Sometimes she would come to the netting that separated the inside from the outside and yell over the noise of other kids to ask if Ben was okay or if he needed anything. Lori worried a lot.

Ben had asked Jenn if he could have a snack a little while ago, and she had said to come back in half an hour. He hadn't looked at a clock, but he had gone down the slide twice and had a really fun play fight with a big boy who had red hair and a Ninja Turtles shirt, and they had shouted Power Rangers moves while throwing balls at each other until a Splash Zone Lifeguard in a bright red shirt came by and said that they weren't supposed to do that, and then both Ben and Ninja Turtle–shirt boy had pretended not to know that they weren't supposed to do that and said sorry. So it had probably been half an hour.

He climbed up the steps, which were purple and made of the same padding that all of the floor was here in the play area, and then waited for an Indian girl wearing a pink princess dress and a sparkly silver Splash Zone Birthday Crown to go down the slide first. Then he hopped onto the slide and whoosh-bounced down after her, laughing as the slide heated and stuck under his clothes and sent him tumbling, so that he rolled into the ball pit with a crash of hard plastic flying everywhere.

He waded out of the ball pit and climbed through the gap in the netting, onto the padded floor that led to the tables where all the grown-ups sat and looked at their phones.

Jenn wasn't at the table where she had been before.

Ben looked around, and after a moment he saw her. She had a group of big men around her. They wore dark suits, and one of them was holding Jenn by the arm. They didn't look like Splash Zone Lifeguards, and Jenn looked scared.

Ben went over to her to see what was wrong.

"Miss Vickers, if you have any information about your friend, you need to tell us right now," said one of the men. "The fact that you're here suggests that her brother, Ben, isn't far away, and it's important that we get him to safety as well."

"Get away from me!" Jenn yelled, and Ben looked around for adults to come help, but all of the adults stood there with blank faces instead. "Leave Ben alone!"

Another man reached into his pocket and took something out, something small that moved in his hand. Ben didn't know what it was, but Jenn pulled against the men, and Ben knew that it was something bad.

"Hey!" he yelled. "Leave her alone!"

The men and Jenn turned to him.

"Run!" Jenn yelled. "Ben, run away now!" And she kicked one of the men in the shins and threw herself down as the other one started to come toward Ben.

Ben tried to be brave, but Jenn was the grown-up, and he was supposed to do what she said, so he ran. He climbed back into the play zone as the men in the dark suits came after him, pushing past the other kids and then climbing nimbly through a little hamster tube to get up onto the next level. Lori always had trouble finding him when he did that.

He peeked out of one of the tiny windows and saw some of the men in the dark suits pacing back and forth in front of the play area.

The other men had taken Jenn to a table, and it looked like they were trying to put something in her mouth.

HAWK

The doorway that Hawk followed Iara through led to a kind of indoor plaza area between the stores, most of which had been filled in with concrete when the water rose. Past a fountain and marble benches, both mostly submerged under the still-rising water, Hawk saw shoe stores and electronics shops and places to buy expensive chocolates, the front facings still bright and attractive, with bare blocks of gray behind the windows.

"We need to . . ." he began, and then broke off, because why would anyone listen to him, anyway?

Maya, treading water nearby, looked over at him. "Do you have an idea?"

He had too many ideas, and that was the problem. Too many ideas and not enough execution.

Tapper splashed back through the water, which was now chest high, sloshing around the closed-off stores. "It messes with your head," he said. "Come on. We gotta keep moving."

Letting the water carry him forward, Hawk looked ahead to where Iara was swimming, so pretty in that swimsuit that matched her bright green hair. She'd kissed him like he meant something. Like he hadn't just been a loser.

"You were right," he said to Tapper. "The miracoral . . . I think it chose us all because we were broken. Like you said."

"What do you mean?" Maya said, at the same time that Tapper said, "So?"

Hawk squeezed his eyes shut, felt his heart hammering. "I had a bad time last year. It was nothing special, you know, but . . . I started doing this . . . thing where I'd take a knife, and I'd . . ."

A hand closed over his own. He looked up to see Iara. He'd forgotten how good her hearing was. She nodded.

"I wasn't gonna kill myself, but it helped to cut a little. It, um . . ." He broke off.

"It let the pain out," Maya finished.

"Yeah." Hawk tried a smile, and Iara squeezed his hand. "Guys in my family don't talk about feelings, and my dad would have thought I was weak, and . . . And then one day I woke up, and I couldn't. I couldn't hurt myself anymore. Couldn't get hurt at all. Just like Iara woke up and was killer in the water, or Tapper—"

"So?" Tapper said again. The girls looked over at him angrily, and he waved them off, splashing water around as he did. "Yeah, my brain is different, and that was hard even before I realized I liked guys—"

"Wait, man, you had a crush on Iara," Hawk said.

Tapper glared. "*You* have a crush on Iara," he said, "and this?" He held up his hand, and it blurred in the air. "Maybe the coral was trying to help, or maybe it was just messing with us, but *that doesn't matter.* I don't get banned from comment threads for what I *am*. I get banned for what I *do*. That's what matters. That's *all* that matters." He looked back toward the entrance, where the guards were swimming through the doorway. They saw them and began yelling. "So you wanna prove them wrong? Do something."

"Prove who wrong?" Maya asked. "The coral, or those guys, or the people back in high school who were mean to him?"

Tapper glared. "Everyone, Blondie. Everyone."

"Dude," Hawk said, "good bro speech."

Tapper actually grinned at him. Then he blurred into the water, going under and cutting a point of white into the rushing water as he arrowed back toward the guards.

"Split them up and take them down!" Hawk yelled, and pulled away from the girls.

The first guard fired at Hawk as he drew close, and the shot, some kind of spear-dart thing, bounced off his chest. Before the guard could fire again, Tapper slammed into him, knocking the gun aside and hammering the guard into the wall. Another guard raised a different weapon, something that crackled with electricity at its tip, and Hawk dove under the water. He saw Iara race past him, knifing through the water, and then she leaped up, and a moment later Hawk saw the guard who'd aimed the electro-thing tumble limply into the water.

He surfaced, saw a guard raising his gun toward where Iara had been, and took the man down with a single punch. Over on top of a bench, Tapper was a blur, hammering on a guard who had Maya wrapped around his face.

"We don't have to beat them!" Hawk called over. "We get Kirk in here, and then run back out, okay?"

"Got it!" Maya called as the guard went down, and then, "Look out!" as a guard tackled Hawk.

It didn't hurt, but the guy was bigger than Hawk was, and even as the memories started to come back, being pinned there on the playing field, everybody laughing, Tapper blurred by him and caught the guard with a punch. It gave Hawk the leverage to get a grip on the man, and he hauled him over his head and slammed him into a half-submerged bench.

Kirk swam through the doorway, his lips curled into a sneer. "This is your plan, children? Punch a few more people and make me *swim farther* before I take you down? Unless *exercise* is the key to defeating me, I think you may be grasping at straws."

Hawk dove under the water and pulled as hard as he could against the current. He couldn't match Iara's speed, but he could cut a path, and he saw Kirk's legs and chest, pulled over out of his path, and angled past him to the door. Then he was through, out of the plaza area and back in the clothing store. Iara darted through the doorway a moment later, flashing him a smile under the rushing water, her hair flaring out like magical seaweed. In a blur of white water, Tapper raced through as well.

And then . . . nothing.

Hawk surfaced along with the others. The water was too high to stand in now, at least for him. "Where's Maya?" Iara and Tapper were looking around frantically.

"Oh, were you leaving?" Kirk called from the other room.

Hawk let the current take him, but he wasn't as fast as Tapper, who shot back into the other room with water spraying out behind him.

Maya was backed up against the fountain, with Kirk coming toward her. "Go!" she yelled. "Get out! He'll get all of us!"

"No chance, Blondie," Tapper muttered, and slammed into Kirk in a blur of white water.

Kirk bobbed around a little, then grabbed hold of Tapper. "Well done, Mister Taylor," he said as Tapper writhed in Kirk's grasp. "That will make all the other kids want to play with you at recess." He pushed Tapper under the water.

Hawk rushed in and punched him, and then punched him again, and then again, yelling in rage, and Kirk rocked back, taking the blows and never losing his smile. "What shall I do with you, Mister Bautista? Shall I pin you down? You're supposed to be big and strong and tough, but you can't even stop me from hurting your friends."

"Stop it!" Maya yelled, and then she was between Hawk and Kirk, her arms circling around Kirk's and breaking his hold on Tapper. "Leave them alone!"

Kirk shifted his hands so that he was holding *her* wrist instead. "I've been looking forward to this ever since we met you, young Finch," he said, smiling eagerly. "Of all the shame and self-hate of you Nix, I figured you would be the best."

"Why?" Maya asked, and blinked, and then looked down at Kirk's hand. "Oh, because of that?"

Kirk's smile froze.

"Um, I was a popular kid on the *football* team, and I left *on purpose* because I knew who I was," Maya said, and squinted. "But *you* don't feel like you're real. You feel like . . . there you are." Her free hand darted into the water and came up with . . .

Hawk squinted. It was . . . something. A feeder, maybe, but a tiny one, something like a crab or a spider, with tons of tiny legs and grasping pincers and a lumpy transparent shell through which Hawk could see its insides working.

"You can't!" Kirk sputtered.

Maya broke free from Kirk's grip and brought her hand down hard on the top of the fountain, which was still above the water level. There was a soft, wet, squishy crunch.

Kirk flickered and vanished.

"How did you know?" Iara asked. Hawk hadn't heard her come up behind him. "I never heard his real body."

"I never saw him," Tapper said, "and I see *everything*."

"I dunno," Maya said, and shrugged. "Maybe you were focusing on him."

"What did he mean?" Hawk asked. "He talked about you feeling ashamed and all, and—"

"Hey," Tapper cut in. "Not our business."

"No, it's okay," Maya said, "see, I was on the football team, and like I was popular and cool and stuff, but I didn't like who I was, so I dropped out and I . . ." She stopped and looked at Tapper. "You knew, didn't you? You can see me?"

"Sometimes," Tapper said, "but also *antimayaer*."

Maya winced. "I always forget to specify full-word-only on search and replace." She smiled at Iara with a little trepidation. "So, um, remember when I grabbed the hard drive data and then gave it to you later? I maaaaaybe made a tiny adjustment. In the files they had on all of us, it, um, originally called me *Matt*."

Iara looked over at Tapper, then back at Maya, and let out a small sigh. "Ah. And you corrected this before giving me the disk."

"Yeah, sorry." Maya ran her fingers through her hair. "I just—"

"*Alemã*," Iara cut in, smiling, "it was yours to share when you were ready."

"Wait," Hawk said, frowning. "So if Maya was *Matt*, you're really a—"

Tapper was very suddenly in front of him. "She's *really* a doofus with terrible opinions about anime and a short attention span," he said, "and you wanna make fun of Blondie for *that*, you go ahead, but otherwise—"

"Dude, chill." Hawk raised his hands. "It's cool. We're cool."

Tapper gave him a long and careful glare before moving out of the way.

"Come," Iara said, "with the guards down and Kirk destroyed, we can flee in safety before Tiamat arrives."

"Too late," came a voice from the doorway, and Hawk turned to see a mass of coiling tentacles slide through, with Tia Lake's torso atop them. "You have destroyed too many of me, and now you have taken the one creature I trusted." She looked down on them, coldly furious. "We shall see if the miracoral screams when you do."

LORI

She lay on the bedroom floor for a long time as the sobs took her. She couldn't have said what she was crying for, only that the tears would no longer stay inside of her, that it felt like part of her came out with them. Her parents. Handler. The friends she couldn't reach, couldn't help.

Finally, sniffling, she pulled herself out of the bedroom. She shut the door behind her. She would remember it now.

She tried her phone, but it was definitely dead. Maybe it would work after charging.

Handler had said that the phone would have new identities for her and Ben.

She stumbled down the hallway, still looking at her dead phone.

Why *and Ben*?

Handler needed her to feed, but Ben was just . . . what? A way to motivate her? A reminder that she was vulnerable, that she had to be careful? That didn't make sense. Why would it have connected with Ben, let Ben remember their parents? That wouldn't motivate Lori. Lori hadn't even been aware of it. Why would Handler try to help a human it had no reason to care about?

It didn't matter anymore, not with Handler dead, or as good as dead. Lori had no powers. She had what she wanted instead. She was a normal girl again, with a normal little brother.

And Handler was dying. Had told her to go.

So she'd do that. She wiped her face, shoved her phone in her pocket. There were Legos on the floor, a plate on the table, and a yogurt cup on the counter. Would someone come in and find them? Not Lori's problem. Her job was to get Ben, get on a plane with her new identity, and get to the mainland. She took one last look at the kitchen, gripping one of the chairs by the back for support.

That was what Handler had said. That was what it wanted. That was all Lori could do, in fact. She couldn't help Handler. She was just a normal human. She couldn't help Maya and Tapper and Hawk and Iara, either, and that was all right. That wasn't her job. They had the miracoral for that, and it was stronger than Handler. It was what the Leviathan that had . . . erased . . . her parents had been chasing in the first place.

She couldn't help her parents. She couldn't *remember* her parents.

For a moment she thought about going back to the bedroom and grabbing one of the pictures. Her hands ached as she thought about it. One of them was gripping the back of the kitchen chair so tightly that her fingers had gone white.

The other was in her pocket, clutching her dead phone.

She grabbed the plate from the table angrily and stalked over to the counter. She dropped it into the sink, breathing hard. She would do what Handler had said. It was the only thing she could do. The others would take care of themselves. Or not. It was a big and unfair world, and terrible things happened to everyone.

If she were lucky, she could recharge the phone, and once it was working, she could get the fake IDs Handler had made. It had been weak, but it had promised it would make them.

It always kept its promises.

Just like it sassed her and encouraged her to kiss Maya and reminded her to be nice to Ben.

Just like it held her when she cried, as best it could.

Not it. *She*.

Lori took a breath, swallowed, and looked up from the sink, and there was the stupid sign.

OUR FAMILY MIGHT GET THERE LATE . . .

Lori stumbled to the door, staggered down the stairs, and came out onto the sidewalk. It was still deserted. The canal was empty, the water calm. There would be no ferries for the next five or ten minutes, going by the normal schedule.

And there, down at the bottom, glowed a patch of miracoral.

Before she could change her mind, she vaulted over the railing and into the water.

The water was cold, but it was only water, and she let it wash over her and pushed out her breath, sinking down to the bottom of the canal as a cloud of bubbles floated up. She opened her eyes, ignoring the sting.

There it was, the miracoral, with its harsh yellow glow that was already turning red as she drew closer.

It didn't do that for normal people. That was something.

All right, she thought at it, *here I am.* Could it hear her? One way to find out.

She pushed herself down closer to it. The angry red glow got angrier and redder, and the crayfish popped out from the little brain grooves of the coral. They probably weren't even different creatures. They were probably just parts of the creature, like Lake and her eels, or like Handler and Lori.

How she'd thought she'd been, anyway.

I'm not leaving, she thought, and pushed herself forward. *Pinch me, shock me, whatever you're going to do.*

There were dozens of crayfish swarming her. They flashed forward, a cloud of claws between her and the coral, and they latched onto her, and it *hurt*, their claws digging in like tiny little electric shocks that—

go away go away go away don't hurt me

—hurt more than anything had ever hurt in Lori's life, and she screamed out more bubbles and shook in the water.

And did not swim away.

I need your help, she thought, and kept swimming forward. *And you owe me! You're the reason the Leviathan took my parents!*

More claws flashing into her, pinching her arms and legs and face, too fast for her to protect herself—

no you are feeder you are like what I fled you will make more come

—and the shocks drove her back, her muscles spasming from the sudden deadening thrum of the electricity.

No! Nobody wants to hurt you! Handler eats things that hurt people, Lori thought as loudly as she could, *and you are going to help it—no, you're going to help* her *and me, so that we can help your Nix.*

She was getting dizzy, and her pulse pounded at the edges of her vision. The crayfish hovered in front of her, hundreds of tiny little legs flicking as they treaded water.

One of them darted forward, then zipped back, as though it

was scared of *her*, and then it crept forward again and touched her very gently on the arm with a tiny little shock.

   explain

12

IARA

Tiamat was massive and terrible, floating into the plaza on a cloud of tendrils that formed her lower body. They frothed the water as she slid toward them, blocking the doorway that was their only path to escape.

"We will not help you, monster!" Iara called, and added a *click* at the end. She heard the feel of the creature, and it was as it had been yesterday in the laboratory. She was not a woman with eels under her control. She *was* the eels. They made up her body, even the parts of her that seemed to be human.

The miracoral might have helped, perhaps, but Iara had dropped it when the puppets attacked. It was back in the clothing room now. It might have been a world away.

"You will," Tiamat called, and her voice was a spike of pain that cut through Iara's mind. With her perfect hearing, she could hear it coming from everywhere, and it was too loud, too much. "Where is the other one?"

"Lori has not come back to us," Iara said, the words flowing from her like water, and she wanted to say more, she knew Lori's address, even, and started to say it, but Tapper clapped her ears, and the pain shot through the voice for a moment, letting her fall silent. At least that meant Lori had escaped, Iara thought with a grim satisfaction.

"Have you discovered anything new from the miracoral?" Tiamat asked, coming closer. Hawk put himself between her and Iara, even as he and the others all spat out answers.

"No."

"Nothing."

"No."

"It's kind of heavy." That was Maya.

"Useless." Tiamat snarled. "I cannot use it, and I cannot destroy it. But I *can* grow the eels inside you as I would inside another of my kind. Perhaps you will prove more helpful once the eels have taken your pain."

"Or perhaps you will die!" Iara yelled. "Now!" And she threw out her keening scream directly at the heart of the beast.

Tiamat collapsed, her human shape falling apart into a mass of sickly yellow-green. Before the pile of wriggling flesh even hit the water, Iara was moving, diving forward with the others close behind.

Tapper ran past her, leaving a plume of white water behind him. He swept into the cloud of eels like a pinball, blurring here and there, leaving crushed bodies behind him. Hawk was there a moment later, crushing the biggest eels in his bare hands. Even Maya leaped into the fray, twisting through the writhing cloud.

Iara struck with all her strength, smashing the blunt faces with blows from her hands. All the while, she kept the keening wail coming, leaving the eels to twist and shudder and giving the Nix a fighting chance.

"There's got to be a big one!" Hawk yelled. He smashed

another one, then lunged at one as large as he was. "Find the one in charge!"

"No no no no!" Tapper's voice seemed to come from everywhere as he flew across the room. "We're fighting blind, Pint-Size! We need to run!"

Iara's voice was growing tired. She crushed another eel, swatted a large one out of her way, and through the cloud saw one in the center of the mass, half again as large as she was. "There!" she yelled, and then forced out one last keening burst.

The cloud of eels shuddered, leaving a gap, and Tapper grabbed Hawk and blurred both of them close. Even with his speed, a wave of yellow-green flesh crashed down toward them . . . only to collapse on Maya instead, as she grabbed hold and pulled the mass of eels out of the way. With a last grunt, Tapper threw Hawk through the closing gap.

Iara's voice failed her, but she saw Hawk hit the massive eel in the middle of the cloud. He gripped it with superhuman strength, and even as the swarm descended on him, he tore it in half, spewing ichor everywhere.

Then the mass coiled around Iara, snaring her arms and legs and throat all at once. One wrapped around her mouth like a gag, and she tried to keen again, but it was too tight, and all she could do was choke. Helpless in the coiling mass, she felt herself rising. A moment later she was out of the water, as were the others, each tangled in a mass of eels that held them fast several meters above the water.

A nest of the eels coiled together above them all, and its color slid to blood red, and then it was the Tia Lake shape again, staring at them all with contempt, human from the waist up and eels below.

"I told you," she said, "and you did not listen. *I cannot die.*" Her face was naked in its grief for a moment, and then she was angry again. "I thought you might be the key, but you are nothing. The Nix are just the miracoral amusing itself while it hides in this world. Broken humans for whom it felt sympathy. You cannot stop me. You cannot even escape me. Let us see whether the miracoral pities you when you lie screaming on my table."

She floated toward Iara, her blood-red fingernails extended. "You annoyed me, dear. We'll quiet you down first."

Iara tried one last keen, but the eel that kept her gagged was too tight. She bit into the sour flesh and growled her final defiance.

Tiamat smiled and raised her hand, fingers curled into claws.

And with a tiny *pop* that only Iara could hear, Lori Fisher blossomed into existence in midair and punched Tiamat square in the face.

BEN

The man in the black suit waded into the ball pit, and Ben didn't know where to go, and the man was really big and didn't care that he was shoving other kids out of the way to get to Ben, and Ben shrank back—

—and then Ben was somewhere else, and *then* Ben was in his living room.

"Hunh," he said after a moment.

He wasn't sure what to do. Was Jenn still in trouble? What had happened with the men who had been chasing him? How did he get here?

A phone on the table buzzed. Ben looked over at it. It had a cover with the Lego RoboDragon on it, and at the top, the name BEN in big letters. He picked it up as it buzzed again, and then turned it over to see what was making it buzz.

Handler: It's okay. You play here and stay safe.

Handler: I'm taking care of Jenn and Lori and everyone else.

"Hunh," Ben said again.

A new phone wasn't as cool as the RoboDragon Rampage set, but it was still nice.

LORI

Lori felt the crack of her fist on Tia Lake's face, solid and satisfying, before she plummeted several meters down and into the water that had half filled the former shopping mall where Lake and her friends were fighting.

It was colder than the water at the canal, but that was all right, because as she went under, she sucked in a breath and felt the shock and chill, and then felt her lungs fill . . . and work again.

Her phone buzzed in her pocket, a single long buzz. *Yes.*

She kicked to the surface and saw the Nix pulling free from the tendrils as Tia Lake shook her head, glaring down at Lori in fury. "So you live, little feeder?"

The words pulled at her, but she didn't fight them this time. "I'm human, not a feeder. But yes," she called back, spitting the words up at the towering half woman above her, "I live. And so does the feeder who takes care of me."

"Impossible," Lake hissed, and dove down at Lori, hands curled into claws and a thousand eels baring their fangs as they descended—

Now, Lori thought.

—and crashed into the water where she *had* been, as Lori watched safely from the doorway. Lake spun as she saw her. "How could it survive? Why would it come back here?"

Lori looked over at the Nix, at Iara and Hawk and Tapper

and Maya, now all of them free as Lake focused entirely on Lori. "Because *she* found friends," she said, "and so did I."

Her phone buzzed, and she fished it out.

Handler: Found them. Corner of the room behind you.

"And you cannot have any of them," Lori added, and the world flashed around her again.

She caught a glimpse of it this time, of that impossible dark expanse. Only this time, the darkness was pushed back not by the shaky light of her phone but by the golden glow that came from Handler's injured side, where a great mass of miracoral clustered around her wound and countless crayfish forms worked in unison to stitch it shut.

She splashed back into the water in a room filled with floating clothes and the remains of guard puppets. Fluorescent lights lit the area, but beneath her, Lori saw the golden glow she had been looking for.

The miracoral, the piece the Nix had taken when they fled from Tiamat's lair.

She dove down into water that was higher than her head, kicked toward the miracoral. It flickered orange, crackling at her approach.

Then it returned to its friendly golden glow, with a warmth that no longer hurt her eyes.

She reached out and grabbed it.

The coral was rough like a pumice scrub, and heavier than she had expected, but it didn't shock her, and no crayfish darted out to rip into her with their claws.

She kicked for the doorway that led outside. Behind her she heard the water froth with Lake's approach, and Lori swam as hard as she could with only one free hand, out of the clothing room, into another room where waterlogged mattresses sat near piles of bloody clothes, the remnants of Lake's testing.

An eel wrapped around Lori's ankle. She looked back, and Lake was there, with her mass of eels writhing around her.

"You are nothing!" Lake snarled, and the eels coiled around Lori.

Lori turned and thrust the miracoral square into Lake's face, and as the light turned red and the crayfish swarmed out to snap and shock, as Lake screamed in pain and the eels flinched back, Lori yelled through the water, "I am small, and I am weak, but I am *not* nothing!"

Lake recoiled, and Lori kicked away and swam again, through the room, to the air lock. She looked back to see Lake again, her pretty face burned from the crayfish. "And neither are you!" Lori added, her voice bubbling through the water. "You were here thousands of years. You could have helped people. You could have made this world better!"

Lake screamed, and the eels all swarmed around her, and then they *were* her, and there were no eels anymore, just a flawless woman in a red dress who walked through the water as though it weren't there, her heels clicking on the floor, her face unscarred again. "For what?" she snapped, her voice sending ripples through the water as she approached. "For the *humans*? You are *things*! I exist in a dimension you cannot even understand, little girl."

"But we're still real," Lori shot back, and swam through the air lock. Whatever had happened to it, both doors were open, and while the flow of water was no longer a staggering rush, it was still coming in strongly enough that she had to force her way through to get outside. "We're real enough for our memories to keep you here."

Lake stepped into the air lock as Lori kicked her way out.

"Trapped," she hissed, wrenching the half-opened door aside. "Broken! Do you know what that feels like?"

"Yes." Lori answered before the words could even force themselves out. "That's what you don't get." Something started to bubble up inside her, and she thought it was a sob, but it came out as laughter instead, laughter that sent little bubbles up and away as she kicked out into the cold open water. "*Everybody* knows what that feels like! Handler, the coral, the Nix, all of us! We all feel *exactly the same way you do!*"

She hung in the open water. Below her was the darkness, inky black, and in it a sound so low that it registered only as a rumbling in the pit of Lori's stomach. A moment later she felt the water grow hot around her.

Tia Lake stood at the edge of the air lock, looking out at Lori. She didn't look angry anymore. She looked sad and . . . something else. Sadder, smaller. Maybe even human.

"How do you make it stop?" she asked softly.

Lori shook her head. "You don't. You find other people and try to help them. You go forward."

The water tasted of blood now, and green bubbles frothed up around Lori as Tia Lake swallowed. "I can't do that," she said. She clutched the edge of the air lock, her fingers digging little grooves into the metal. "I want it to go away. *I* want to go away, but I can't, not as long as they remember me."

Lori looked down, where through the darkness she felt a sense of motion, of something huge. Tiamat's main body. When she looked back up at Tia Lake, the other woman's eyes were hard and set again. "The miracoral would not call the Leviathan for me. Perhaps your little feeder will call it for you." She glared. "Why are you smiling?"

"I feel sorry for you," Lori said, even as the water below her swirled. Finally she added, "You don't have to do this."

"I do," Tia Lake said.

Below Lori the *real* Tiamat rose, its great maw wide like a chasm, ringed with hundreds, thousands of eels that coiled around it in a writhing dance. It was too large for this world, and Lori hung in the water over that gaping impossible maw, feeling the heat of the green bubbles rising from inside it, and thought, *Now.*

She drew the miracoral out again and held it up.

And in her hand it blazed a perfect white and screamed.

The piercing wail cut through the water, cut through Lori, cut through the very world, and it was pain and fear and loneliness all mixed together and forged into a crystalline sound that shone pure beyond measure. Every sickly green bubble hissing around Lori popped, and the water went cold again. Nothing in this world or any other could ignore that sound.

Tiamat, the great beast, stopped dead in the water.

A moment later the Leviathan came.

It had no form. It was not a thing as much as it was an *effect* on the world. Tiamat's impossible maw, too huge for the entirety of the ocean, dwindled and shrank and fell into nothingness, and the current from its movement slammed into Lori with the force of iron. She spun dizzily, clutching the miracoral with both hands now, her legs flailing, and then she slammed into the side of the building, not far from the air lock, and the water breath was shoved from her lungs by the impact.

Standing in the air lock, Tia Lake looked down at her.

The flawless face smiled softly.

"Thank you," she said, and then her form slid away into a dozen eels that in turn slid away into the darkness, receding and dwindling as though being pulled somewhere Lori could not follow.

She barely heard it, coughing and struggling to breathe, and with her free hand, she grabbed for the edge of the air lock, but the current slammed into her again and tore her away, and she hurtled down into the darkness, spinning. There was no Tiamat, not anymore, but the thing that had taken her, the Leviathan, had drawn Tiamat into its jaws with a great inhalation that threatened to suck Lori down with it.

Lori thrashed desperately. The air lock was a tiny beacon of light far above. The miracoral had gone dark, hiding in her grasp, too small again for the Leviathan to notice now, but the current still pulled her down, down, down, and she didn't know how far it was—it was too large for this world, and distances meant different things—but she knew Handler couldn't pull her away, not without revealing itself as well, so she kicked and pulled with one arm, fighting back toward that light.

It wasn't enough.

The current was dizzying, and she could sense it now, the Leviathan, still hunting, still searching, opening its jaws to pull in everything nearby, feeder and human and part of the world alike.

This is how the water rose. This is how my parents died. Ben, I'm sorry. I don't know if you'll remember me, but I tried to keep you safe. You and the Nix and everyone. I tried.

She shut her eyes as the darkness overcame her.

Then, with a rush of bubbles, something grabbed her arm, and a voice yelled through the water, "Rrrblhere!"

Lori opened her eyes and found Tapper holding her with one arm. His other arm blurred, as did his legs, frothing the water as he pulled against the current.

"We have you!" came Iara's cry, and then she was there on the other side of Lori, catching her other arm and swimming hard, the two of them heaving to pull her up.

Iara reached for something with her free arm, and Lori looked up. There was Maya, stretched out impossibly far toward them, both arms reaching, and Iara and Tapper shouted with effort as they pulled against the current, pulled Lori up, and grabbed Maya's hands.

Up in the air lock, metal groaned, and Lori saw Hawk holding Maya's legs, straining with all his might.

They all hung in the deep water there for a moment, the Nix holding Lori up as the Leviathan pulled her down.

Then, with a low twisting groan, the air lock doorframe sagged and began to break free—

Pretend for a moment that you're not good at this. Pretend you've been trying as best you can, and some days you're tired, and some days you're scared, and some days you have no idea what you're doing. Pretend you came here to hide, and because you felt sorry for a microbe on a plate, because it hadn't had any more luck than you had.

Pretend that microbe saved you, and now it was in danger, and so were its friends, and you're still not sure about a lot of things, but you're sure about this: You and the microbe and its little brother, you don't know where you're going, and you might get there late.

But you'll get there together.

—and as the air lock doorframe broke free, massive jaws sprang out of nowhere to lock around the edge, holding up the frame, and Hawk, and Maya, and Tapper and Iara, and Lori, who looked up at Handler, so huge and scary and so tiny compared to the terrible darkness below her, and thought to her, *Thank you.*

They all hung in the water there for a moment, straining against that impossible current.

And then, with a sigh that shook the world, the water went back to normal.

Dizzy and exhausted, Lori felt air on her face, and as her vision cleared, she saw that she was looking at the shops of Reef Square from the middle of the little harbor. They had cleared the chasm.

Tapper and Iara were still beside her, breathing hard, and a moment later Hawk and Maya surfaced as well.

"So *that* was superdangerous and dumb," Maya said, "and I'm not sure, but I think I dislocated some stuff, wait, no, never mind, it's back."

"That Leviathan thing was big," Tapper said, gasping.

"Big enough to destroy Tiamat herself," Iara said with satisfaction.

"You didn't . . ." Lori caught her breath. She wanted to laugh. She wanted to cry. "You didn't have to—"

"Yeah, we did," Tapper cut in, glaring, and jerked his head at Maya. "Your girlfriend would never've let us live it down otherwise."

"Besides," Iara added, "heroes take care of each other."

"And you're kind of the worst swimmer on the team," Maya added. "Um, no offense."

"Lucky for you we were all there with superstrength and stuff," Hawk added, grinning.

Lori's phone buzzed in her pocket, a single long buzz for "yes."

She looked at them all, her wonderful, imperfect, broken new friends.

"Lucky for me," she said, and splashed over to pull Maya into a kiss as the ferries began honking at them.

FRIDAY

EPILOGUE

LORI

"I mean, she's just *gone*," Hawk said on the couch in Lori's living room the next day, clicking on his phone. "Look, the entry for the god of good dragons is still Bahamut—"

"Appropriative," Iara said from beside him, and elbowed him.

"Hey, I didn't write it. But look, the evil one, which I'm pretty sure *used* to be Tiamat—"

"Or Takhisis, depending on which of the worlds you're in," Tapper added.

"Wait, worlds?" Hawk looked over at him. "D and D does space?"

"No," Tapper snapped, "Dungeons and Dragons does not *do space*. Okay, there was Spelljammer, but that doesn't count."

"Anyway," Hawk finished, "my point is that the evil dragon god is now some kind of snake thing called Falak." He showed them his phone, where a fiery snake creature was visible next to a listing of armor class and hit dice. "The Leviathan wrote her out of existence *completely*. No religious stuff, no historical stuff, nothing."

"Good," Maya said, and took a bite of pizza.

"So why do we remember it?" Hawk asked.

"Our connection to the miracoral," Iara said. "It lets us see the truth of the world, just as Lori's tie to Handler does."

"What about the building?" Tapper asked, and as everyone looked at him in confusion, he gestured irritably. "The one we broke into? It was the Lake Foundation, so what is it now?"

Iara brightened. "I investigated that yesterday. It is something called the Angler Institute."

Lori dropped her pizza. "Really?"

Iara nodded, tapping on her phone. "They do studies of the miracoral to ensure that it is used safely and responsibly without harm, and they are also working on new medical treatments."

"Hmm," Lori said, and then a knock at the door interrupted her.

She got up, pulled it open, and was immediately engulfed in a hug. "Hey!" Jenn said after a long moment. "So everything is okay?"

"Um . . ." Lori's phone gave one long buzz for "yes." "Yeah." She'd talked with Ben about what had happened, glossing over it enough for Ben to be okay with *sometimes that is going to happen and try not to worry about it.* "How are you?"

"Oh, man, I feel like such a tool!" Jenn shook her head. "The one time you need help, and I lose him in the stupid play area."

So she didn't remember. That was probably okay. "It happens," Lori said. "Hey, these are some friends that I met from work." She gestured to the others. "Guys, this is my friend Jenn."

"Hey, Jenn," said Ben, who was playing a video game with the headphones on, "do you want to see the Pokémon game I got on my new phone?"

"Totally," Jenn said, and waved at everyone, who waved back. Behind Jenn's back, Lori made desperate eye contact with everyone. She didn't *think* anyone was going to start talking about Tiamat immediately, but . . . her phone buzzed.

Handler: Chillllllllllll.

"Yeah, yeah." Lori plonked down by Ben's seat at the table, where several baby carrots sat studiously uneaten next to the crumbs that were all that remained of three pieces of pizza. "Our job is done, so we're celebrating. Since you took care of Ben, you get a piece too, if you want."

"Jenn, this is Sylveon," Ben said, and held up his phone, which showed a deer-looking thing. "He can attack people with kisses, just like Maya and Lori!"

"Um," Lori said, and grabbed a carrot desperately from his plate.

"Oh, *really*," Jenn said, and looked from Lori to Iara, who pointed to Maya, who in turn raised her hand.

"Gardevoir's got the kiss attack too," Tapper said, "and since it's psychic/fairy, it's better for—"

"Noooobody caaaaares," Maya said in a singsong voice, and Tapper shook his head, laughing to himself.

"Anyway, Maya is prettier," Ben said magnanimously.

"Wooo!" Maya reached over and high-fived him.

Jenn smirked at Lori. "You could have told me."

Lori found herself flushing. "I didn't want to make it weird."

"You're my friend, dumbass." Jenn poked her. "And now that your job is finished, we're still going shopping, so you can impress your girlfriend." She grinned at Maya, then lowered her voice. "Should we buy some flannel, or . . . ?"

"Hey," Hawk said, "so, um, speaking of, did you two talk

about Maya being, uh . . ." Iara elbowed him again. "You know, I was just trying to, okay, shutting up!"

"Oh, about Matt stuff?" Maya asked.

"We talked about Maya's *past history*," Lori said, and took Maya's hand as she came back to her seat at the table, "and we are good." They'd talked about it while Ben had been at day care—where a strangely relaxed Mister Barkin had had no recollection of Lori decking him and had been happy to take Ben back in the middle of the day.

"Okay, cool. That's cool." Hawk nodded. "I mean, I figured you'd be cool, because you're chill, but, you know . . ." He shut up when Iara leaned over and kissed him.

As everyone talked and laughed, Lori's phone buzzed again.

Handler: So hey btw

Lori: The Angler Institute?

Handler: Okay, putting reality back together is tricky.
Handler: Especially when the Leviathan has torn a great big hole in it.
Handler: Institute maaaaaay also be opening an on-site magnet school

Lori: A school for who?

Handler: Oh, you know.
Handler: Gifted kids with aquatic-animal-related powers and stuff.

Lori: Were you going to run this by me?

Handler: We could use the help, kid.
Handler: Tiamat wasn't the only nasty thing crawling around this world.

Lori: Right. You're still here.

Handler: :(

"Lori, you okay?" Maya asked, and reached over to stroke her arm. A smooth touch, warm and gentle and soft, and it still gave Lori goose bumps.

Handler: The Nix could use the help too.
Handler: Their families are safe now, but money's tight for some.
Handler: I haven't sent the invitation e-mail yet
Handler: Wanted to see if you were okay with it

Lori looked up at Maya and smiled.
"Yes," she said. "Yes, I am."
Then she leaned in and kissed Maya as all of their phones chimed to tell them they had new mail.

ACKNOWLEDGMENTS

Every novel is a team effort, and this one is no different. Thanks to David Hale Smith, Liz Parker, and everyone at InkWell for continuing their amazing job with all of the legal stuff I will never understand, leaving me critical time to look up the biology and behavior of various sea creatures. Thanks to Annie Nybo and everyone at Margaret K. McElderry Books for being not just understanding but enthusiastic about a novel whose pitch was "anglerfish teen girl superhero" and for helping it be the best interdimensional anglerfish novel on the market. Thanks to Jenn, Ritzy, Adri, Cookie, and Cara for showing me where things clunked in the early drafts. Thanks to Karin for doing that and *also* being an awesomely supportive, nonplatonic life partner and *also also* soloing the boys on a lot of nights and weekends so that I had time to write this.

Thanks to Greg Rucka for cuffing me gently on the head when I started overthinking things, to Matthew Inman at *The Oatmeal* for his wonderful write-ups of both the anglerfish and the peacock mantis shrimp, to Jason Portan at *Rejected Princesses* for introducing me to the wonderful legend of Iara, and to Sylvia Feketekuty for liking Starro more than anyone ever needed to.

Finally, thanks to everyone who doesn't feel like they fit in, whether it's because of how you look or how you think or who you're attracted to or anything else. Thank you for being who you are. You may not fit in, but you don't have to. Be you, as hard as you can, because you matter, and you have something to offer this world.

We are all in different places on our shared journey, and we might get there late.

But we'll get there together.